JUSTICE
ON A
MIDNIGHT
CLEAR

—～—

JUSTICE
ON A
MIDNIGHT
CLEAR

STAR OF JUSTICE SERIES

BRUCE
HAMMACK

CHAPTER ONE

"It's Thanksgiving Day, I'm eight months pregnant and you want to check out a call about a gunshot that a Riverview officer already said he'd handle." CJ turned her head to give her husband a hard stare. "What's wrong with this picture?"

David turned the wheel on his unmarked SUV and pulled onto the white concrete street of Riverview's newest subdivision. "This won't take long, and I'm not answering the call about the gunshot." He rolled his window down to listen. "It's probably a deer hunter a mile from the nearest house. All I want to do is check out the new homes."

"You're not fooling me. You don't like to visit people in hospitals."

"Guilty," said David. "I'm saving myself for when you deliver our little tax deduction."

CJ tried to get comfortable, but that proved impossible with no slack in the seat belt. "Let's make this quick. One drive-through, then to the hospital to see Margaret for a few minutes, and then home."

1

With an eyebrow raised, David said, "I know someone who ate too much turkey and dressing."

There was no need to contradict him. She'd overindulged and her soon-to-be-born baby didn't appreciate the cramped quarters, made even more so by an overstuffed stomach. She covered a belch that tasted like sage.

A single blacktopped driveway looked out of place as it snaked from the subdivision to the horse ranch and home of Judge Kraft. The house reminded her of a southern plantation with Romanesque white columns and wide porches.

"By the way," said CJ. "Did Tig Murphy ever surface?"

"What made you ask about him?" asked David, with a little more inflection in his question than necessary.

She pointed. "Seeing that backhoe brought him to mind. I don't like unsolved murders and I'm not convinced the people you work for are interested in finding him."

"We've been over this a hundred times. Captain Crow is under instructions not to spend any more time or money looking for him. There's nothing I can do about it, even if I wanted to."

"Which you don't."

A county dispatcher's voice disrupted what was turning into a family dispute. "All units near Riverview Regional, respond to shots fired at the six-hundred block of Lexington Downs Drive in the new Ridgemont subdivision. One victim reported." The dispatcher then broadcast the sheriff's call numbers with instructions for him to "public service" her. Cop talk for calling on a telephone.

"Get out your phone," said David.

CJ had already reached for her purse. David had the microphone in hand. He tried to give his badge number, but had to wait as radio traffic picked up. In the meantime, he increased his speed and turned onto Lexington. He reached fifty-five before leveling off at the base of a rise at the end of the four-hundred block. Once the radio was quiet, he gave his badge number and broadcast that he was on the scene. Grabbing binoculars and a hand-held radio, he threw open his door and moved to the side of the road with the most trees and disappeared from sight.

It always amazed CJ how tense moments stretched time and amplified sounds. She heard every chirp and squawk of birds and the rustle of fall leaves. There were no sirens being carried on the wind yet. Thanksgiving afternoon was one of the worst times to expect a quick response.

After several long minutes, David emerged from a clump of trees and jogged to the vehicle. "It's Judge Kraft. He's beyond help. I need to get some gear."

CJ piled out and lumbered to the rear of the vehicle. David opened the back and grabbed his body armor. After donning the vest, he pulled out the assault rifle he carried in a hard-side case. "Call the sheriff and tell him we need at least two perimeters set up, three would be better. I think the shot came from the lone finished home at the base of the hill. Also, there're bloody footprints leading down a side street." He pointed. "They look like they're headed to that house standing by itself." He cast his gaze in the direction of the recent death. He paused mid-task and looked at her. "Don't get curious and look over the hill. It could be an ambush."

CJ nodded, even though her first inclination was to issue a protest. David's experience as an army sniper in the Middle East made him well informed when it came to potential ambushes. Her priority had to be taking care of herself and the son they would soon welcome into the world. "Do you want me to call Captain Crow?"

He nodded. "Tell him it's a single shot from about a hundred yards with a high caliber rifle."

"No chance of a stray shot from a hunter?"

David shook his head. "Thick trees in all directions." He

3

double checked the extra clips in his vest. "Tell Sheriff Gladstone I need help to clear the house. As soon as I get three more people who know what they're doing, I'll go in."

He took the time to give her a last word. "Remember what I said. This could be an ambush. Stay where you're safe."

"I'll take care of me. You look after yourself."

She relayed all pertinent information to the sheriff in a brief, succinct conversation. A couple of minutes later, the first siren approached, followed by a symphony of wails, warbles, and yelps, still some distance away.

Her next call went to Captain Crow and was routed to voice mail after several rings. The ball was in his court now.

It wasn't long before a baby-faced deputy sheriff arrived with lights pulsating and siren blasting. CJ held up a hand for him to stop. He piled out of his car, one hand hovering over his holstered gun. "Who are you?"

"CJ Harper. The assistant chief of police at Agape Christian University."

"This doesn't look like a university vehicle." The young man hooked his thumbs in his vest and gave her a narrow-eyed stare.

"It's my husband's, David Harper. He's a DPS sergeant and special investigator with the Texas Rangers. You must be new."

"Started three days ago. Is there something wrong out here?"

"Someone shot a state district judge. His body is on the other side of the hill."

The young man's Adam's apple bobbed up and down. "Holy smoke. Shouldn't we go secure the crime scene?"

"That's what I'm doing. Securing it from a safe distance."

A sheriff's department pickup truck approached. A wide man with chevrons on his sleeves bounded out and closed the distance with long strides. His cowboy hat dipped as he nodded. "CJ, what's the situation?"

"Judge Kraft's body is on the other side of the hill. One shot. Fatal. David's somewhere between here and the house at the end of this street. He's waiting for backup to help him clear the house. I talked to the sheriff about getting perimeters set up."

"I'll help him clear the house," said the patrolman.

The sergeant shook his head. "You're not supposed to be on patrol by yourself, let alone breach and clear a house at a murder scene. Go to the front entrance of the subdivision and don't let any civilians or press in. Tell every officer that comes to call me. I'll decide who goes on perimeter and who needs to help clear the house. If they can see the house at the end of Lexington, they're too close. I'll stay here for now."

CJ wondered if the young man was going to cry, but he accepted the assignment and was soon out of sight.

"Were we ever that young?" asked the sergeant.

Before she could answer, CJ's phone came to life. Ominous music meant the call originated from only one source, Captain Crow, David's supervisor with the Texas Rangers. She pushed the green icon and the blustery voice caused her to wince.

"Doesn't that husband of yours ever keep his phone on?"

CJ bristled, but was quick to respond. "He's sneaking through a grove of trees on his way to clear a house where he thinks a killer might be. Do you want me to go track him down and tell him to turn on his phone?"

"I'm not in the mood, CJ. Give me what you know."

"Judge Weldon Kraft was shot once from a hundred yards away. The sheriff's trying to set up a double-perimeter, but the response time is pitiful. David and I were first on the scene, but he told me to stay back. He's afraid it could be a murder/ambush."

5

After a single expletive, the Ranger captain asked, "Any chance this was an accident?"

"David says no."

"Anything else?"

"Bloody footprints leading from the body."

"Was his wife or anyone else with him?"

"Unknown."

"Find out by the time I get there. FBI is on their way, too."

The phone made a multi-note sound when he cut off the call.

CJ looked at the sergeant. "If I didn't respect the old goat so much, I'd tell him to go swim in a septic tank."

A highway patrolman slid his black and white SUV to a stop and scurried toward the sergeant and CJ. She knew him from her years as a state trooper. His service record in law enforcement and as a Marine was exemplary.

"CJ, long time no see." The trooper smiled as his gaze drifted down CJ's belly mound. The twinkle in his right eye told her a smart comment was on the way.

"Don't say it," she cautioned. "I'm well aware of the fact that I'm pregnant. David said he needs three people who know what they're doing to help him clear a house. Why don't you two find one more and help him?"

CJ already had the maps program out on her phone. "Approach the house from the south. There are plenty of trees on that side to give you cover."

Both men jogged to their cars.

Sirens sounded like a large pack of coyotes coming from all directions. The response had been slow, but was now in full bloom. A glance at her phone told CJ eighteen minutes had passed since the first call came from the dispatcher, an eternity when seconds mattered.

The next minutes passed with the speed of a drugged

sloth. CJ, a highway patrol lieutenant, and a deputy sheriff waited in the November sun. An ambulance joined the line of vehicles waiting to top the hill. David's voice came over the radio. "House clear. Securing crime scene."

Instead of driving, CJ said, "Let's stay on foot."

The three topped the hill and stopped in unison.

"What the..." said the deputy.

"That beats anything I've ever seen," said the lieutenant.

CJ swallowed hard at the sight. Below them, about forty yards away, was the body of Judge Weldon Kraft. He sat upright in the road with his head dipped forward on his chest.

"Get out your phones," said CJ. "You two film and I'll take still pictures."

The three moved forward at a slow pace, which suited her fine. While they covered the distance, she racked her brain to explain the strange sight. By the time they arrived, she had the answer.

CJ and the lieutenant made a wide circle around Judge Kraft while the deputy stayed even farther away, taking a wide-angle shot of the two veterans going about their grim duty.

"I don't get it," said the deputy in a voice that broke the mood of respect for the judge. "How is he sitting up?"

CJ didn't speak until she and the lieutenant were standing with the deputy. "David told me he saw something similar once. It's caused by hydrostatic shock. I'm sure you've both seen rounds fired into ballistics gel. When you watch in slow motion, you can see a shock wave of kinetic energy ripple through the gel. That stuff mimics the human body. Judge Kraft dropped where he stood. His legs and rear end formed a triangle that kept him upright."

The lieutenant nodded in agreement. "Let's get the area

taped off. How far would you say, CJ? Fifty yards in all directions?"

"Because it's a state district judge, I'd say all the way from our cars in one direction and past the house in the other."

"I agree," said David. He'd come up on CJ's blind side. "On my way to the house, I came across fresh tire tracks in a low area that caught silt from the last rain. That area is being taped off, too."

CJ turned to look where David pointed. The sun reflected off a window on the second floor, causing her to squint. "Did the shot come from the house?"

"From that direction," said David. "Let's get out of the crime scene."

CJ's ringing phone brought her attention away from the grim sight. "Yes, Sheriff." David moved close to poach on her conversation. She pulled the phone away from her ear so he could listen.

"Judge Kraft's wife was with him," said the sheriff. "She's at a doctor's house on a street parallel to where you are. Every warm body I can find is setting a perimeter. Could you take a statement from her, CJ?"

"Happy to help."

When the call ended, David said, "That explains the bloody footprints."

"At least the sheriff *asked* for my help," said CJ. "Captain Crow didn't give me that option."

CHAPTER TWO

C J parked behind a Riverview County patrol car on an eyebrow shaped driveway. The white concrete was so new it remained unblemished from stains of oil or transmission fluid. Not three miles from Riverview Regional Hospital, the dwelling and its counterparts seemed perfect for doctors and other professionals who didn't mind tacking a hefty mortgage onto their mountain of student loan debt.

She'd met Christine Kraft a few times and knew her to be involved in all things equestrian, especially the local rodeo club. Otherwise she only knew her as Judge Kraft's wife, a perky, beautiful blond, who seemed as comfortable in tight jeans as she was in the latest fashion.

The front door swung open and CJ looked down on an adolescent-looking man of Asian heritage.

"CJ Harper, assistant chief of police at ACU. Sheriff Gladstone asked me to stop by." The badge and accompanying credentials hung inside a leather case on a lanyard draped around her neck.

"Please, come in. I'm Dr. Thomas Gee."

"How is Mrs. Kraft?"

"As you would expect. I gave her a light sedative."

"Is she able to speak to me?"

Dr. Gee was already moving toward a hallway leading off the foyer. "I believe it would be of significant benefit to her. Despite what most people think, talking about a traumatic event as soon as possible after its occurrence is the most therapeutic thing a person can do. The problems come when people try to bury the memories." He paused. "Mrs. Kraft and the officer are in my office. First door on the right. I'll be in the living room if you need me."

A uniformed sheriff's deputy opened a door before CJ could knock. "Am I glad to see you."

"Hello Beula Mae."

Two things stood out concerning the woman standing at the door. Her eyes, while a beautiful blue, were so large they gave her small face the look of a bull frog in a constant state of surprise. The second characteristic that made Beula Mae memorable was her voice, and not just the Texas twang. By her own admission, her voice never grew past the way it sounded when she was seven years old. High and soft, it served her well in disarming recalcitrant inmates and diffusing volatile situations. It also made her the object of endless mimicking.

CJ asked, "How did you get out of jail today?"

The deputy tented her hands on her hips before explaining. "Sergeant Brown bribed me into taking his shift on patrol. He's such a football nut he couldn't bear not watching the game this afternoon. I worked my normal shift and then took over for him at 2:00 p.m. Poor feller, it all backfired on him. He'd no more sat down to eat when all this broke loose. He had to throw on his uniform and is now somewhere looking for whoever did this horrible thing. Since I was the first female to arrive on scene, they told me to see what I could do for Mrs. Kraft. Poor thing, I can't believe..."

CJ had neither the time nor the inclination to listen to Beula Mae rattle. "Did you ask her about the shooting?"

"Nah. I knew someone with rank would be along for that. All I've done is wag my tongue."

"Thanks." CJ paused before proceeding. "Texas Rangers and the FBI will be along soon. I'm sure they'll want to talk to you. Plan on it being a long night."

Over her shoulder, CJ heard Beula Mae squeak. "Lordy, Lordy, what a three-ring mess this Thanksgiving turned out to be. Serves me right for volunteering."

Beula Mae began introductions, but Mrs. Kraft cut her off. "I know CJ. We've met a few times and we use the same farrier." She gazed at CJ and spoke with a subdued voice. "Weldon always spoke in glowing terms of you and your husband."

CJ nodded an acknowledgment of the compliment and of their limited relationship. "I'm very sorry for your loss, Mrs. Kraft."

"Please, call me Chris."

"Ok, Chris. I'm sure you know why I'm here and why it's important we hear what happened. If you don't mind, I'll record this."

"I understand."

"Let's all take a seat and get comfortable." CJ turned her head to Beula Mae. "Why don't you have a seat at Dr. Gee's desk." Chris settled in a wing back chair while CJ wrestled the chair's twin to within an arm's reach of the widow.

"This may sound strange," said CJ. "But I want you to start with waking up this morning and tell me everything you can remember about the day."

Training and experience had taught CJ not to barrage Chris with questions about the shooting right off the bat. It required time and getting into a rhythm of speaking to relax a person. Safe, mundane things were the best place to start.

The narrative of Chris's day began. "Let's see, I woke up at my usual time, 5:15. Weldon had stayed up late doing his thing, so he was still sleeping when I got up."

CJ turned her head and raised an eyebrow. It was enough for Chris to understand she required a more thorough explanation.

"Legal stuff. He was writing an opinion, or researching motions—you know, judge stuff."

"Ahh," said CJ.

"I threw on some jeans and a sweatshirt and went downstairs for my morning coffee. I then went to the barn to feed the horses."

With each statement, CJ nodded her head to show she understood and to encourage the flow of speech. Her simple requests for elaboration eventually led the bereaved widow's speech to shift from halting to a steady recital of the day's events. The more details CJ could pull out of her, the better the chance Chris would remember little things that could make a big difference in solving the case.

By the time the new widow finished her tale of cooking the Thanksgiving meal, it was time for CJ to delve into more sensitive questions.

"What time did you serve the Thanksgiving meal?"

"At one fifty-five."

"That's very exact. How—?"

Chris answered before CJ could finish her sentence. "The game started at four. I wanted to have a nice relaxed meal with Weldon and Kevin before kickoff."

"Refresh my memory," said CJ. "How old is Kevin?"

"Nineteen. He's in his sophomore year at Texas Tech."

"How's he doing?"

"I'm not sure how to answer that. His grades are good, but he hates Lubbock. He complains about it every time he comes home."

"Then why did he choose to go to Tech?"

"Weldon didn't give him any choice. He wanted Kevin to go to his alma mater. It was Tech or nothing."

Chris fixed her gaze on CJ and asked, "What is it about teenage boys and their fathers?"

"Other than disagreeing about college, how did they get along?"

Chris crossed her legs and arms. Defenses had gone up like a draw bridge.

"Kevin and Weldon haven't seen eye-to-eye since Kevin was in middle school."

"Was it more than the normal father-son problems?"

"Much more. Kevin and Weldon looked like mismatched bookends. Weldon was the tall, dark, handsome college football player who succeeded at everything he put his hand to. Kevin tried hard to be like his father, but he got an overdose of my petite genes. He's finally filling out but was always so skinny that he couldn't live up to Weldon's expectations in sports." Chris heaved a sigh. "It all began in the seventh grade. Kevin broke an arm playing football. In the eighth grade, it was his leg. I put my foot down and told Weldon that was enough."

CJ shifted in her chair after the baby gave her a good kick. "And things went downhill from there?"

"Straight downhill. I'm sure you'll find this out in your investigation, but Kevin's been arrested for possession of marijuana."

"I can see how that would upset Judge Kraft. Do you think Kevin takes any other drugs?"

"His grades are too good for him to be on anything hard. He told me he uses marijuana, but not much. He justifies his use with his belief that it's inevitable the marijuana laws will change. He never drinks; he can't stand alcohol."

"Did the two of them argue often?"

"This may be an exaggeration, but it seems all they did was argue. Have you ever seen two bulldogs latch on to a short length of thick rope? That was Weldon and Kevin. My son may not have inherited Weldon's size, but he got every bit of his father's stubborn streak."

"So, Kevin came home this week for the holidays. How was it between him and his dad?"

"Kevin stayed at school as long as he could and even stayed an extra night with a friend in Lubbock. He arrived home late Sunday night, and has been in and out all week, mostly out. Last night, Weldon played prosecuting attorney with Kevin. I felt so sorry for him." Chris lowered her head and added, "But that was nothing compared to today."

"Oh?"

"Weldon searched Kevin's room this morning while he was out visiting his best friend. A baggie with a couple of marijuana cigarettes were in Kevin's sock drawer. Weldon flushed them down the commode. As usual, Kevin arrived late for lunch today. Weldon was fit to be tied and confronted him the minute he walked in the door. It was quite a scene. Kevin stood up to Weldon, and the battle began."

"And?"

"It got physical. Weldon isn't used to people talking back to him. He slapped Kevin. Hard. Kevin came right back at Weldon with cursing and accusations that he must have buried for years. He challenged Weldon with what he sees as hypocrisy. It was quite a row. Anyway, Weldon pushed Kevin hard enough that he lost his balance and fell over a coffee table. That was all Kevin could take. He left and I haven't seen him since."

Beula Mae shifted in her chair, causing both women to cast their glances her way.

"What happened next?" asked CJ.

"Weldon went to his office. I locked myself in our bedroom and cried for half an hour. After that, I washed my face and tried to salvage what I could of the Thanksgiving meal. I fixed Weldon a plate and took it to him. An hour later, I went to get him for our traditional walk after holiday meals. It keeps us from going back for that second piece of pie." Her brief smile turned to tears. "It kept us..." She stopped and gently blew her nose.

"What time did the two of you leave your home?"

"Seven minutes after four. I remember because Weldon said he didn't want to be gone over forty-five minutes. He wanted to be parked in his chair before the game started."

"Did you notice anything unusual or out of the ordinary as you began the walk?"

"Like what?"

"Anything. I noticed a sign by the road leading to your home."

"Oh, that. Weldon is..." Chris' eyes shifted downward and whispered. "I still can't believe he's gone." She inhaled a deep breath and righted herself. "Weldon was hearing a case involving oil well fracking. Some guy that drives an old van has been putting signs in our yard and around the neighborhood for the past week. I tried to take them down before Weldon could see them. If he had seen them, there's no telling what he might have done."

"Do you still have any of the signs?"

"I took one down today. It's in the garage behind some boxes."

"I'll need to get it from you," said CJ.

"You don't think..." Chris' voice trailed off.

"We need to explore all possibilities. Do you know the guy driving the van?"

"No, but I bet you do. The van has ACU student parking stickers on the back glass."

CJ searched her memory. It didn't take long. "Was it a white cargo van?"

Chris nodded.

"About 15 years old?"

"Uh-huh."

"You're right. I know it, and the owner."

CJ had suspect number one locked in her mind. It was time to press Chris for more information. "Let's get back to where we were. You took dinner to his office, then returned an hour later and told him you wanted to go for a walk."

"That's right. It had been a trying day, and we needed to get out, even though neither of us felt much like it. We walked without talking for at least twenty minutes, stopping at various homes to check their progress."

"Refresh my memory," said CJ. "Aren't you developing this subdivision?"

"I bought fifteen-hundred acres with inheritance money after Kevin was born. We built our home and set aside a little over two-hundred acres for my horses. It's a long, narrow strip of land that borders the north side of the subdivision. The rest we sat on until three years ago. With the new hospital right down the road and so many people moving to the state, I saw the need for new, upscale homes. Because I owned the land outright and because of Weldon's position, the banks were more than willing to finance the project." Chris scooted forward in her chair and became more animated.

CJ encouraged her by asking, "How are sales?"

A sparkle came into Chris' eyes. It seemed for the moment the happenings of the day were forgotten. "Couldn't be better. The construction company I started is building as fast as we can. From here on out, everything is pure profit."

"And how is your horse business?"

Chris shrugged. "Not as good as I'd like. It's an expensive venture."

CJ thought of the initial cost and ongoing maintenance of her and David's two horses and nodded in agreement. She also suspected Chris downplayed the profits. Her horses were known for their quality and demanded top dollar.

"What did you and Judge Kraft do after you examined the homes under construction?"

"I wanted to check on the last house we completed. It's the white stone at the end of the cul-de-sac. So, we walked on. We crested the hill and came down it a way. I confronted Weldon with his violence. That's when we stopped. He stared straight ahead, looking at the house at the end of the street. He didn't answer or respond to me for a long time. Then he turned toward me. The next thing I knew, Weldon dropped to the ground, and I heard the crack of a rifle."

"Chris, I know this is difficult, but I need you to think very hard and try to remember. Did you notice anything unusual about the house?"

"Like what?"

"Anything."

"No, nothing about the house but..."

"Yes?"

"That white cargo van was parked on the side of the street, in a low spot."

Beula May squeaked out, "Oh, my Lord."

CJ remained expressionless and asked Chris, "Where were you standing in relation to Weldon?"

"I was beside him. Well, a few feet away."

"How far?"

"I don't know. Perhaps four feet."

"Facing him or facing the house?"

"I must have been facing the house and the van, but I was looking at Weldon out of the corner of my eyes."

"Did you see anyone in the van?"

She shook her head instead of answering.

"Are you sure? Think hard, it's important."

"I was looking at it, but I wasn't really seeing it. You know what I mean? At the time I was trying to keep my family from falling apart."

"And then what did you do?"

Chris hung her head again. "You may think me a horrible person, but I did nothing. I froze. There was so much blood and Weldon..."

"It's all right," said CJ. "Take a deep breath."

Tears fell in a torrent.

CJ allowed Chris to compose herself before she proceeded. "What did you do next?"

"I turned and ran. Dr. Gee's was the nearest home."

"You didn't have your cell phone with you?"

"I didn't think about it."

"What about Weldon? Did he bring his?"

"I don't know. Now that you mention it, I guess he did. He's almost always on call. But there was so much blood. So much blood."

CJ patted Chris on her knee. "That's all for now. Let's get you home."

Chris dabbed her eyes. "I need to find Kevin. He won't answer calls or respond to my texts."

CJ sent Beula Mae to thank Dr. Gee as she and Chris went outside. Chris climbed into the passenger's seat while CJ excused herself to have a last word with Beula Mae.

Out of earshot of Chris, and with the front door closed, CJ placed a hand on Beula Mae's forearm. "I need to talk to you."

"Uh-huh?"

CJ stood to her full height of six feet tall and looked down at the wide-eyed officer. "I know you're itching to tell everyone that you know who shot Judge Kraft. Right now, the only people who know about the white van are me, you, and Mrs. Kraft. For your own good, I'm asking that you keep this to yourself until we question the owner of the van. I have plenty to get a search and arrest warrant, which will happen tonight as long as the suspect doesn't get rabbit and run. I need to know I can trust you not to tell anyone what you heard, unless it's one of your supervisors. Can I count on you?"

"Sure you can," responded Beula Mae, acting offended that CJ would have to ask.

CJ gave Beula Mae one more hard look. "Do you remember Betty Ogletree?"

"Uh-huh."

"Tell me what she did."

"The sheriff caught her spreading gossip about Lieutenant Jackson and a female prisoner."

"Which turned out not to be true," added CJ. "And what happened to Betty?"

"She's working at a convenience store."

CJ nodded in agreement and concluded, "One more thing."

"Yes, Ma'am."

"Follow me to Judge Kraft's house. I need you to collect every stitch of clothing Mrs. Kraft has on. You'll need to watch her the whole time, even while she changes clothes. I'll explain to her why we have to do this."

CJ turned to David's SUV and took a step.

Despite the reprimand, Beula Mae said one more thing. "Assistant Chief Harper?"

"Yes, Beula Mae?"

"There's something I need to tell you."

"Yes?"

Beula Mae shuffled her feet as her tiny voice became even

smaller. "This may be nothing, but Mrs. Kraft left the office once while I was with her. Next to Dr. Gee's office there's a half bath. Mrs. Kraft said she needed to wash her face."

"Is that all?"

Her eyes opened even wider than usual. "They must have skimped on insulation when they built this home. I could hear her talking on her phone."

"Ahh. Could you hear what she said?"

"By the time I got my ear next to the wall she'd hung up."

"Thanks. That may be important."

CHAPTER THREE

CJ wheeled David's vehicle into the driveway of the Kraft's home and found a burgundy-colored car already parked there. Two occupants emerged. The sight of them caused CJ to whisper, "Thank you, Lord." The duo of Father Broussard, the lone Episcopal priest in Riverview, and his wife was a welcome sight. Mrs. Broussard made haste to Chris and enveloped the widow in her arms. Her husband offered an inadequate, but heartfelt, "I'm so sorry."

He turned to face his wife. "Honey, take Chris inside. I need to speak with Mrs. Harper. I won't be long."

With an arm holding her tight, Mrs. Broussard guided the widow into her home. CJ motioned for Beula Mae to follow them inside.

While the women made their way to the front door, CJ inspected the clergyman she knew only by reputation. Five foot nine, two hundred pounds, receding brown hair, bifocal glasses, clerical collar over a black shirt.

"I'm so glad you're here," said CJ.

A half nod was the clergyman's only response before he asked, "How is she?"

"About as good as we could hope for, all things considered. Dr. Gee, a new internal medicine specialist and a neighbor, gave her a mild sedative. I spent a good thirty minutes with her, going over what happened."

"Good, good. That's the part I hate most, having to ask a person to relive a traumatic event."

At that moment, CJ noticed two black SUVs stream past on the main road leading into the subdivision. Captain Crow and the FBI agents had finally arrived. Arriving late would likely escalate the senior captain's typical dark mood to pitch-black. She imagined her blood pressure rising just thinking about it.

"Well, I better be—"

A question from the priest interrupted her attempt to leave. "What can you tell me about what happened? I'm sure you understand I don't want to say or ask anything that will cause more pain."

CJ refocused and said, "I'll give you the Cliff's Notes. This is for your ears only."

The priest nodded in agreement.

"Judge Kraft died from what appears to be a single shot from a high-powered rifle. It occurred on the last street in this subdivision. Chris was with him, only a few feet away." CJ let the priest take in the sparse details then added, "It had already been a very rocky day for the entire Kraft family, especially between Kevin and Weldon."

"Ahh."

It wasn't what he said, but how the priest acknowledged CJ's words that caused her to ask, "Am I right in believing this was not the first you've heard of their domestic problems?"

"Both Weldon and Kevin have powerful wills."

"Previous violence?"

Closed eyes and a nod confirmed her suspicions.

CJ continued. "Kevin left this morning after a physical confrontation with Judge Kraft. It appears he doesn't want to be found."

"You might check with the Martins. Marty Martin was Kevin's best friend before Marty went to A&M and Kevin went to Tech. I assume they're still close buddies." He searched her gaze. "Are you thinking Kevin might be a suspect?"

"Right now all we're doing is gathering facts and information."

Not wanting to linger on speculation, CJ resumed her story of the day's activities. "You knew there was trouble between Kevin and Judge Kraft. How would you describe the relationship between Chris and her husband?"

"You place me in a tough spot. Chris confided in me about personal matters, but not before I assured her our conversation would remain private." He paused. "I've always found Chris to be open and forthright, but only if she believes the person she's speaking to is trustworthy."

Despite being on maternity leave, her conversation today with Chris Kraft was probably not her last.

CJ BROUGHT David's state-issued SUV to a stop as close to the mobile command center as she could get, which was almost a block away. The MCS was an over-sized gooseneck trailer converted into a single room bristling with maps, computer screens, communications equipment, a conference table with chairs, and a fair amount of riot gear stored in the front section. The foldout handrail was a welcome sight, and she used it to haul herself up the three steps. Once inside, she nodded a salutation to Captain Crow and the sheriff. She then shook hands with the two FBI special agents as David made introductions. He pulled over a metal folding chair for her to sit on and elevated her feet onto a second chair.

Captain Crow wasted no time. "What did you find out?"

"Long version or short?" asked CJ.

"Keep it short for now, but I want a detailed report emailed to everyone here by 5:00 a.m."

CJ dove in without hesitation. "We need a search warrant for the apartment and van of Noah Epstein. He's an ACU postgraduate student." She reached into her pocket and pulled out a piece of paper. "Texas plates, HA-5762. He lives in apartment 1245 of the Pines, which backs up to the west parking lot of the biology building. He usually leaves his van in that parking lot and cuts through the hedge to his back door."

Dressed in a dark blue suit, white shirt, and tie, the younger of the two FBI agents interrupted. "How do you know so much about this Noah Epstein guy?"

All eyes shifted to the federal agent. The looks he received were like those reserved for middle school students who asked stupid questions.

CJ answered without skipping a beat. "Noah's well known to most everyone in Riverview. He's what you might call a professional protester. It doesn't matter what the cause du jour is, you can count on him being obnoxious. At present, he's our most vocal radical environmentalist. Judge Kraft was in the middle of a fracking case and things weren't looking good for the environmental plaintiffs."

While rubbing her protruding midsection, CJ kept talking. "Mrs. Chris Kraft, the judge's widow, told me Epstein has been planting protest signs around the neighborhood, even in Judge Kraft's yard. Mrs. Kraft said she saw Epstein's van parked down the street from the site at the time of the shooting."

David interrupted. "The van left tire marks in a muddy spot. We'll be able to match the tire impressions."

CJ picked up her narration. "Mrs. Kraft also stated there were no other vehicles or people in sight."

All eyes shifted to the sheriff. He had already pulled out his cell phone.

The one-sided conversation was cryptic. "Captain, we need two warrants. One for the apartment of Noah Epstein and the other for his van that should be on the ACU campus." He recited the license plate and the address for the warrants. "Get over to Judge Hawthorn's house. For justification put something to the effect that Mrs. Kraft identified Epstein's van down the street at the time of the shooting." Muffled words came from the sheriff's phone.

"That's right, take him into custody and don't worry about telling the little snot why. Put him in an interrogation room and don't let anyone talk to him. I'll be down with Rangers and the FBI to do the interview. And coordinate with John Sylvester. If the van is on university property, have them do the search and impounding."

As the sheriff gave instructions to his captain, CJ was speaking with her boss and friend, John Sylvester, chief of the Agape Christian University Police Department.

"John, have you heard about Judge Kraft?"

"Are you kidding? Bea called me. I swear that woman knows about things before they happen."

Before he could elaborate, CJ got to the business at hand. "We have a suspect. Noah Epstein. Mrs. Kraft saw his van parked near the crime scene. It was the only vehicle on the street."

John made no comment, so CJ continued. "Captain Lewis from the S.O. is getting warrants for Epstein's apartment and van. The S.O. will take him into custody and search his apartment. If they find his van on campus, they'll be calling you to do the search."

"I changed clothes as soon as Bea called. I'm on my way to campus now."

Once all phone conversations ceased, Captain Crow prompted CJ to complete her report on the interview she had with Chris Kraft. She shifted in her chair and said, "The second thing of interest Chris said had to do with problems between Judge Kraft and their son, Kevin. The relationship between the two has been rocky for years. Today they had a blow up that resulted in violence. Nothing real serious, but Kevin bolted afterward and hasn't responded to Mrs. Kraft's attempts to contact him."

CJ took in a breath and shifted again. "Beula Mae is with Mrs. Kraft. She'll know if Chris got in touch with him. Reverend Broussard and his wife are also with Chris. He confirmed a longstanding feud between Judge Kraft and his son."

The sheriff stepped away and keyed his radio. Beula Mae responded with a negative report on locating Kevin Kraft.

At that moment, Riverview's chief of police, dressed in full camouflage, stepped into the command center.

"Sorry I'm late for the party. I've been in my tree stand all afternoon trying to get that buck that's dodged me for the last two years. What can I do?"

David caught the chief up on the pending detainment and searches. The chief looked at Sheriff Gladstone as if begging for something to sink his teeth into.

"How 'bout you send a couple of units to help Captain Lewis with the search of Epstein's apartment?"

"Also," said David, "we need to find Kevin Kraft."

"Father Broussard said he might be with Marty Martin," said CJ.

"Don't the Martins live in town?" asked David.

26

The chief answered, "Jim and Sally live on Cimarron Avenue. I'll send a unit. Where do you want Kevin when we find him?"

"Send him home," said David. "I'd like to talk to him there."

Police radio traffic increased. At the same time, the sheriff's cell phone rang. The upshot of the call and radio chatter was that the search of the woods behind the white stone house proved to be a bust. The sheriff directed his sergeant to tell his patrolmen to maintain the perimeter.

After this second flurry of activity, Captain Crow turned to CJ. "Anything else about Chris Kraft?"

"There is one more thing. I asked why she didn't call for help instead of running to the nearest home. Mrs. Kraft had her cell phone with her. Her husband likely had his too. She broke down crying when I asked her why she didn't call."

David spoke up. "That means either Mrs. Kraft was in such a state of shock that she didn't remember having her cell phone on her, or she didn't want to use it. It could be she wanted the shooter to have time to get away."

The senior FBI agent spoke next. "I'll get the phone records."

"No need," said CJ. "Her phone is in David's SUV in an evidence bag." She shrugged. "Sorry, a contraction distracted me and I forget to bring it in with me."

"Anything else?" asked Captain Crow.

"Beula Mae heard Chris make a phone call from inside the bathroom of Dr. Gee's house."

Captain Crow turned to David. "Get the phone. I want full financial records on Judge Kraft, Mrs. Kraft, Kevin Kraft, and that Epstein character. Also, background reports, and I mean complete, down to the last detail. Blake Cruz will be here at first light. He'll be your direct supervisor."

Captain Crow then turned to CJ. "After you email your report, you're off the case."

CJ stiffened, "But—"

"But nothing. Look at your ankles and feet. You had to catch your breath after climbing three steps. I'll not be responsible for anything going wrong. You're already on maternity leave from ACU, and now you're on leave with me." He cleared his throat. "After you email that report."

The Ranger captain turned to David. "There are plenty of state troopers in the area. Get one of them to take CJ home."

CJ stood, spun, and made as hasty of a retreat from the trailer as she could. David exited before her and offered to assist her down the stairs. With a wave of her hand, she communicated his help was neither needed nor appreciated. He radioed for a trooper to report to the command center.

The state forensic team arrived and took David away from her. Alone, she stood outside the mobile command center. Kicking a rock didn't make her feel any better.

CHAPTER FOUR

S till sulking about her dismissal from the scene, CJ issued a single word of thanks to the state trooper who ferried her home. After an obligatory pat on the head to Sandy, her shepherd-mix dog, she mumbled a one-sided conversation with herself as she walked from the driveway, past the swimming pool, and onto the back porch.

"Kicked to the curb. That's what high-and-mighty, big shot Texas Ranger Captain Crow did to me. First, he tells me to drop everything to come help him, and then he says, 'Hit the trail, fatso.' He's lucky I didn't give him an extra-large piece of my mind. And that husband of mine; you'd think he might have said something. But no, not a word. When he gets home, he and I are going to have a long talk. On second thought, it will be a short talk. I know just what I'll tell him. 'Grab a blanket and hit the couch.'"

Laughter floated from the living room as CJ stepped through the back door. She took the time to go to her bedroom and secure her five-shot .38 Special. Returning, she found the living room furniture rearranged in a circle. Little Davey, an eighteen-month-old, was being chased from couch to chair, to loveseat, to recliners, to another chair and back to the couch.

"Hey, Miss CJ, I didn't hear you come in. Is Mr. David with you?"

Like her son's, the nineteen-year-old college student's carrot-colored hair could use a brush. Both were permanent house guests who held the status of quasi-adopted.

CJ wagged her head to show a negative response and asked, "Another game of the good knight versus the evil queen?"

"Davey the Defender is about to turn the tables on the evil queen and send her to a faraway land."

On cue, Davey turned and grabbed one of Nancy's thin legs. Both went to the carpet. The sight and sounds of mother and child laughing and rolling on the floor had a transforming effect. Thoughts of the brutality she witnessed earlier in the day faded when Davey the Defender pinned his mother to the carpet. CJ's world, right this minute, turned small and safe and filled with laughter.

Davey rose from his conquest and ran to where CJ stood. He grabbed a leg and hugged with all his might. CJ placed a hand on his mop of red curls and whispered a short blessing.

He looked up with eyes wide and outstretched arms.

"Come sit beside me on the couch and tell me all about it," said CJ. She kicked off her shoes and allowed them to fall where they may.

Nancy chimed in. "After you visit for a few minutes, it's bedtime for you, young man."

Nancy brought the room back to order as little Davey chattered, and CJ listened with rapt attention, her feet elevated on an ottoman. Nancy made her way to where the duo sat and pushed a thumb into a swollen ankle. She said nothing, but lifted her eyebrows in displeasure.

It took a while, but Davey ran out of words and yawned.

Nancy met his protest about going to bed with a hard stare. It was enough to inform him it was time to read. Defeated for the first time today, Davey the Defender shuffled off with his bottom lip pushed out. Nancy guided him with gentle pressure on the back of his head and asked, "What story do you want to read tonight?"

"Anks-iving," replied Davey. Next to wrestling, following along with pictures as someone read to him was Davey's favorite pastime.

"Thanksgiving," said CJ. *Out of the mouths of babes...*

An indeterminate amount of time passed as CJ allowed the peace of her and David's home to surround her like a warm blanket. She willed herself to recite a familiar list of things she was thankful for. Without thinking, she rubbed the mound where a flat torso had been eight months prior. Her words of comfort to their son ended when Nancy rejoined her.

"Davey didn't last long." She plopped into a chair. "Will Mr. David come home soon?"

"There's so much going on right now. I doubt I'll see him until tomorrow afternoon at the earliest."

"Aunt Bea called and told me you might not be home tonight. I'm glad you got off your feet."

"I didn't have a choice. They put me out to pasture."

"Good. Are you hungry?"

"Did Bea send something home with you?"

"My knees buckled under the weight of what she sent. We're set for several days with Thanksgiving leftovers. How about a full plate?"

"It's too late for that. Any pie?" asked CJ.

"There's pumpkin, pecan, apple, chess or sweet potato."

CJ wrinkled her brow in concentration as she weighed the choices against her physical condition. "I can justify a small slice of sweet potato pie more than the others."

Nancy rose from her chair. "Whipped cream on top? There's a container of Lite Cool Whip."

CJ threw caution to the wind. "Why not? Thanksgiving only comes once a year and Lord knows I've walked enough today. And while you're at it, could you see if there's any coffee left from this morning? If there is, put it in a mug and microwave it."

Nancy returned with a full plate of turkey and trimmings for herself and CJ's modest slice of pie. "Davey went to sleep before I could turn the third page."

"You wore him down."

"He had a very full day. Aunt Bea went into full Christmas mode after you and Mr. David left. For three hours she had everyone help bring boxes out of storage."

"Bea loves to celebrate holidays."

Nancy waved her fork and talked between bites. "This goes way beyond celebration. I think she might be diagnosable."

While CJ examined the crumbs on her plate, Nancy asked, "It's a little late to be drinking coffee, isn't it?"

"I have reports to write."

"You need sleep more than homework."

"Don't worry. I'll have plenty of time to sleep since they kicked me off the case."

"Good."

CJ bristled. "That's twice you've said 'good.' Are you against me, too? This is the most important case I've ever been a part of, and they pulled the rug out from under me. It's like they banished me to a sanitarium."

Nancy countered by retrieving her cell phone and snapping a photo of CJ's swollen ankles and feet.

"What are you doing?"

"I'm making sure you don't do anything to harm yourself or the baby. If you don't want me to send Dr. Norquist a text with this photo attached, you'll follow her instructions. You need to watch what you eat, keep your feet elevated as much as possible, and not get into stressful situations. If you hadn't talked her out of it, you'd be on full bed rest right now."

"This is blackmail," said CJ.

Nancy grinned. "Admit it, Miss CJ, I have you over a barrel, and it's for your own good."

CJ let out a huff. "I know everyone is right to keep me away from work, but a case like this only comes along once in a lifetime." She shrugged. "Oh well, I helped David get the ball rolling on the investigation. That will have to be enough."

Nancy stuffed in another bite of gravy-covered dressing, chewed, and swallowed. "This is so good." She stabbed a bite of turkey with her fork. "Do you think they'll find the killer soon?"

"I hope so. I'd like to put everything dealing with law enforcement behind me and focus on my Christmas baby."

"But you're not due until early January."

"There's no way this baby is going to wait until next year." CJ put her feet on the floor and scooted to the edge of the sofa. "Give me a hand up. I need to get to work on those reports."

THE SLAM of the back door caused CJ to crack open the lone eyelid that wasn't buried in a pillow. She raised her head, moaned, and glanced at the digital clock on David's nightstand. Only two hours had passed since she slid between the sheets. She'd met the 5:00 a.m. deadline, but only by fifteen minutes. The laptop lay on the unruffled side of the bed.

Unlike her husband, who could go two full days with only an occasional nap, sleep deprivation left CJ muddle-minded and in ill humor. She'd pay for the all-nighter, and so might anyone who interrupted her overdue slumber.

On this November morning, it was David who steered into dangerous waters. Grumblings mixed with low growls as he stomped into the bedroom on his way to the master closet. Boots fell heavy.

"Can you make any more noise?" shouted CJ.

"Go back to sleep," came the command from the closet.

"How can I with you making that racket?"

The jangle of a belt buckle and the rustle of pants sliding off first one leg then the other mixed with muted mumbles. The clatter of items hitting a hard surface and the slamming of a drawer preceded David's exit from the closet. CJ felt the baby jump when the bathroom door rattled in its frame. The pounding of the water in the shower lulled her into a light sleep. She jerked awake when a can hit the tile floor followed by a sharp expletive.

"I might as well be on a New York subway." CJ heaved herself to her left side, facing an east window. The angle of the sun was perfect for a shaft of light to slip through a crack in the curtains. Her eyelids slammed shut, but not for long. Too tired to get up, she flopped back into her original position on her right side and tried to go back to sleep. No luck. Her mind and her body were on different wavelengths.

Thoughts of the previous day flooded in. One memory rose up and flashed before her. She was standing at the crime scene, looking at the white stone house at the end of the cul-de-sac. Bright sunlight reflected off one window above the front porch. She didn't notice it at the time, but the other windows looked different. Only the one window reflected the sun with intensity, like the beacon in a lighthouse.

David emerged from his shower and shave wearing a bathrobe and a scowl. Before he could turn into the oversized closet to dress, CJ stopped him. "Come here. I remembered something from the crime scene."

He shuffled to the edge of the bed but did not sit. "What?"

For a split second CJ considered confronting her husband about the harsh tone of his one syllable question. For once, her better judgment overrode her desire to have her say.

"You need to go back to the white stone house at the end of the street," she said in an even tone. "Check out the first window on the left above the front porch."

He sat on the bed and swiveled to look at her. "I did. They were all latched."

CJ nodded. "Look at it from the outside. The sun's reflection flashed bright from that window but not the others. Something's different about it."

David's gaze drifted to the door of their bedroom, looking but not seeing. His gaze shifted back to her. "If it turns out to be what I think it is, you just saved an innocent man from being indicted for murder."

CJ extended a hand toward her husband. "What do you mean?"

"After you went home last night, things got testy. The chief played the jurisdiction card and told Sheriff Gladstone the city police would search Epstein's apartment and arrest him. It turned out that the van wasn't on university property so ACU police had no say, either. It was all done by the city cops. They found a spent .308 casing in the van. The chief arrested Epstein himself, called the press, and set up a news conference. Of course Epstein lawyered up. I never got the chance to interview him. The only thing he's saying now is how he's going to sue the City of Riverview for all it's worth."

"No wonder you came in mad. Why didn't Chief Satterfield wait until we had more evidence? The trajectory report from forensics will show where the shot came from."

David lifted a shoulder and let it fall. "Headlines, I guess. Things haven't been going well for him. The city council and the mayor are making noises. They want someone new. If this thing blows like I think it will, the chief may not be in Riverview much longer."

David rose from the bed. "I need to get going. I'll look at the window and send you a text of what I find."

Four hours later, CJ awoke and checked her phone. Nothing. As she placed it back on her nightstand, a text alert sounded. *Wanted to let you sleep. Screen on window cut from frame. Small dent on the bottom of the metal frame. Lab boys testing. Good catch.*

CJ put together the pieces. The shooter gained entry into the house, probably through the garage door. They're simple to open, even for a novice thief. He then went upstairs, raised the window, and cut the screen out along the frame. Then, he rested the rifle's barrel or stock on the metal frame, waited for the moment Judge Kraft stopped, and took the shot. The rifle bucked up and slammed down against the frame, producing a dent in the aluminum.

CJ grabbed her phone and called her husband. "Whoever shot Judge Kraft wasn't a pro, was he?"

"Probably not. A professional would have steadied his aim with either a fold down bi-pod or something soft to place under the barrel. It's the mark of an amateur to rest it on the window frame."

CJ had one more thing to say. "It makes no sense that Noah Epstein would leave his van in plain sight while he went into the home and took the shot."

"Beauty and brains. That's why I love you. Get some more rest."

A loud yawn came out before CJ could stop it. As David chuckled, she formed her next question. "How do you explain the shell casing in Epstein's van?"

"The suspicious side of me wonders if someone planted it there. Or it could be as simple as he picked it up some time ago while walking through the woods. With him not talking, it's hard to find out."

"Before you go," said CJ. "What's the latest on Kevin Kraft? Have they found him?"

"Kevin and his best friend, Marty Martin, went to a deer lease near Uvalde. They're on their way back. Highway patrol officers are monitoring him. I'll interview him as soon as he's home." David's next words came out in a rush. "Gotta' go."

Settling back into a fluffy pillow, CJ abandoned hope of more sleep. Even though Noah Epstein was in the vicinity, he seemed an unlikely killer. That left her to wonder who shot Judge Kraft, and why? Could Kevin Kraft have killed his father in a fit of rage? What about Chris Kraft? Would the killer be as elusive as the buck sought by Riverview's chief of police?

Too many questions and CJ needed to stay in bed. "How can I help David?" she whispered to the empty room.

CHAPTER FIVE

David waited for Kevin in the driveway of the Kraft home. "I want you to know how sorry I am about your dad. Believe me, I know what you're going through."

Kevin nodded. "I need to let Mom know I'm home. Do you want to come in?"

"I'll wait here for you. Your mom knows I'm here and that I need to talk to you."

Tentative steps took Kevin to the front door and into the family home. He didn't tarry long inside. When he returned, his cheeks were pink and his eyes red-rimmed.

"This is a hard time for you, and I understand how you feel, but I need to ask you some questions," said David.

Kevin lashed out, "How could you know how I feel?"

David squared his shoulders. "The summer before my senior year of high school, I came home to find my mother's body in our home. I was out having fun with my best friend when the killer broke in."

Surprise crossed Kevin's countenance. After a long pause, he asked, "How did you deal with it?"

"A lot worse than you're going to. Your mom has already arranged for you to talk to someone on Monday morning."

"A shrink?"

"Not a psychiatrist, but she is a qualified psychologist. It's Bea Stargate."

"Aunt Bea?"

"You know her?"

Kevin nodded and even cracked a weak smile. "When I was in middle school, our life-science teacher was fresh out of college. She knew her stuff, but was a mousy thing with zero self-confidence. She was supposed to teach us about the birds and the bees but was so embarrassed she broke out in hives before she could get past the introduction. The principal had mercy on her and called Aunt Bea to come to her rescue."

Bea Stargate, their neighbor and a professor at ACU, had a real knack with young people. Most people didn't know the homespun woman with a penchant for deer hunting had her Ph.D. David had to ask, "Did you learn about the facts of life?"

"I learned more in fifty minutes than I did in all my high school classes combined. Along the way, she had us laughing so hard I'm surprised we didn't wet our pants. I'll never forget her."

Kevin's smile made David think. The unusual thing about grief is that laughter has a way of kicking in the door when you think all you can do is wail, scream, or curse. Kevin learned only a few hours ago that his father was dead. David needed sleep. Yet, there they sat, a sophomore in college and a veteran lawman, smiling at each other as if nothing had happened, at least for a few fleeting moments.

Like an ebbing tide, grief flowed back into Kevin. David noticed the change and got down to business. He followed the pattern CJ used and asked Kevin to recount Thanksgiving Day, beginning with when he first awoke. All descriptions of the day's events matched what Kevin's mother told CJ. He needed to press harder.

"I see the bruise on your face. Your dad tagged you pretty good," said David.

Kevin shrugged.

"How did that make you feel?"

"How do you think? I was mad. I'd had enough and needed to get away."

"So you went to see Marty?"

"Yeah, it wasn't the first time I'd been to Marty's house after Dad got rough with me."

"How long were you at Marty's?"

"His mom is one of those women that thinks food will cure anything. She insisted I have the Thanksgiving meal with them. While we were eating, Marty's dad suggested we go to the deer lease and allow things to calm down."

"Near Uvalde?" asked David, even though he already knew the answer.

Kevin nodded. "It's so far out in the sticks I doubt they'll ever have cell phone reception."

"Let's not get ahead of ourselves," said David. "Tell me what you did after you and Marty made plans to go to the deer lease."

"I headed home while Marty packed his gear and his mom filled a cooler with leftovers."

"I take it Marty brought along his rifle?"

"Sure."

"What does he shoot?"

"It's an off-the-rack Marlin 30-30 with a six-power scope. Not much to look at but he does all right if it's not a long shot."

"And you came home alone to pick up your rifle and hunting gear? Marty didn't come with you?"

"I knew Dad would tell me I couldn't go, and there'd be another fight. I didn't want Marty in the middle of our mess."

"What time did you get home?"

"I don't know. Around four-fifteen, I guess. Nobody was home when I got here. I didn't waste time. I grabbed what I needed and left."

"What rifle did you take?"

"I have a .308. It's a SAKO A7."

"Nice rifle."

"Dad bought it for me for my fifteenth birthday. He took me to Alaska to break it in on caribou."

"Did you and your dad hunt a lot when you were growing up?"

A look that blended distant fond memories and recent regrets crossed Kevin's countenance. "Dad and I didn't agree on much, but when we went hunting or fishing, we had an unspoken agreement to not talk about anything else."

"Did you and your dad do something together regularly?"

"Even with his schedule, we managed to get out together at least once a month until I was going into my junior year of high school." Kevin cast his gaze downward. "He kept offering, but I begged off after he told me I had to go to Tech. I was so mad at him for not letting me go to A&M that I didn't want to be around him."

Kevin's chin quivered. David needed more information on recent events, so he steered the questions away from past unpleasant times. "And you left the house yesterday afternoon, about four-thirty?"

An affirmative nod.

"You didn't go looking for your parents to tell them where you were going?"

"I didn't care. I guess I wanted to hurt both of them. All I wanted was to get out of town as fast as I could."

David made a mental note to come back to this point.

Kevin went on without prompting. "I went back to Marty's. We loaded his gear and hit the road."

"Did you make any stops along the way?"

"Only to take a leak on some county road in the middle of nowhere."

"No stops for gasoline?"

"I drive a Prius. I filled up the day before Thanksgiving."

"What did you do at the deer lease?"

"It was way after dark when we arrived. No electricity. We built a fire and stayed up talking for a couple of hours."

"What did you talk about?" asked David.

Marty shrugged. "The usual—what was going on with the people we graduated with, girls we met at college, how our classes were going, how much I hated Tech and how much Marty loved A&M. We also talked about going to Mexico."

"Did you talk about the fight you had with your dad?"

Kevin shook his head left and then right. "Marty's real good about taking my mind off what goes on when I come home."

Again, David made a mental note to delve deeper into the Kraft's home life.

"And today?"

"We didn't want to hunt before we sighted in our rifles. Neither of us had fired a shot since last year when we went over Christmas break. A game warden found us while Marty was finishing his shots. He told us something bad had happened to Dad, and we needed to get back to Riverview. I got stopped twice for speeding by state troopers but they just told me to slow down when they found out who I was and why I was driving so fast."

David backtracked to something that caught his ear. "Why did you and Marty want to go to Mexico?"

"Marty and I made a bucket list of things we want to do before we get married and settle down. One of them involves tequila shots and Mexican señoritas." He shook his head and looked at the ground. "Who were we kidding? We'd have backed out. We always do."

David was more interested in Kevin's reaction to the next question than he was in the answer. "Is your rifle in your car?"

"Yes." Kevin's response was matter of fact.

"Did you clean it before you packed it?"

"I haven't taken it out of its case since I sighted it in this morning."

"How many shots did you fire?"

"Three. The pattern was all in the ten ring at a hundred-and-fifty yards."

"Were you prone or on a bench?"

"Prone. My front stock has an adjustable swivel bi-pod."

"What scope do you have on your .308?"

"It's a Nightforce ATACR, 5 to 25 by 56."

David nodded in approval. "That's a lot of gun and scope for shooting whitetail."

"Dad and I went after moose and elk before I quit hunting with him. For whitetail I only make neck shots. Unless he's standing just right, you're bound to ruin a shoulder."

David watched for another reaction. "I need to take your rifle with me."

Kevin didn't flinch. "I figured you would."

David tilted his head. "Why is that?"

"I had a lot of time to think on the ride home. I had motive, means, and the opportunity to kill my father."

"Did you?"

"No." Kevin paused. "Do you think I did?"

Normally David would have dodged this question, but fatigue clawed at his mind like a cat trapped in a closet. He responded after heaving a sigh. "No, Kevin. I don't believe you did."

"If you don't mind me asking, why don't you think I killed my dad?"

"Several things, but I'll give you two. To begin with, you and Marty always back out of going to Mexico."

"What does that have to do with anything?"

"You may talk a good game when it's you and Marty, but there are boundaries you won't cross."

"I guess we need to take Mexico off our bucket list," replied Kevin. "And the second?"

"You loved your dad too much to kill him. There's something that happens between a father and son when they spend time together hunting and fishing."

Tears formed in the corner of Kevin's eyes. He blinked to keep them from falling. "Those hunting and fishing trips are all I thought about today."

A hush fell over the driveway. David led the way as the two stepped toward the trunk of Kevin's car.

"One more thing," said David. "How do you get along with your mother?"

A slight twitch caused a muscle in Kevin's right cheek to move. "All right, I guess. She's busy with her horses and building out this subdivision."

"Did she and your dad have problems?" asked David.

Kevin kicked a pebble off the driveway. He then paused several more long seconds before answering David's question with one of his own.

"Mr. Harper, how messed up were you when you found your mother?"

David's head jerked back. "That's a strange question, Kevin. Why would you ask me that?"

Kevin pushed on. "I bet it left you pretty screwed up, didn't it?"

"It did, but—"

Kevin didn't wait for David to complete his thought.

"What do you think it would do to a twelve-year-old if he walked in on his mom with someone other than his dad? And not only that, but he knew for a fact his mom was still carrying on with the same guy?"

David knew he should ask who the man was, but something stopped him. Instead of causing more grief, David extended his hand. When Kevin shook it, David drew him into his chest and wrapped his free arm around him. Kevin's heaving sobs took several minutes to subside.

This left David with big unanswered questions. Who was Chris Kraft's paramour, and was that person, or the two of them, responsible for the judge's death?

CHAPTER SIX

The setting sun displayed a kaleidoscope of colors before it grew tired and slipped below the horizon. The day had crept by in slow motion for CJ. She whiled away the hours reading, watching a plotless movie, looking at her swollen feet, and, most of all, thinking.

For viewing the sunset, she moved to the front porch swing. From over the hill, she heard the final construction noises come from her father-in-law's half-built home. CJ turned sideways to prop her feet in the swing and used a walking stick to nudge it into motion. Sandy, her K9 companion, was the only one privy to her complaints of boredom. When the dog turned and went to the other end of the porch to lay down, she realized even her faithful friend had her limits about complaints.

The black SUV heading down the gravel lane connecting their home to the farm-to-market road caused CJ to change her conversation with her dog. "Sandy, there's Daddy."

Sandy jerked upright and sniffed the air. Then, as if shot from a cannon, she launched herself in a full sprint toward the oncoming vehicle, excited yelps paving her way. Like a motorcycle policeman giving a dignitary an escort into town, Sandy ushered David to the rear of their ranch-style home.

By the time CJ made her way to the back porch, David was out of his SUV, giving Sandy a lackluster rub on her ears. She met her husband on the back porch and presented him with a hug, a quick kiss, and a sideways glance. "You look like you could sleep for a month."

"It's been long days and nights. Can you make me a turkey sandwich?"

"Wouldn't you prefer a hot meal? We have plenty, and it won't take but a few minutes to pull out the leftovers."

"Just throw some turkey between two slices of bread."

Once inside, David hefted himself on a barstool, rested his chin in the cupped palms of his hands, and massaged his temples. "I know you're off the case, but could you do a little phone investigating for me?"

CJ had her back turned to him pulling a mélange of sandwich makings from the refrigerator and placing them on the counter. "What do you need?"

"I spoke with Kevin Kraft today. He told me his mom has been having an affair with someone since he was twelve. He's so torn up about what happened to his dad, I didn't press him for details. The last thing I asked him was if he heard a shot while he loaded his car to leave town. He said he did. When it dawned on him that he heard the shot that killed his father, it pretty well unhinged him. While hatred boiled over in him, his dad was dying."

CJ hung her head. "That's horrible."

"I shouldn't have asked about the gunshot. It was an afterthought, and a cruel thing to do. I didn't think it through." David sucked in a breath and opened his eyes. "I figured you and Bea could find out about his mom easy enough."

CJ turned toward her husband and tented her hands on

her hips. "Do you think all Bea Stargate and I have to do is sit around gossiping?" She turned her back while continuing the lecture on gossip. David's sandwich grew from meat and bread into a three-course meal stuffed between slices of whole wheat. Only when she turned to present her master-piece did she realize David had left the room.

She left the sandwich on a plate and went to the bedroom. In the army, David learned the art of sleep-when-you-can. Today, he'd taken the skill to a new level. Fully attired, boots and all, she found him stretched out on their king-size bed. Other than prying off his boots, CJ left him alone.

The sound of a second vehicle caught her attention. In no time, Nancy filed into the kitchen, carrying a sleeping toddler. "I'll put him in his bed," she whispered. CJ allowed the duo to pass, but not before she gave the child a kiss on the head.

Nancy returned and launched into explaining her day's activities. "We went to Aunt Bea's and helped put up more decorations. I'm suffering from sensory overload. She's moved from having the spirit of Christmas to full-blown crazy. She even hired a decorator to customize the inside of that overgrown mansion. To top it off, she flew in a Holly-wood prop guy for the exterior and special effects inside and out. While we were there, a truck arrived with two opening-night-of-a movie spotlights. They put one in the front yard and the other is going somewhere in town. Doesn't that beat anything you've ever heard?"

"I guess that's what ultra-rich people do to make Christmas special."

"I wouldn't have believed it if I hadn't seen it with my own eyes. You'll see after dark. It's one of those spotlights like you see in old movies about the Germans bombing London in World War II. I bet it's twenty feet in diameter. They're supposed to test it tonight."

"Why in the world would Bea want such a big spotlight?"

"She said it's going to be the crowning touch on her Christmas Eve celebration. She's hiring an advertising airplane to haul a banner of Santa's sleigh full of toys and eight reindeer. The spotlight is to illuminate Santa in the night sky as he goes about making his deliveries."

CJ couldn't help but smile. "It'll be something people talk about for a long time."

Nancy pushed her lips to one side. "I wonder if Christmas crazy is a diagnosable mental disease?"

The excited teen spied David's abandoned meal. "Now that's what I call a sandwich. Who's it for?"

CJ shrugged. "Whoever wants it. I made it for David, but he flamed out."

Before CJ could finish her sentence, Nancy took a huge bite and groaned in ecstasy. With mouth full, she mumbled, "Mind if I take this with me? I need to study."

"You're studying over Thanksgiving? I thought you'd take a break."

Nancy chewed and swallowed before she tried to answer. "I need to stay ahead. Finals are coming up and I never know when Doc Steele will need me on a farm call."

CJ glanced toward the hallway leading to Nancy's bedroom. "Finals slipped my mind. How are things looking for the semester?"

The question was a waste of words. CJ knew Nancy didn't make B's.

Nancy backtracked from the hall to the kitchen. "I'm doing okay." She pulled out a barstool and sat down. "How is Mr. David's investigation into Judge Kraft's murder going?"

"To tell the truth, I'm in the dark. Since they placed me on maternity house arrest, I'm not in the loop."

Nancy asked, "Nothing? Mr. David always tells you something."

"Well, not much. Before he went into hibernation, he said he spoke with Kevin Kraft today. Based on that conversation, he gave me an assignment. I should be able to find out what he needs to know without leaving the house."

Nancy took a more reasonably sized bite, pushed it to one side of her mouth and asked, "Can you tell me what you need to find out?"

CJ hesitated. Even though Nancy was an adult with a child to care for, it was difficult to see her as more than a college student. Thin as a fence post, with tendrils of red hair framing a cute face and a pixie nose, she appeared younger than her nineteen years. That impression dissipated once she spoke. Nancy could hold her own with her professors, let alone anyone else.

"Well? Can you tell me or not?" asked Nancy, after CJ's silence went on too long.

"It involves some tawdry gossip about Judge Kraft's wife. Are you sure you want to know what I need to find out?"

Nancy kept a straight face. "Do you mean the affair between Mrs. Kraft and Gil Wright?"

All CJ could do was squeak out, "Uh-huh."

Nancy continued as if she were reciting a chemistry formula instead of the details of peccadilloes. "Don't look so surprised. When I'm making farm calls with Doc Steele, I hear a lot of things I shouldn't. You wouldn't believe what the ranchers talk about. Believe me, the beauticians and customers at Curl-Up-and-Dye have nothing on those old coots. I keep my ears open and my mouth shut. What those men talk about is enough to straighten my hair."

CJ came to her senses. "Did you say Gil Wright, our farrier?"

"Yep. He puts shoes on half the horses in the county. By the way, you need to call him. Your horse is due and David's horse has a split hoof that needs tending."

"And you say that Gil Wright and Chris Kraft are an item?"

Nancy corrected her. "I'm not saying I know anything for certain. What I am saying is, according to local ranch gossip, those two have been using hay for more than feeding horses."

Nancy finished her sandwich and left to absorb who-knows-what kind of knowledge. CJ decided the back porch swing would be a better spot for serious thinking. She hoisted her puffy ankles and swollen feet to the swing, remembering too late that she left her push stick out front.

She thought about how much work David faced in researching financial reports and doing background checks. Yes, it was important, but it would consume his time. That meant he needed her help to do some interviews before the trail grew cold. "I'll take it easy," she whispered. "But if Captain Crow thinks he can sideline me from this case, he needs to think again."

She reached for her phone.

CHAPTER SEVEN

T he Saturday morning following Thanksgiving began with clouds as gray and thick as CJ's mood. David had grabbed a couple hours' sleep and worked again until 2:00 a.m. Three more hours of slumber left him still worn thin, but that's when his day began. Gathering financial records and detailed personal information on Judge Kraft and the growing list of suspects proved to be a source of major frustration with banks and businesses closed. He surfaced from his home office in a foul mood and went back to bed.

CJ took stock of her own frayed emotions and found the source to be rooted in her confinement. She'd always enjoyed near-perfect heath and her previous pregnancy didn't last long enough for the symptoms of hypertension to manifest. She looked down at her puffy feet and grunted out a blast of disgust. "Another month to go and I look like a bowl of bread dough allowed to rise too long. My wedding band doesn't fit, and I'm wearing ugly diabetic shoes and support hose. I retain water if I even look at a salt shaker."

The ringing of David's phone brought her feet down from the living room couch where she'd spent the night. Moans came out as she reached for the noisy device on the coffee table. The caller ID told her Texas Ranger Blake Cruz wanted to speak to her husband.

"Hey, Blake. He's still asleep, but I'll be glad to wake him."

Blake chuckled. "You sound too willing."

"When he got in late yesterday afternoon, he only slept two hours before he tried to start on background research. He was grouchy as a centipede with a blister on every toe. I made him take Tylenol at 2:00 a.m. They worked, but his snoring drove me to the couch."

"Let him sleep. I wanted to talk to you about the judge's wife, Chris. You seem to know her better than David. What's your impression of her?"

CJ didn't want to admit to Blake that part of the reason she didn't sleep well was because she couldn't get Chris Kraft out of her late-night pondering. "She's pretty, smart and savvy in business."

"That much I got from the Internet. What about her relationship with the judge?"

"Not great. I found out something that could be important. I would have told David last night, but he went down for the count and woke up grumpy. Anyway, it seems the local farrier, Gil Wright, has been in a relationship with Chris for years. At least that's the rumor going around."

"What's your source?"

"Nancy. She goes on farm calls with Doc Steele, and retains everything she hears. It seems to be common knowledge."

"Do you know where this guy lives?"

"Somewhere west of town."

"I'll try to pay Mr. Wright a visit today."

"I spoke with him last night," said CJ. "He's coming out next week to shoe our horses."

"When?"

"Monday morning."

The phone went quiet for a few seconds. "You and David know him. Why don't you two talk to him?" He paused. "That is, if you can get out of bed. The way David talks, you shouldn't be doing much of anything."

"A talk with Gil won't hurt me."

CJ was still holding the phone when Blake said good-bye and David entered the room. Flopping in a chair, he dug crusties out of the corner of an eye.

"Who was that?"

"Blake."

"Is that my phone?"

She nodded. "I took it so you could sleep. He wants us to interview Gil Wright when he comes out Monday morning to shoe our horses."

David yawned without covering his mouth. "Why?"

"Gil is Chris Kraft's lover."

"Says who?"

"Nancy, and half the ranchers in the county."

David's scowl told her the news didn't sit well with him. "When did you know this?"

"Last night."

"Why didn't you tell me?"

CJ stood and walked toward the kitchen. "Because you told me I looked fat."

"I did not," said David with words that came out like the crack of a whip.

She turned to face him, lowered her chin, and stared. "Comparing my ankles to bratwurst wasn't the kindest thing you've ever said to me."

David looked out the window. "Did I say that?"

She nodded. "I wrote it off to lack of sleep, but you'll get the couch if it happens again."

Nancy's voice came from the hall. "Let me know when it's safe."

"Come in," said CJ. "I'm leaving."

"Where are you going?" asked David, in the same snappy tone.

"To our bedroom and then to the other side of the hill. I want to look at the progress your dad and Alice are making on their new home."

"Be careful and watch where you step. Better yet, stay in the truck."

Anything else David might have said bounced off the bedroom door as it closed. CJ had heard enough.

After making the bed, she settled in the recliner she used for reading and quiet times. A spiral notebook served as a catch-all for random thoughts, the occasional cartoon she might draw, ideas for birthday and holiday gifts, and anything else that crossed her mind. Today, she used it to jot down the names of suspects and motives. They came in no particular order and she understood before ink met paper that most, if not all, would lead to nothing. Investigations worked that way.

The first name was that of Chris Kraft, the judge's widow. Probably not the killer, but she might be an accomplice. The local rumor mill found her guilty of infidelity with Gil Wright. She wrote his name on a separate line and drew an arrow back to Chris. The rumors would need to be verified. She concentrated on Gil for a few minutes and wrote a dollar sign. A more comfortable financial future than shoeing horses was an excellent motive for latching on to a rich widow.

Next, she scratched down the name of Chris' son, Kevin. Beside his name she wrote RAGE. Again, she allowed her mind to go wherever it wanted. Under Kevin's name, she wrote Marty Martin, Kevin's best friend. She drew another line with an arrow between them. She remembered how much Kevin wanted to change schools. It was a stretch, but she'd been to crime scenes where people died for lesser reasons.

Noah Epstein's name went on the page next. Try as she may, she couldn't see him murdering the judge, even though Chief Satterfield had him in jail for it. The press wasted no time in finding him guilty, too. Noah was a pain in the neck, but he was a self-proclaimed pacifist. He impressed her as the type of person who found enchantment with the sound of his own voice. He loved to wind people up. Epstein's joy came in arguing for causes, and it didn't matter which one.

"Four suspects so far," said CJ to herself in a whisper. "There's bound to be more before we find the killer. After all, Judge Kraft put a lot of men and women in prison." Then it occurred to her why Blake wanted her and David to interview Gil Wright. It was going to take a tremendous amount of manpower to sift through the stacks of court cases the judge presided over. Someone needed to eliminate people who thought the judge gave them a raw deal.

On the next line, she wrote CRIMINAL CASES. After another minute of thinking, she added, CIVIL CASES. Perhaps there was someone, or multiple people, that believed the judge had been less than even-handed in passing judgment. She started a list of the things that could upset people enough to kill. It didn't take long before the task overwhelmed her. After writing CHILD CUSTODY, she abandoned the list.

"There could be hundreds of people with a motive." She closed the notebook and put it back in a drawer. "Time to get outside and clear my mind."

It always amazed CJ how much David was a carbon copy of his father in looks and mannerisms. The gray around his father's temples, and being three inches shorter than David's 6' 3", made identification easier from a distance.

The first words out of Bob Harper's mouth showed how much father and son thought alike. "Shouldn't you be home with your feet up?"

"Bob," chided Alice, "is that any way to welcome my favorite daughter-in-law?"

As was her custom, Alice took CJ by the hand and gave it three soft pats.

"Sorry," said Bob. "I've never been a grandpa before. It's like I'm reliving what it was like in the last month before David was born." He shifted his gaze to CJ. "Any more complications?"

"Nothing serious. I'll see Dr. Norquist this coming Friday. From here on out I'll have a weekly appointment."

She didn't come to talk about swollen body parts, so CJ changed the subject. "Show me the progress."

Alice took over. "Let's start with the barn."

It always took CJ aback to see Alice Cummings-Harper wearing jeans and a tan Carhart jacket. As president of Agape Christian University, the petite, silver-haired woman dressed for success. Today, a baseball cap advertising a farm and ranch supply store hid most of her hair and added an extra touch of incongruity.

Bob took over once they reached the barn. "I took most of the design features from your barn and incorporated it into ours, with a few modifications. It has the full bathroom, so I can shower if I get too dirty working on old cars. I also added a washer and dryer. As you can see, we put in four roll-up doors running down the side. That's the biggest change I made. You never intended your barn to be used to restore old cars."

"A lot of the building materials are already in the barn," said Alice. "Bob has them arranged in the order needed for construction to proceed."

Bob rolled up all four doors. The first two bays held neat rows of roof trusses. The next two held an assortment of electrical and plumbing supplies, dry wall, cabinets, bath tubs, and what looked like a thousand boxes containing things to bring a home to life.

"What I'd expect from an engineer," said CJ. She turned to look at the wooden skeleton of the new home, laying on a gray slab. "It looks like trusses are next in line to be installed."

Bob rocked back and forth from the heels of his work boots to the balls of his feet. "Weather permitting, they'll start Monday." He looked outside at the gray clouds. "Let's hope they can. I'd like to have everything dried in before the baby comes."

Alice moved close to CJ after a damp wind almost took her hat off. "We're not in complete agreement on the flooring or paint scheme."

"I thought David and I would come to blows over paint colors. We agreed to let Bea's designer choose, and we made a pact that we would never say if we like it or not."

"It may come to that," said Alice as another stiff breeze came from the north. "Let's get inside the barn. There's something I need to ask you."

Once inside, Alice pulled her hands from her jacket pockets and breathed warm air into them. After returning them to the pockets she said, "I wanted to ask you about Noah Epstein. The press seems to believe he's responsible for Judge Kraft's murder. What do you think?"

"Not likely. Between you and me, Chief Satterfield jumped the gun in arresting him."

Alice gave a worried look at the ground. "I thought that might be the case. I had two closed-door meetings with Noah last year. He's a free-thinker and misguided in some of his ways, but I can't picture him using violence. Non-violent tactics to bring about change are more his modus operandi. Pushing and even stepping over boundaries of legality, I expect. But physical harm isn't in the profile I have of him."

"They have other suspects," said CJ. "I tried to make a list of them this morning, and had to stop. Think about how many cases Judge Kraft ruled on. Each one had a winner and a loser."

Alice raised her gaze to look at CJ. "I hadn't thought of that. I restricted my focus to Noah. The Dean of Student Affairs wants him expelled as soon as possible. I'll advise him to hold off."

CJ nodded her agreement. "If evidence shows that Noah had nothing to do with the murder, he'll be ready to file lawsuits against anyone he perceives wronged him. He'll start with Chief Satterfield and the city, but he may not stop there."

Alice gave her head a firm nod. "There's nothing to be gained by making a hasty decision and much to lose."

CJ glanced outside as mist fell. "I should get home to my growling husband."

Alice put a hand on her forearm. "We'll pray for David. I fear he'll wear himself out trying to solve this one." She squeezed. "At least you're not involved. You have a much more important assignment."

Bob joined them. "We were going to pick up construction trash, but it looks like a rain-out. Thank goodness we have the barn to keep everything dry." He looked at CJ. "Something's been nagging at me about the last big case you and David worked on."

"Tig Murphy?"

"Yeah. Is he still missing?"

CJ cast her gaze once again to the site where the new home would be. "I mentioned the case to David the day of Judge Kraft's murder. The warrant for Tig's arrest is still active, but nobody's looking for him."

"Why not? He's responsible for several deaths."

"I've asked David the same question several times. He never gives me a decent answer."

Bob shoved his hands in the pockets of his jeans. He shook his head but said nothing else.

"Do you have a theory?" asked CJ.

Bob took in an over-sized breath. "From what I know of the Rangers, they don't stop looking until they're convinced the person they're after is in jail or dead."

Bob had put into words what CJ believed to be true. Someone buried Tig Murphy in East Texas, just not in the spot David and the Rangers had looked.

CJ asked, "Why are you asking about Tig?"

"If he's still alive, he could be a suspect in killing Judge Kraft."

A slight chill ran down CJ's back and caused her to shudder. Alice must have seen it. "You need to get out of this cold, damp weather."

CJ didn't disagree, but wanted to respond to Bob before she left. "I'll talk to David about Tig Murphy again. I doubt there's a connection between him and Judge Kraft."

"Go put your feet up and have that son of mine take care of you."

"I'll tell him you said for him to do that very thing."

"Don't do that. The way you get him to do something is to tell him not to do it."

Plans rattled around in her mind as CJ drove home. She'd ask David about there being any possibility Tig Murphy might have killed the judge. Next, she thought about paying Noah Epstein a visit. On Monday she and David would talk to Gil Wright and see what long-term plans the amorous farrier might have with Chris Kraft. Based on what he said, she'd plan her next step.

CHAPTER EIGHT

Both David and CJ followed their normal routines on Monday morning by starting their day before dawn. Nancy dragged herself to the breakfast table a little after daybreak with her usual bed-head and economy of words. Downing a cup of coffee helped to oil the hinges of her jaw. "Davey didn't sleep well last night. Tummy ache. It might take a stick of dynamite to get him up this morning."

"Let's let him sleep as long as we can," said CJ. "They'll feed him at the early childhood development center."

David added, "Pack his clothes. They can change him out of his pajamas after you get there."

"I hate to do that," said Nancy. "I always feel like I'm neglecting him when I don't spend time with him in the morning."

CJ waved away the complaint. "You had all Thanksgiving break with him, and not a single farm emergency with Doc Steele."

The sound of tires on gravel caused CJ to look out the window of the breakfast nook. "Gil's here early. You two finish your breakfast. I'll go out."

"It's too early to think about food," said Nancy. "I'll get bridles on the horses."

Crowned with a baseball cap, CJ met the vintage pickup and trailer as Gil wheeled into the area near the corral. She greeted him and received a tepid response. Perhaps Gil didn't like early mornings any more than Nancy.

It wasn't long before Nancy came with CJ's horse. She made note of the girl's erect posture, determined bearing, and confident stride. Gone was the slump-shouldered teen wagging a baby on her hip, convinced she deserved nothing better than a minimum wage life laced with heavy doses of public humiliation.

The roan mare stood fourteen hands high. A snort revealed the temperature had dropped enough in the night to see breath, but no frost had formed on the roof of the barn.

Gil placed both hands on the small of his back and squared his shoulders before he moved to his trailer. He acknowledged Nancy with a nod of his head and an almost silent, "Mornin'." He donned a pair of leather chaps that covered his faded jeans, lit the propane burner under the coals in the forge on wheels, unloaded a rolling cart containing his tools and retrieved a tripod hoof stand.

"Walk her around. I need to see if anything needs correcting."

Nancy led the mare about fifteen yards away, retraced their path and retied the mare to a post. "How does she look?"

"She's a little turned in on her left front, but not much. It'll be an easy fix."

Gil moved the rolling cart and tripod stand to within arm's reach of the horse, and stroked the mare's right shoulder. He lifted her right front leg and pinned it between his knees with his back hunched over. After grabbing what looked like large metal pliers, it took Gil mere seconds to pry off the first shoe. He gave it a three-second examination and pitched it in the cart.

All the while, he never spoke a word. Nancy broke the silence. "You can't reuse the shoe?"

By this time, Gil had already reached for a new shoe. "Too much wear."

According to the clock on CJ's phone, the entire process of replacing the shoe took eleven and a half minutes. Gil placed both hands on his knees and, with a grunt, pushed himself to a vertical position before moving to the next hoof.

After the third shoe, Gil raised himself to a crooked standing position and broke his self-imposed silence. "Nancy, would you go to my truck and bring me the medicine bottle on the front seat?"

"Are you all right?"

"I need a little help from the farrier's best friend. And bring me that thermos of coffee, if you don't mind."

Gil shook out two pills and swallowed them with coffee.

As Nancy traded the mare for David's gelding, CJ tried to pry open a conversation. "You sure know your way around horses."

"Horses' hooves are 'bout all I know."

"You must love it."

Gil's shrug was noncommittal.

"I hear you do a lot of work for Mrs. Kraft."

"She has a big operation." He took a long drink of coffee and looked toward the river.

Once Nancy performed the same routine of walking David's horse while Gil examined him, she secured the halter rope and excused herself.

CJ realized her best way to gain information was to act dumb, talk a lot, and look for reactions. She launched into a rambling soliloquy, looking all the while for Gil to respond. "Isn't it awful what happened to Judge Kraft? I mean, who could do such a thing? David is about to pull his hair out. I think this is one case that has him stumped. I talked to Mrs. Kraft the day her husband was killed. I hadn't seen her in a while. She's a beautiful woman. I can't imagine me ever getting my figure back. Don't you think she's a looker?"

Gil's face didn't change. "I guess."

CJ plowed on. "And, poor Kevin. Did you know he and his dad had a big fight the day someone shot the judge?"

For the first time, Gil's eyes registered interest in her words.

"That's right." CJ nodded a bit too much. "They had a blow up on Thanksgiving Day. Kevin and a friend went to a deer lease down in south Texas. Did you know Kevin was standing in his driveway packing his rifle in his car when the shot rang out? He remembers hearing it."

Gil's full attention was now on her. It was brief, but CJ thought the corner of Gil's mouth twitched.

She kept talking. "You must know Kevin pretty well. I mean, since you do so much work out there shoeing their horses. David says he's okay. What do you think of him?"

Gil's face remained hard. "Spoiled rich kid."

"That doesn't surprise me. I don't know about you, but I have little patience for kids who get everything handed to them. Growing up on a farm, you and I know the value of work."

Gil's response was to take a last sip of coffee and spit it out, like it had soured in his mouth. "I have a full day ahead of me. Do you know what's wrong with that right front hoof?"

"It looks like seedy toe to me and Nancy. He already threw the shoe."

"Will anyone ride him much in the next few months?"

"Not much, if any."

Gil moved toward the horse. "If it's seedy toe, I'll open up the hoof and leave the shoes off."

CJ's diagnosis was accurate. A fungal infection had worked its way an inch and a half up the front of the hoof and caused a split. After cleaning and trimming the hoof, Gil used the nippers to cut a V-shaped groove in the hoof's front and then probed with a nail. After determining how far up it went, he used his hook-blade knife to elongate the V until he hit solid hoof. A hand held Dremel tool rounded off the edges.

After removing the three remaining shoes, Gil trimmed and cleaned the other hooves. He struggled to straighten himself to his full height and leaned to the left as he walked. Another pill went from the bottle to his mouth, swallowed with a fresh swig of coffee.

CJ pulled a wad of twenty-dollar bills from her jacket pocket. Following some last-minute instructions on hoof care, Gil tipped his hat, and shoved the wad of bills in the front pocket of his jeans without counting them.

As he cleared the driveway, David joined her. "Not very talkative, was he?"

"Tight as a clam. It could be because of a guilty conscience. He's not a fan of Kevin Kraft. Thinks he's a spoiled rich kid."

"That's one thing Kevin and Gil have in common—mutual dislike." David ran a hand down his clean-shaven face. "Is it possible Chris and Gil could have planned to take out Judge Kraft together?"

This was an angle CJ had considered and partially rejected. "That seems unlikely, but you'd better not rule it out yet."

"Anything else?"

She turned and hooked her arm in David's and nudged him toward the house. "Gil's taking some sort of prescription pain killers. He's eating them as if they were baby aspirin. I think his days as a farrier are numbered."

When they reached the back door, CJ stopped. "I thought you were going to help me interview him."

"You didn't need my help to get information out of Gil. A pregnant farm girl isn't as intimidating as someone wearing a gun."

CJ rubbed her belly. "Speaking of carrying a pistol, I'm at a loss for how to carry mine. I can't get a belt around my middle. Stretchy pants show every bulge. My shoulder holster doesn't fit anymore, and there's no way I can stuff these feet in any type of normal footwear, which rules out a boot holster. If I don't have my purse with me, I don't have a gun."

"You shouldn't need one if you're here resting." David opened the back door and allowed her to precede him.

Not wanting to argue the point, CJ moved on to another topic. "What's the chance of me talking to Noah Epstein?"

A tilted head preceded David's next words. "Not good. His lawyer gave him strict instructions not to say anything to anyone."

She thought about asking David for the name of Noah's attorney, but decided against it. There were plenty of sources for that piece of information and there was no rush. Noah wasn't going anywhere until someone found evidence to clear him.

After a last half cup of coffee, David left to meet with Blake Cruz to begin what promised to be a long day of interviews and fact gathering. CJ saw Nancy and Davey off to spend their day at the university, which left her to her own devices. It only took one call to Beula Mae, the talkative jailer, before she had the name of the attorney representing Noah Epstein.

She punched in the number for a local law firm and

listened to three rings before she heard the crisp voice of a woman announce, "Law offices of Snell and Snell."

CJ gave her name and asked to speak to Wendy Snell.

"I'm sorry, she's not available. Would you like to leave a message?"

"This is regarding Noah Epstein. She'll want to take the call."

The receptionist changed her story. "Please hold."

A honey-and-cornbread voice came on the line. "CJ. I thought you were on maternity leave. Did they drag you back to work on the case?"

"Not officially, but I wanted you to know I spoke with my mother-in-law about Noah's status with the university. They're taking no action until more evidence comes in."

"Why not? Everyone else wants him sitting on death row."

"Only the people that don't know Noah. He and I have had several long and interesting talks over the years."

"Did you put in a word for him with Alice?"

"All I did was tell the truth. I don't think Noah has it in him to kill anything bigger than a gnat."

"What about the shell casing? I have to defend him when a jury's going to be looking at that and the cops will testify they found it in his van."

"What does Noah say about where it came from?" CJ held her breath, hoping to get an answer.

"You know I can't tell you what I discuss with a client."

CJ released her breath. She assumed this would be the attorney's response and came prepared. "I know you can't, but listen to what I'm thinking and tell me if I'm crazy or not." She took in a deep breath. "Noah hates guns and is a staunch opponent of gun ownership. Right?"

"Yep."

"Noah loves any cause that has to do with animal rights and that applies double to hunting and fishing. Right?"

"You're doing good so far."

"Noah would love to see some hunter get arrested for illegal hunting. Right?"

"There's no doubt about it."

"He might even collect evidence to prove someone was breaking the law."

"Keep talking, CJ. This is getting more and more interesting."

"If I could talk to Noah, I might find out where the shell casing came from and what he was working on."

A boisterous laugh came from the phone's speaker. "You were doing so good until your last statement." She paused. "Let me talk to my client and see if there's anything to your theory. If there is, I'll let you know."

Wendy hesitated before she spoke again. "Even if he can explain the shell casing, it won't get the charges dropped."

"I know, but it might be enough to get his bond reduced."

"You may be right. By the way, has the funeral home announced the date for Judge Kraft's funeral?"

"David said the governor got involved and expedited the autopsy. The date and time will be announced by noon today."

"Thanks for the call," said Wendy. "It's not every day a defense attorney and the police work together to get an innocent man out of trouble."

"I wouldn't have called if I didn't believe he was innocent."

CJ put the phone on her nightstand. She realized there was nothing left for her to do until Wendy called her back, or she attended a funeral. Another day of entertaining herself in an empty house.

What if she was right about her theory? What if Noah was gathering evidence about a hunter shooting game illegally? Who would he like to see in trouble? The problem was, there were so many. Even Bea and Billy Paul were avid hunters.

Her thoughts became fuzzy, and she slipped into sleep. She woke up with a face etched on her mind. It could well be the person Noah was targeting. She picked up her phone and placed a call.

"Maria. This is CJ. Could you stop by the house after you get off work today?"

CHAPTER NINE

The funeral for Judge Kraft took place on a cool Wednesday afternoon, made even more uncomfortable by a stiff northwest wind. CJ walked with her arm laced in David's as he anchored his best felt Stetson with his left hand to keep it from cartwheeling across the parking lot. A good portion of her long brown hair wrapped around her chin before they found shelter inside the Episcopal church. She excused herself to find a mirror and repair her mane.

David issued a loud whisper as they entered the stately sanctuary. "I'll be in the back row so we can see everyone come in." CJ nodded. It was a long shot, but sometimes funerals proved to be windows to a killer's soul, and they ignored the need for caution. Perhaps other people's grief brought a sense of accomplishment, or closure, or sadistic pleasure to twisted minds. CJ pondered the psychology of violent criminals, but not for long. She'd determined a long time ago that human motivation and behavior were beyond her pay grade.

Once back inside the sanctuary, she found David right where he said he'd be, waiting for people to arrive. She sat beside him and let her gaze take in the beautiful architecture of the old building.

Three times as long as it was wide, the sanctuary was nothing like more modern churches. There was no raised platform for cameras, no theater lights, or smoke machines. This was old-school, high church, complete with pews made more comfortable with two-inch thick seat pads covered in celery green. The pews emptied onto carpeted aisles, one in the middle, and one along each side. Stained glass windows, each one bearing the family name of a long-departed church benefactor, and a scene depicting a biblical milestone, looked down with elegant stillness.

The men from the funeral home came with a huge spray of flowers for the coffin and a photo of Judge Kraft on a tripod to stand in front of the casket.

David surveyed the near empty room and whispered. "I can't see as well as I'd like to. I'll stand in the alcove." He pointed, and CJ nodded in agreement. From the inconspicuous vantage point, David could remain standing and view the faces of all who entered.

Dignitaries, state and county officials, fellow judges and other officers of the court filed in and sat among parishioners and friends. Muted conversations rose and fell to the strains of hymns played on the church's pipe organ. A familiar face entered and caught CJ's eye. She drew David's attention by clearing her throat and looking his way. He nodded an affirmation that he'd noticed, too.

Prompted by an usher, Gil Wright yanked a sand-colored cowboy hat from his head and smoothed his hair with the palm of a thick hand. His cowboy cut jacket looked new, inexpensive, and uncomfortable. The buttons of his white shirt strained in their buttonholes and still bore creases from the factory package. Even if he had tried to wear a necktie, it's doubtful the top button would have reached. Unlike the jacket and shirt, Gil's double-starched blue jeans had a crease sharp enough to cut your hand on. The jeans fit snug until they gathered over the instep of a pair of snake skin boots.

CJ continued to gaze at him and concluded Gill looked as out of place as a vegan at a steak house. Maybe he hadn't seen the inside of a church in a month of Sundays, or perhaps his discomfort had more to do with a guilty conscience. She and David had already decided they'd have a talk with Gil if he went to the graveside service.

Nobody else captured her interest.

The service progressed in true Episcopalian fashion—formal, liturgical, and reverent, balanced by touching personal remarks from Reverend Broussard and eulogies delivered by three others. Judge Kraft's supervising judge, a judge from the Supreme Court of Texas, and a former Red Raiders football teammate spoke in that order. Between the three of them, a picture of Judge Kraft's life came into focus. Intelligent, strong in all ways, and dedicated to the fair administration of the law as he understood it were the sentiments projected by the two judges. The football teammate painted Judge Kraft in a much more human light. Yes, he was hard working and, to quote the former roommate, "disgustingly smart," but Weldon Kraft was also a fun-loving undergraduate who didn't mind playing practical jokes. He recalled how Weldon had fallen hopelessly in love with a beautiful blond rodeo queen.

"Weldon didn't know which side of a horse to mount when he met Chris, but he pursued her with reckless abandon. He spent a full semester learning all he could about everything related to horses and the world of rodeos. She took pity on him after he told her he would quit playing football and become a steer wrestler, if that's what it took to win her." The friend stated he wasn't sure if it was love that drove Chris to marry Weldon, or if she didn't want to be responsible for all the broken bones he'd receive.

A few low chuckles could be heard across the crowd.

Chris raised a tissue to her eyes. Kevin attempted to hold his emotions in check. Sitting between his mom and his paternal grandmother, who sobbed through most of the service, he looked like he'd determined to be 'the strong one.'

With the benediction recited, people filed out of the church and either prepared for the procession to the graveside or went on about their day. Two city police cars stood at the ready, emergency lights activated.

Instead of joining in the procession, David and CJ took a circuitous, but faster, route. They wanted to get in place before the throngs arrived. David chose a promontory well away from the white tent.

"Why did you park so far away?"

"You're staying here." He pulled binoculars from under his seat and handed them to her. "The wind is brutal and I don't want you getting sick. I need to talk to Gil, and I need you to look for anyone who wasn't at the church."

CJ shrugged. "Just as well. My coat won't button, and I've been on my feet enough today."

David leaned into CJ to give her a customary parting kiss and a pat on her distended midsection. She stiffened. "Another contraction?"

CJ took a deep breath and exhaled through pursed lips. "They haven't been regular, but they're getting stronger. The doctor said it's expected from here on."

"Maybe it wasn't a good idea for you to come. Do you want me to take you home?"

"I'm fine. Go talk to Gil. Turn up the heat on him and see what bubbles out."

David anchored his hat the best he could, opened the door, and stepped into a brisk breeze. CJ scanned the area. Nothing looked out of place. The three-sided tent popped in the wind and held an inadequate number of folding chairs.

The new hole in the ground was trimmed in fake grass and topped by a mechanical contraption that held the casket.

She watched as David descended the slope and positioned himself opposite the front of the tent, on the far side of the grave. A surprising number of people had braved the chilly wind to pay their last respects.

CJ considered the sight unfolding in front of her. A traditional graveside service is ninety percent waiting for everyone to arrive and ten percent reading from a minister's manual. This one proved to be no exception. The brief service began when Father Broussard opened a smallish black book. All she could hear was the whistle of wind.

Nestled in their SUV, CJ alternated looking through binoculars and lowering them to gain a more panoramic view. Toward the end of the service, she raised the field glasses a last time. Car by car, truck by truck, SUV by SUV, she scanned the rows to see if anyone else was playing long distance voyeur. She swiveled in her seat to look over her shoulder. "What the...?"

The truck had arrived undetected because she had to turn at an awkward angle to see it. Hard to do in her present state. She raised the binoculars and focused them in time to see someone looking at her through their own binoculars. A cowboy hat tilted down, the binoculars fell away, and the truck threw up a cloud of gravel and dust. Bushy evergreens blocked any chance of seeing the license plate. The driver had chosen his hiding place well, a lone gap in the trees where he could see but avoid detection.

CJ went into full pursuit mode. She raised herself up and over the center console and plopped down sideways in the driver's seat with her head against the window and her shoulders resting against the driver's door. Her legs were bent at the knees with feet in the passenger's seat, but that's as far as she got. Her plan to swivel her body hadn't considered the baby. Her right hip rested against the seat back while her mid-section pressed on the steering wheel. In an effort to return to the passenger seat, her elbow leaned against the horn. It erupted. She jerked it away with her free right hand and held it so it wouldn't again disrupt the solemnity of the service.

CJ scolded herself aloud. "Of all the stupid... Here I am trapped like a mouse in a sticky trap. I can't get up, I can't reach for my purse to call David, and the door handle is out of the question. And now that guy, whoever he is, will be in the next county before David can help me. What else can go wrong?" At that moment, a contraction took her thoughts from anything else but her child.

"Lord, I'm sorry I asked that last question. I didn't mean it. Please don't let this baby come today. David is too busy. Mama can't come for at least another week, and Aunt Bea needs to get through Christmas before she'll be of any help."

CHAPTER TEN

The short honk of the horn caused David to take a glance at their SUV. Nothing looked amiss, so he focused on the job at hand. Just as he suspected, Gil had positioned himself at the corner of the tent where he could see Chris Kraft. During the service, he tried to catch her attention, but she stared straight ahead.

The family made a last pass by the coffin. Chris placed a single yellow rose on it, lingered a moment and, with head erect, stepped toward the limo. Gil moved to intercept her. She tried to walk past him, but he grabbed her arm. She gave him a look that could freeze boiling water. David tried to read her lips and thought she said, "Not here. Not now." With that, she sidestepped him and walked on.

Kevin Kraft, following behind his mother with his grandmother clinging to his arm, wasn't so diplomatic. He released his grandmother and stepped toward Gil. All the loss, pain, and grief spewed like a shaken carbonated drink. One last step and a neat right cross landed Gil on the seat of his double starched jeans.

"Perfect," said David to himself. "That's what I needed to give me an excuse to rake Gil over the coals."

Before Gil could get off the ground, David was on him. With a firm grip on the lapels of his coat, he jerked Gil to his feet. "You're coming with me. Don't say a word until we're clear of everyone or I'll have you back on the ground and handcuffed."

Gil rubbed his chin and tried to focus. He complied and kept up with David's quick pace. After about seventy yards of fast walking, David circled behind an evergreen that blocked the view of anyone attending the funeral.

A second and longer honk of a car horn registered with David, but not enough to keep him from dealing with Gil. He stared at the man with a trickle of blood coming from the corner of his mouth. "What do you think you're doing?"

"Heck if I know. That kid hauled off and hit me. Why don't you ask him?"

David's nostrils flared. He squared his shoulders and raised his right hand with the first finger extended. He poked Gil in the chest, which caused the man to take a step back. The step and poke repeated itself several times with the next few questions.

"Why did Kevin hit you?"

"I don't know."

"Why did you come to the funeral? Is it because you're having an affair with Christine Kraft?"

"Who told you that?"

"Half the people at the funeral know about it. Don't play dumb. I want to hear it from you."

"What of it?"

"How long has this been going on?"

"A long time. Years."

"Did Judge Kraft know about it?"

"I don't know."

"Yes, you do. Don't even think about lying to me. I can read you like a book."

"Okay, he knew. But he didn't care."

"Did you shoot Judge Kraft?"

"What? No. I'll swear on a stack of Bibles. I was in Austin having a burger and a couple of beers. I've got a room full of witnesses and credit card receipts. Check it out."

"I will." David switched gears. "Do you think Chris Kraft is in love with you?"

"I don't know."

"Guess."

"She might be. I mean, we've been seeing each other for a long time. Look," countered Gil as he squared his shoulders and planted his feet. "I've had about enough of this. Arrest me or let me go."

David had pushed Gil as far as he was going to be pushed and poked enough to bruise him. It was time to lighten his tone and tactics. "Do you think Chris had her husband killed so she could be with you?"

"Of course not. You don't understand." It was Gil's turn to change his defensive tone to one that sought understanding. He looked David square in the eye. "Chris is a woman with needs that weren't being met."

"Explain."

With his hands open in front of him, Gil continued. "Judge Kraft may have been a real stud in college, but he developed prostate cancer not long after Kevin was born. Surgery was the only option."

"Are you saying Judge Kraft couldn't perform after the surgery?" asked David.

"I'm not a doctor or a psychologist. He either couldn't, or wouldn't. Get it?"

David's nod was enough for Gil to continue. "Chris told me it was a pride thing. He was an all-or-nothing kind of guy.

Once he couldn't perform like he once did, that was the end of the road for his sex life. That left Chris with unmet needs."

"Which you were more than happy to fill," added David.

Gil shrugged his shoulders. "If not me, she'd have found someone else."

David took a step back and continued. "Perhaps you and Mrs. Kraft planned the judge's killing together."

"That's crazy."

"Then who killed Judge Kraft?" asked David.

Gil's voice and demeanor lifted with confidence. "I don't know. Some newspapers say it's that kid from the university. Reporters on television think it was someone Judge Kraft sent to prison, or some drug cartel set it up." Gil paused. "Or maybe that crazy kid of hers. I hear he left town right after the shooting. You just saw how violent he can be."

David played along and let out a long sigh of defeat. "Sorry about jerking you around." David looked back at the retreating limousine. "This case has me tied in knots. You wouldn't believe the pressure I'm getting."

"Am I free to go?"

"Let the people clear out first. That was quite a scene you caused. It would be wise if you kept a low profile for a while. If your alibi doesn't check out, expect a visit."

———

CJ's HEAD and shoulders flopped down level with the seat. "Don't stand there. Help me out."

Shocked into inaction, David recovered and hooked his arms under CJ's and gave a tug.

"Wait. Move the seat back. I'm wedged in."

David's giggle morphed into something more. CJ snapped at him, "David Harper, if you drop me, I swear, I'll..."

David let out a loud cackle. "You look like a beached

whale." With a good pull, he extracted her from her four-wheeled tomb.

CJ gained her footing and quick stepped around the front of the car as David barraged her with, "How in the world did you get in such a bind?"

A gust of wind caught her hair and whipped a substantial amount into her mouth. CJ combed it back with her hands. "Five-year-old white Silverado pickup, half ton. The driver watched the funeral through binoculars. He made me before I saw him. I was going to follow, but moving from the passenger's seat to the driver's side over the center console doesn't work when you're near full term."

David hopped in and drew out his cell phone. He waited until CJ was inside. "How long ago?"

"Since the service ended."

"License plate?" asked David.

"Couldn't make it. He left in a cloud of dust."

"Description of driver?"

"All I saw was binoculars and a hat that he tipped down to cover his face." She paused. "Or, her face."

"You don't even know if it was a man or a woman? Why didn't you honk?"

"I did. Twice. Did you notice we're in a cemetery at a funeral for Judge Kraft? I didn't think people would appreciate me leaning on the horn."

David put his cell phone in a cup holder on the center console. "Whoever it was is long gone, and there's no shortage of white Silverado pickups in the county."

A turn of her head and a melting stare at her husband followed a huff of disgust from CJ. "Did you call me a beached whale?"

"Uh..."

CJ prepared to give her husband a double portion of what

she thought about that remark when the next contraction hit. "Yikes."

"Is it bad?"

CJ's response was a deep, cleansing breath and a firm nod of her head.

"Hospital?"

She nodded again.

DAVID'S PHONE call on the way to Riverside Regional Hospital alerted the hospital's staff. They were waiting to wheel her in when the SUV came to an abrupt halt under the covered portico. Nurses had CJ out of her clothes, into a drafty gown, and hooked up to monitors for her and the baby in no time. The ER doctor wasn't familiar to her, but he had a friendly, pudgy face and red cheeks. CJ thought he'd make a good Santa in another thirty or forty years.

"When did the regular contractions start?"

"About forty-five minutes ago."

"What were you doing?"

This was the question CJ dreaded. How do you tell a doctor you were trying to move over the center console of a SUV so you could chase a potential killer?

She told the story in as few words as possible. The jovial doctor's stomach looked as if it was having spasms when she relayed the part of David having to pull her out like a cork from a bottle.

The doctor controlled himself, checked the monitors, and warmed the stethoscope with his hand. After listening to her and the baby, he straightened himself up to his full height, which wasn't over five foot eight. "Have the contractions been steady most of the day?"

"Not really. Not until I got stuck. That's when the real pain started."

"Are the contractions stronger now?"

"They're easing up."

He took a step back. "The fetal monitor will tell us what's going on. Right now, everything points to false labor, but we'll keep you here an hour or two to make sure."

David came in a few seconds after the doctor left. "Is this the big day?"

CJ's words came out in a tone that spoke of disappointment. "The doc thinks this is a false alarm. Hold off calling anyone."

David chuckled. "Too late for that. Bea and Billy Paul followed us here from the cemetery. They're in the waiting room."

"That means your dad and Alice will be on their way."

David nodded, "And a few more, if I'm guessing."

CJ pushed the button on her bed control and brought her shoulders up a few inches. "Call Nancy. There's no need for her coming. Also, you'll need to send everyone home." She took in a big breath and let it out. "I feel so silly for crying wolf."

Time passed, and the contractions became more widely spaced. An hour into the wait, the familiar figure of Detective Maria Vasquez appeared in the room. "No baby today?"

"He's stubborn like you, Maria. He won't come out until he's good and ready."

With CJ now sitting almost straight up, she and Maria weren't far from looking at each other eye-to-eye. Maria may have been short in stature, but she made up for it with an extensive history of mixed martial arts training and fights. Like dynamite, Maria packed a lot into a small package.

"How are things on campus?" asked CJ.

"Slow. Finals are this week and the lazy students are

waking up to the fact they need to study. That means they're not getting into as much mischief."

David spoke over his shoulder as he left the room. "I need to call Blake and tell him it looks like I'll be available to help for a while longer."

Once she and Maria were alone, CJ said, "I'm glad you came. I have a couple of things I need help with."

"Good. I hate not having much to keep me busy. Sorry I didn't get out to see you the other day when you called."

CJ crooked her finger and motioned Maria to come closer. She lowered her voice. "I heard from Noah Epstein's attorney. He claims the shell casing they found in his van came from under a deer stand near the municipal golf course. He doesn't know who the hunter is, but thinks it must be a city official because it's on city property."

Maria had a blank look on her face, but only for a few seconds. "Do you think Noah was trying to catch a poacher?"

CJ nodded.

"That would make sense," said Maria. "If he could embarrass an official of some sort, that would make his day."

"It might also go a long way to proving the shell casing didn't come from the gun that killed Judge Kraft."

A twinkle shone from Maria's brown eyes. "And all I need to do is find out who's hunting near the golf course?"

"You're the best detective the university has," said CJ with a sly smile.

"I'm the only detective." Maria took a step back. "Sounds like fun. I'll have to find good places to hide and I can only work on my off hours." She gave her head a firm nod. "I can't stand Noah, but I hate the thought of innocent people being convicted even more. What else?"

"In the next day or two, I need you to come with me to talk to the man who helps Judge Kraft's wife with her horse operation. His name is Alejandro Vega. He's a Mexican national that lives in an apartment over their horse barn. David, Blake, and the FBI have already talked to him, but I want to make sure they didn't miss anything. It's my understanding he speaks Spanish and very little English. I want us to take a run at him."

"When?"

"Saturday morning. I'll call Chris and set it up."

"Don't make it too early. I'll be in the woods near the golf course until about ten o'clock."

CHAPTER ELEVEN

It was pushing ten-thirty on Saturday morning when CJ and Maria found Chris Kraft at the sixth door of a twenty-stall horse barn. She wore rubber boots, jeans, and a slouchy gray sweatshirt. Her blond ponytail stuck out the back of a baseball cap and she wore no makeup.

Using a scoop shovel, Chris scraped up mounds of horse manure and clumps of urine-soaked hay from the stalls and pitched them to the center walkway. Dung and ammonia odors rose like an invisible cloud from a fetid pond. With head down, Chris pitched a pile that grazed Maria's boots.

"Sorry. I didn't see you."

"No harm," said Maria through gritted teeth.

CJ spoke to avoid an even more awkward moment. "Thanks for seeing us. I didn't expect to find you mucking out the stalls."

"This is Alejandro's job, but ever since..." Her voice trailed off. She squared her shoulders and looked at CJ. "I've had trouble sleeping. Working until I drop is all I've found that helps. Do you mind if I keep at it while we talk?"

"Not at all," replied CJ. "I'll get out of the line of fire."

She moved to a corner of the stall, while Maria took another corner, out of harm's way. As usual, Maria remained quiet, leaving the talking to CJ.

"You mentioned Alejandro. Is he here today?"

Chris kept working. "He's exercising a high-strung mare and will be along once he gives her a good workout."

CJ was glad the ranch hand had other chores to attend to. She wanted that interview to be between Maria and Alejandro.

Chris looked up. "Alejandro does most of the work with the horses. Building out the subdivision occupies most of my days."

"Was he working here on Thanksgiving Day?"

"He works every day. Did you notice the stairs? I built the barn with two one-bedroom apartments. The front one is my business office, and the back one is Alejandro's."

Chris glanced up. "I take it you want to interview him."

"Since he lives here full time, he might have seen or heard something."

Chris kept her head down. "It's a good thing you brought an interpreter. He speaks limited English."

CJ couldn't think of a delicate way of asking the next question, so she did the best she could. "How long has Alejando worked for you?"

"Four years."

"And before that?"

"I found him working horses on a ranch west of San Antonio." Chis looked up. "If you're wondering if he's legal, Weldon made sure he had a green card. It wouldn't do for a state district judge to get caught hiring an undocumented alien."

CJ allowed silence, save the sounds of lifting and pitching muck, to fill the barn. It didn't take long before Chris said, "I knew you'd come. I'm surprised it took so long. I guess you had to let the others have the first crack at me. Am I right?" Chris stilled the shovel, glanced up at CJ, and answered her own question. "Yeah, I'm right."

Chris went back to work and spoke without prompting. "You have a reputation for being plain spoken and everyone says there isn't a dishonest bone in your body. I've heard you can spot lies and deception almost as good as your husband. My attorney advised me not to speak to anyone unless he was present. Well, that's not the way I'm wired. The only thing I want is for whoever killed Weldon to wait for life's end on death row. My withholding information from you might impede an arrest and conviction. I only wish you could help more with the investigation."

It was a sudden shift of the conversation, but not unexpected. CJ had seen it before in people experiencing life-altering trauma. Eventually, they needed to talk. The mere act of rattling on about things was Chris's attempt to find the new normal.

"Kevin had three sessions with Aunt Bea. She encouraged him to go back to his earliest childhood memories of his father and work his way forward. At each step, she helped him remember and find words for his feelings, both good and bad. According to Kevin, he held nothing back, including walking in on Gil Wright and me before he was a teen. He also told her what he thought of our ongoing affair, which always took place upstairs."

Chris threw a final scoop of wet straw and said, "Let's move on to the next one."

After repositioning themselves, Chris continued talking, all the while scooping and pitching. "In order for you to understand what's been going on with me and Gil, I need to give you some background. I grew up on a ranch outside Decatur. It was a big spread with plenty of cattle and horses, and quite a few oil wells. Daddy was a sweet old buzzard who taught me everything I know about horses and business. He knew how to make money but didn't know women. He didn't marry until he was in his mid-forties.

"Mom was twenty-two, beautiful and a gold-digger. She played her cards right and kept her extra-marital affairs quiet. A couple of years after I was born, she paid a ranch hand to rough her up. Not too much, just enough to have Daddy arrested. After an uncontested divorce, Mom got half the land and some of the oil rights. Daddy kept the rest of the land, the rest of the oil wells, the horses, and cattle. He also got me. I was on a pony by the time I could walk, and barrel racing when I started school. Horses and rodeos have always been a big part of my life. I thought nothing else mattered until I met Weldon."

Chris made quick work of the stall and motioned the duo to move to the next one. Once again, she put her head down, concentrated on work, and talked at the same time. "Like I was saying, things changed after Weldon and I started dating. He was a member of a fraternity and he introduced me to a lifestyle that I didn't know existed. He took me to formal affairs where I had to dress up in something more than jeans or rhinestone-studded rodeo outfits. Most people think the guys that join fraternities are just a bunch of drunks who party their way through college. Some of that was true, but it wasn't true of Weldon's fraternity. About half of them were on athletic scholarships and those who weren't were smart and came from well-to-do families. Those young men were going to be the businessmen, bankers, attorneys, and professionals of the next generation. They banded together as much for future benefits as for the social aspects of college life. It didn't take me long to realize how strategic Weldon was."

With another stall completed, Chris headed for the next one where she resumed her testimony. "I saw you at the funeral. You heard Weldon's former teammate say how hard

Weldon chased me. It's true." Once again, Chris went to work. "Like I said, Weldon was always strategic in his decisions. I had my mama's looks, and my daddy's brains and work ethic. I was just what Weldon was looking for, an ornament for his arm and a woman who could fit in with ranchers, oil men, bankers, or state senators. Weldon was going to be a success, and in his mind, I was going to help him get where he wanted to go."

A half-smile crossed Chris's face as she took a break. "Then something happened that took both of us by complete surprise. We fell head-over-heels in love. He was looking for someone to help him realize his professional and political goals. I wasn't looking for anyone, but Cupid's arrow was in deep before either of us knew what hit us. I don't think we could have been more in love."

Chris grabbed her shovel and continued working with head down. "Daddy died in February of my senior year. Weldon and I married two weeks after we graduated that same year. Mama got drunk at the reception and had a big fight with husband number four. She's on number six now. With each one, she's lost a few oil wells. She's down to just enough to keep her in gin and in her house."

Some of the aroma of the ever-growing piles in the center walkway hitchhiked on a newfound breeze that flowed through the open doors at each end of the barn. By the time they reached the next stall, Chris was ready to talk again. "Daddy left me the ranch and the livestock and the oil wells, but by that time, my life was with Weldon. I sold it all and put my degree in finance to good use by getting hired at an investment firm. We watched our money grow, and I helped put Weldon through law school. After he graduated, we looked around the state to see where we might want to live and work. Riverview seemed the best choice, so we packed up and made our way to central Texas. Land was still pretty cheap. I bought as much as my inheritance would allow and paid for our home. That's when I started raising horses. Everything Daddy taught me paid off and still does."

She seemed to be watching a movie of her life. "We had the world by the tail. Weldon made a name for himself as a lawyer and I was building my reputation as a businesswoman and horse breeder. Then Kevin came along. Life couldn't have been better."

Chris' voice took on a melancholy tone. "After ten years, ten months and five days of marriage, the doctors diagnosed Weldon with prostate and testicular cancer. The only treatment option offered was surgery. After the operation, everything changed. His perception of manhood meant everything to him." Chris' eyes clouded. "He called himself a eunuch, only a shadow of the man I deserved. That's when he pulled away in every way, and dedicated himself to his work."

With tears coming down her cheeks, Chris attacked the waste with her shovel. "I tried for years to convince him that all I wanted was him, no matter what had changed. He was too proud, or ashamed, or whatever. Things were never the same between us."

Instead of moving on, Chris stared at CJ. "You want to know why I started having the affair with Gil Wright, and why it continued all these years, don't you? I'm a strong woman, but not that strong. I can handle not having the physical part of marriage, but I couldn't take Weldon checking out emotionally."

She cast her gaze to the end of the barn. "Imagine if David had the same surgery as Weldon. After the operation he says, 'I'm damaged goods and you only deserve the best.' Then, he never touches you or wants you to touch him. He doesn't talk to you, or confide in you, and buries himself in work. How would that make you feel?"

CJ didn't answer, but the question hit her hard. Compassion rose in her.

"You already know Weldon chased me in college until he caught me. Even after he knew I was his, he continued to chase me. Once a week he sent me flowers. Every day he would leave me a note telling me how much he loved me. On our anniversary, he would get down on one knee and propose to me all over again. He didn't need to chase me, he had me heart and soul. But he did, and I loved him all the more for it."

Chris' voice lowered to a whisper. "Then, everything stopped."

Quiet seconds ticked by. "Why did I have an affair with Gil Wright? The answer came to me a few nights ago. It's as simple as it is stupid. I wanted to make Weldon so jealous he'd run Gil off and take me in his arms like he used to and tell me he'd never let another man have me."

Chris came back from that place of deep introspection. "I've been rambling. Ask me what you need to."

CJ nodded her acceptance of the ground rules. "Are you in love with Gil Wright?"

"No. I tried to make Weldon want me again. It didn't work and I see now how silly it was for me to think it could. Gil is one dimensional and a very inadequate substitute in every way."

"Do you think Gil is in love with you?"

"If he is, he'll be disappointed. I've contacted a new farrier. I don't want Gil around anymore, and I know Kevin hates him."

"That's all the questions I have," said CJ.

"You didn't ask me if I killed Weldon, or paid to have him killed."

"I didn't need to."

Chris put her head down and threw two more shovels of dung before she stopped. "Can I ask you a question?"

"Go ahead."

"Did you ever do something you were so ashamed of you believed you were beyond redemption?"

"Not really, but David has, and we walked through it together."

"Was it as bad as what I did to Weldon and Kevin by having the affair with Gil?"

"It was worse. A crooked sheriff and a scheming judge falsely convicted David's father of murdering his wife, David's mother. For sixteen years David believed his dad was guilty, and for sixteen years he abandoned him."

Chris nodded her head. "I remember reading about his dad." All became dead quiet as Chris asked, "How did he deal with the guilt?"

"It still bothers him, but not like before. Somewhere along the line it changed from guilt to regret, like an open wound turns into a scar."

"Do you think Kevin will ever forgive me?"

"He wouldn't have decked Gil Wright at the funeral if he didn't love you and wasn't trying to protect you. My guess is you getting rid of Gil will show Kevin you love him and you two can move on."

"Any other advice?" asked Chris.

"Forgive yourself, and talk to Bea Stargate."

Alejandro's arrival thwarted a reply from Chris. He came in, leading a chestnut mare that jerked its head and snorted. Chris told Alejandro to put the horse in its stall and cooperate in answering questions.

CJ understood more Spanish than she could speak. It was time for her and Maria to play the Hispanic-cop, gringo-cop game with Alejandro.

CHAPTER TWELVE

A t five foot seven with boots on, Alejandro Vega wasn't a big man. Years of sun, wind, and hard work gave him a weathered look. He reminded CJ of a mesquite tree with its dark, rough bark. He wore the standard uniform of a ranch hand in the cool December weather: cowboy boots, blue jeans with a red bandanna peeking out of the back right pocket, a wide belt with a leather holder for a lock-blade knife, chambray shirt, a work-stained insulated vest, and a grimy felt cowboy hat.

Maria whispered. "Let's talk outside. The *barrio* I grew up in didn't smell as bad as this barn."

When CJ nodded, Maria instructed Alejandro to meet them on the north side of the barn. The sound of the stall door closing behind the two women meant they wouldn't have long to wait.

Maria took the lead in the Spanish-only conversation with CJ looking on so she could study Alejandro's reactions to questions. She'd ask questions, but they'd go through Maria for translation.

Maria began by showing her badge, identifying CJ, and

asking Alejandro what other police he'd spoken to about Judge Kraft's murder.

He didn't appear to be surprised about being questioned, or by Maria's first question. "How many police have talked to you so far?"

"*Muchos hombres.*"

CJ had already read David's copy of Blake Cruz's report of Alejandro's interview. It stated Alejandro had almost no contact with Judge Kraft, and the ranch hand spent Thanksgiving afternoon away from the property. He had a dozen people who were watching television at a bar in a nearby town ready to back up his story.

Maria asked what show was on, and Alejandro answered without blinking.

So far, so good. No signs of excessive nervousness or deception.

Maria turned up the heat by telling Alejandro he was wrong about what was on television. Instead of arguing, he said he might be wrong, but she should check. He then gave details of the soccer game they watched.

CJ asked Maria to find out about Alejandro's history and to be more specific about how much interaction he had with Judge Kraft.

The history given was specific, brief, and void of details or dates. Alejandro's left hand went over his right forearm when Maria asked him about the year he came to the United States.

Maria then delved into the man's life story, where he came from, his experience with horses, and how he came to Chris Kraft's attention. He answered each query with quiet confidence.

"What about your family? Still in Mexico?" asked Maria.

He spoke a brisk, "*No familia,*" then looked away.

There it is. Maria found the soft spot.

Maria didn't miss the deception and looked ready to

pounce. CJ pulled her up short by saying, "Thanks, Maria. Tell Mr. Vega we appreciate him taking time to talk to us."

Maria's squinted eyes told CJ she wasn't buying the story about it being time to leave, but she complied all the same.

Once back in the car, Maria huffed, then said, "I could have broken him down."

"You know he's lying, and I know he's lying, but why?"

Maria shrugged, "I don't know."

"I like to know the answers to questions before I ask them. You did a great job of identifying that he's hiding something concerning his family. It will be easy enough to find out if he's sending money back home to support someone."

"You're going to make another phone call, aren't you?"

CJ reached for her phone. This would be a good time to see if training Maria to be a detective was paying off. "Who would I be calling?"

"Your husband, but that's not the real question."

"What is the real question?"

"Who will *he* call?"

CJ couldn't help but smile. "Who will that be?"

"His new friends at the FBI. There are limits to what state law enforcement can do. The FBI can find out things like that."

"You're on a roll. Don't stop."

Maria nodded with confidence. "You're gathering all the information you can before we talk to Alejandro again."

"I always said you had the most potential of any officer I ever trained."

CJ spoke about the present and the near future. "Never overlook the ones that fit into the landscape. They know things you wouldn't expect them to, and they almost always know more than they're willing to say. Be patient, do your homework, and don't press them too hard. Then, when you're ready, reel them in."

David answered CJ's call with a voice laced with concern. "Are you in labor?"

She held the phone away from her ear and laughed. "That's not why I'm calling. Maria and I just spoke with Chris Kraft and her ranch foreman. Have you done a full background on Alejandro Vega yet?"

"Blake worked on that one. He has an airtight alibi."

"I know, but I think he might have missed something. Alejandro told us he has no family. He's lying."

"Are you sure?"

"He may not have family in Texas, but Maria and I will both bet he's sending money back to Mexico."

"I'll check. If it turns out he is, I'll get Blake to contact the FBI."

CJ covered the speaker on her phone and winked at Maria. "I wish I'd thought of that."

"What was that?" asked David.

"I was telling Maria I wish we'd thought to call the feds."

David lowered his voice. "If the two of you are finished sleuthing, go home and put your feet up."

"Not before I take Maria out for lunch. Bye."

Maria gave a snort of disgust. "You married people play too many games."

"Games can be fun," said CJ. "You'll find out some day."

"Never."

"ALL YOU WANT IS A SALAD?" asked Maria when they arrived at Pepe's Pizza.

"No, I want a large meat lover's special with a triple order of cheese, but all I'm allowed to eat is a salad with no salt, and very little dressing."

"Yuk."

CJ didn't contradict her. They placed their orders. A personal pan Hawaiian with jalapenos for Maria and the salad bar for CJ.

"Any progress on finding who's hunting near the golf course?" asked CJ once she settled with her mound of salad.

Maria held her hand out and wiggled it back and forth. "Some. I scouted the woods this morning. With the nice weather we've been having, I knew golfers would be out. That meant the chances of a hunter being there were next to zero. I did find three tree stands."

"That could mean there's more than one hunter."

Maria's shoulder shrug communicated she wasn't sure. "The stands are nothing but two-by-four scraps nailed into the trees for steps and a couple of boards to sit on between two level branches. They're all painted in the same green and brown camo pattern."

CJ swallowed her first bite of salad. "Someone's going to a lot of trouble trying not to get caught. If Noah Epstein found a shell casing under one of those stands, he'd love to catch whoever fired the shot."

Thunder rattled the windows of the pizza parlor, and most of the patrons shifted their gaze to the windows, including Maria. "There's the cold front. Right on time. It's supposed to rain this afternoon and taper off to a sprinkle later tonight. Misty rain all day tomorrow."

"The biggest buck I ever killed was on a wet, nasty day," said CJ. "The rain and cold will keep the golfers away tomorrow morning. Other than getting wet, it could be a good day for you."

"I'll be there before first light."

"Be careful."

Maria waved off the warning. "I found places to set up behind each stand and far enough away I won't be spotted. There's only one road that comes close to the woods. I set up a trail camera to record any movement along that road."

The next roll of thunder, louder than the first, preceded the splatter of rain against the windows. The front door swung open, and a man removed his rain-dappled cowboy hat. He looked to be in his late twenties, of medium height, and he wore the uniform of a state game warden.

"Do you know that guy?" asked CJ.

Maria swiveled in her chair to catch a look. "Never seen him."

"Go ask him to join us."

"Why?"

After a wordless stare, CJ answered the question. "Professional courtesy. It doesn't hurt to know people you might work with someday."

Maria stood, but hesitated. "He'll think I'm coming on to him."

Before exasperation set in, CJ said, "For a girl that isn't afraid to get in the ring and trade blows with men twice your size, you sure are timid. Tell him the assistant chief of police at ACU would like to meet him."

CJ watched as Maria closed the distance, spoke a few words, and pointed toward the table. When the man arrived, CJ looked up at a smiling face and two of the cutest dimples she'd ever seen.

He stuck out his hand and asked, "Are you CJ Harper?"

CJ nodded and shook his hand. "I assume you're our new game warden. I see by the nametag your last name is Moreno. What's your first name?"

"Thomas." He looked down like he'd made a mistake. "Tommy. I go by Tommy, but my given name is Thomas. Thomas Moreno."

"Join us, Tommy. The shy one's name is Detective Maria Vasquez."

CJ shifted her gaze to Maria, who stood transfixed, staring at those dimples. "Are you planning on eating your pizza standing up?"

Maria all but fell into her chair. Tommy lowered himself, while alternating his gaze between CJ and Maria.

Then he fixed his gaze on CJ and spoke before things got too awkward. "I was told you lived in Riverview. I've wanted to meet you ever since you made national news and they selected you as a Ranger."

A server arrived with a menu and a glass of water. "Do you know what you want, sir, or do you need a few more minutes?"

Game Warden Tommy looked at CJ's plate of salad. "Is that all you're having?"

"Not by choice. My obstetrician has me on a strict diet. If it tastes good, I can't eat it."

He turned to Maria. "What about you?"

Maria looked like she was washing her hands. Then she sat on them. "What about me?"

"What are you having?"

"Pizza."

Tommy grinned. "What kind?"

Maria hesitated, looking as if her brain had short-circuited. She recovered and blurted out, "Hula girl with jalapenos. I mean Hawaiian."

"I never tried it with jalapenos. Sounds good." He instructed the server to bring him a medium.

Maria must have found enough courage to try talking again. "They make 'em big here. You're going to take half of it home with you."

"Good. That way I'll have a meal for tomorrow. I'm hoping to hit the ground running."

"Where are you staying?" asked CJ.

He looked out the rain-streaked windows. "For now, I'm in a hotel along the freeway. I need to find a place, and the sooner the better."

CJ rarely made snap decisions, but this would be a good deed, and David wouldn't mind. Besides, it would be fun to watch how it played out.

Before CJ could spring it on Tommy, the server placed Maria's pizza in front of her. She pushed the pan toward Tommy. "Go ahead. Dig in. We'll share until yours arrives and you can pay me back."

He spoke in a serious tone. "That won't be fair. My pieces will be bigger than yours. I'll get gypped."

Anger flashed in Maria's eyes, until Tommy roared with laughter, pointed a finger at her and said, "Gotcha'."

Maria's scowl morphed into one of her seldom-issued smiles. It went all the way to her eyes and showed off how pretty she could be. With the pizza between them, their conversation flowed. CJ ate her salad and wondered how many more Hawaiian pizzas with jalapenos those two would share.

By the time their words stalled, CJ had a plan. She looked across the table, catching Tommy's attention. "What are you doing tomorrow morning?"

He shrugged. "I thought I'd look for an apartment."

After a dismissing wave of her hand, CJ said, "I thought you said you want to hit the ground running. Maria needs help tomorrow morning catching someone deer hunting on posted land right beside the city golf course. It also might have something to do with a suspect in Judge Kraft's murder case."

The dimples went away and Tommy sat erect. "Tell me about it."

As he dove into another slice of pizza, CJ revealed the

plan involving Maria creeping through the woods and catching an illegal hunter. She did most of the talking, but Maria threw in excited comments as well.

By the time CJ paid for the meals, Tommy was all-in on hunting a hunter the next morning. "I wouldn't miss the chance to catch this guy, even if it means I have to stay in the hotel all week."

"You won't need to do that," said CJ. "Your problem of temporary lodging is solved. You can stay at our farm until you find an apartment."

He leaned back. "I can't impose on you like that. Especially since you're so close to having a baby."

"No imposition at all, you'll be in the barn."

It was Maria's turn to laugh at his wide-eyed reaction. "Don't worry, you'll be in an awesome fifth-wheel camper that stays inside the barn. Full hookups."

"And an extra bathroom and shower in the barn and your own washer and dryer," said CJ. "David and I lived in the RV while we built our home."

Tommy grinned. "You've got yourself a tenant. Just until I can find an apartment."

CJ stood and gave her head a firm nod. "It's settled. You'll be the next temporary resident in the barn, and you and Maria will be in the woods tomorrow looking for your first arrest in Riverview County."

Maria jabbered all the way to CJ and David's property. She then insisted on making Tommy's bed with clean sheets and made sure he had plenty of towels.

Rain pelted the county until well after midnight when David slid into bed. CJ woke up long enough to tell him about the latest occupant of their travel trailer and Maria and Tommy's plans for the early morning.

"Are you playing matchmaker?"

"What if I am? Maria needs to loosen up. He's the first

man I've ever seen her give a second look. It must be his dimples."

"If they can eliminate Epstein as a suspect without causing too much of a stink, then play matchmaker all you want."

CHAPTER THIRTEEN

I t was such lousy weather the next day that CJ decided not to change out of her maternity pajamas. Nancy left for classes before eight. She'd leave little Davey in child care all day to give her time to cram for finals. David was at the local highway patrol office, doing background checks. That left her alone, with nothing to do but put her feet up, talk to her dog, and wait for the baby to grow a little more. A perfect day to do next to nothing. In fact, the only thing on her calendar was to be dressed in time to welcome Tommy to his new temporary home.

Then her phone rang.

"We got him," said Maria, sounding a little subdued.

"That's great. Any trouble?"

"Yes and no." Maria kept talking. "We split up. I showed Tommy where to hide behind the first stand. I went to the third one. Tommy heard him park, but didn't know where he went until we heard the shot. It came from the middle stand. We met there and followed the trail to the eighth fairway."

"Good grief. Did he shoot a deer on the golf course?"

"Just outside the hazard line. It didn't run far before it dropped."

"Where's the suspect now?"

"In cuffs."

"Do you know who he is?"

"Yeah, and he's being a real jerk. In fact, he told us we were making a mistake we'd both regret."

"It sounds like he needs a trip to jail to cool off."

The phone went quiet, but the sound of an approaching siren came through the phone's speaker.

"Maria. Talk to me. Do you need backup? Are you still there?"

"Is there any way you can meet us at the county jail?"

"I can if I have to."

This didn't sound good. Maria wouldn't have asked if there wasn't something wrong.

Then, Maria shouted and the phone went silent. CJ waited until Maria came back on, sounding a little out of breath. "He kicked Tommy in the knee. I sort of lost it and I might be trouble."

"Is he hurt bad?"

"He can still breathe through his mouth."

CJ threw her head back and looked up at the ceiling. "If he attacked Tommy, it's the guy's fault. You'll be all right."

"I'm not so sure."

"Why not?"

"I kicked the wind out of him."

"He'll be alright. Give him a few minutes then take him in."

"Well..."

"What else did you do, Maria?"

"You know how it is. One move follows another. I think his nose is broken."

"Tell me who he is."

105

"It's Chief Satterfield."

Something like a ball of cement settled in CJ's stomach. "You broke the nose of Riverview's chief of police?"

The baby must have sensed her stress and let loose with kicks and punches of his own. A contraction followed.

"Take him to jail. We'll figure out what to do there."

"Tommy's calling for an ambulance. It might be best if you met me at the hospital."

Another clump of cement hit bottom.

CJ had another thought sprint through her mind. "Go back to the stand and get the brass from the shot he took."

"We already have it. Tommy knew right where to look."

"I'll call David. He'll be waiting for you at the hospital. I'll be there as soon as I can. Make sure you get Tommy checked out, and take pictures."

CJ rubbed her distended midsection and walked to the bedroom at the same time. She manipulated her phone as she scanned the closet for something to wear.

David's words held both excitement and concern. "Do I need to come home? Is it time?"

"Meet me at the hospital."

"I don't want you driving if you're in labor."

CJ walked out of the closet. "Slow down. It's not me that needs a doctor. It's Chief Satterfield. Maria and Tommy arrested him for shooting a deer at the golf course. The chief kicked Tommy in the knee and Maria took strong offense to it."

David chuckled. "I wish I'd been there to see it." His tone became more somber. "What about the casing from the shot?"

"Tommy has it. I'm sure they have the rifle, but I didn't ask."

David became quiet, which wasn't a good sign. He broke the silence by saying, "I need to call Blake and Captain Crow to let them know what you've done now. I thought we talked last night about not stirring up a stink?"

"It's a gift. Trouble finds me, even when I'm home on maternity leave."

David changed his voice to an even firmer tone. "Don't come to the hospital. I'll take care of everything and give you a full report tonight."

She stomped her foot, pressed the disconnect button, and walked back into the closet. By the time she stopped looking at the racks of clothes, she allowed her shoulders to drop. "He's right. I'd be in the way. Maria's a big girl. This will be an experience she and Tommy will laugh about some day."

CJ's PHONE came to life again. Bea Stargate's name and smiling face appeared on the screen.

"What in the name of little green apples is going on? I heard Maria beat up and arrested the chief of police."

"That's not the entire story. The chief killed a deer at the city golf course and kicked the new game warden who caught him. You know Maria. She's not one to back down from a fight."

"Lord, have mercy. The chief tangled with the wrong wild-cat. It won't be long before we're introducing ourselves to a new chief of police."

"Do you think so?"

"Put money on it."

"Aren't you supposed to be teaching a class?"

"Starts in two minutes, and I'm three minutes away. Got to go."

The phone went silent. Everyone had somewhere to go and something important to do, except her. Times like this made being house bound unbearable. For the past eleven years, she'd responded to other people's emergencies. Now she pictured herself as a bird with its wings clipped, unable to fly.

After pouring herself a half cup of decaf coffee, she moved to a chair in the living room that overlooked the west pasture. Cows grazed on the far side of a white fence that separated the front yard from a field. Rain from land-hugging clouds dripped from the leaves of live oaks.

Before melancholy turned her world a darker shade of gray, she thought about what she could do to further the investigation. Many of the suspects were being downgraded to persons of interest. Her mind settled on Alejandro Vega. David hadn't given her an update on him. She stared out the window and whispered. "If David's report is what I think it is, Maria and I will need to pay Alejandro another visit. If she can stay out of trouble long enough."

She didn't realize that Sandy was standing by her side until the dog yawned, ambled to her doggy bed by the fireplace, made three circles and settled down for a nap.

"Not a bad idea, girl." CJ went to the couch, grabbed a book off the coffee table, and propped up on pillows. She didn't know when she nodded off, but the book was lying on the floor when she awoke.

The rest of the day was uneventful until Nancy and little Davey arrived, both cross and hungry. It proved to be an easy fix for the toddler. All it took was a dry diaper, a bottle of milk, and a few goldfish, and he was ready to explore the living room again. Nancy cut off a few slices of cheese, placed them between crackers, added a soda, and her blood sugar climbed back to a normal level.

Maria and Tommy arrived in separate vehicles, he in his state-issued truck and she in her Honda Accord. They, too, looked tired. The sheepish look on their faces told her the day had been trying.

"Tommy needs to unload his stuff," said Maria. "Is the barn and trailer open?"

"All ready," said CJ. "Would you like something to drink?"

Maria shook her head, and Tommy followed suit. "Thanks, but not now," he said. "What I could use are a couple aspirin, or Tylenol."

CJ nodded. "Maria, go look in my bathroom cabinet. There're all kinds of pain relievers to choose from."

Tommy sank down in a chair and rubbed his temples.

"Long day?" asked CJ.

He lowered his hands and raised his chin. "I wanted to hit the ground running, but I think it ran over me."

"When did you last eat?"

"I had a sweet roll early this morning. Nothing but coffee since then."

"Things will look better after you've had a good meal."

The back door opened and David came in carrying plastic bags emblazoned with the name of a local barbecue restaurant on them. "I hope everyone's hungry tonight."

David put the sacks on the counter and focused on Tommy. "Have you unloaded your gear?"

"Not yet."

"They arrived less than five minutes ago," said CJ.

Maria came back in the room, handed a bottle of generic acetaminophen pills to Tommy, and went to the kitchen cabinet containing glasses.

Tommy watched her every move. The corners of his mouth turned upward when she returned with the water. He thanked her, popped two pills in his mouth and washed them down. "I'd better get my truck unloaded."

"I'll help," said Maria.

"Supper in twenty minutes," said David.

Once the door closed, it left husband and wife alone to catch up. CJ led off by asking, "How bad was it?"

"Not bad, if you like a circus." He chuckled. "Let me put my pistol in the safe and I'll give you more details."

David returned and began pulling containers from the bags. "I'll put the meat in the oven to keep it warm."

After a full day of silence, CJ needed a decent conversation, and wasn't in the mood for incomplete answers. She raised her voice. "Well? Are Tommy and Maria in trouble?"

Again, David chuckled. "It depends on who you talk to. The chief and a couple of his captains were ready to arrest them. I think Riverview's mayor wants to give them a medal."

"Did you get involved?"

"Not much. I got everyone's story and relayed both sides to the mayor. Two city cops tried to get the chief released to them at the hospital. That's when I stepped in and told them Tommy and Maria were the arresting officers and they needed to back off."

"I'm surprised they did," said CJ.

"Maria and Tommy weren't about to be bullied by a couple of locals. She saved the day by reminding them she had her body camera on and was recording."

"Good girl. I don't know about a medal, but she deserves a promotion."

David's eyebrows lifted. "Do you think she's ready to take your place?"

CJ pulled out a barstool and sat down. The real question wasn't whether Maria was equipped to step into the position, but whether *she* was ready to step aside. It had occupied her thoughts since Doctor Norquist put her on bed rest. Her world spun with changes. In some ways, it was being torn apart and put back together, but what would it look like?

David didn't press for an answer. Instead, he pulled plates from the cabinet and set about placing them on the table.

To change the flow of the conversation, CJ asked, "Is Chief Satterfield in jail?"

"Released on a PR bond. In the end, cooler heads prevailed, but that didn't keep a news crew from getting footage of the chief being escorted into the county jail for booking."

"That will keep tongues wagging until Christmas. What else happened?"

David moved to the silverware drawer and spoke as he pulled out knives, forks, and spoons. "Noah Epstein's attorney called me after she heard about the incident. The chief shot the deer with a .308. I'd already sent a state trooper with the rifle and shell casing to the crime lab in Austin. If the brass matches the one found in Epstein's van, she'll file for a dismissal of all charges."

"More egg on Chief Satterfield's face."

David doled out the silverware. "And one more reason for the city to fire him."

Nancy came in, rubbing her eye with a balled fist and yawning. "I fell asleep reading to Davey. What's for supper? I'm starving."

"Fried bologna sandwiches with no cheese or bread," said David with a straight face.

Nancy stuck her tongue out at him.

Maria opened the back door and stepped into the kitchen, with Tommy close behind.

"That was quick," said CJ.

"All he brought was enough clothes for a week."

Tommy took over. "I'll need to go back to Hamilton to get my things after I find an apartment." His dimples made deep divots in his cheeks. "Of course, that may hinge on me getting fired."

David shook his head. "You didn't do anything wrong. Think what would happen to you if you'd overlooked the crime, and the press got hold of it."

"It's kind of a fluke that I'm here at all. I wasn't supposed to start until after Christmas, but they sent me to help with the manhunt after the judge was killed. I bet I've already met most every rancher and farmer on the west side of the county. There's some rugged country out there."

"Why don't they leave you here for good?" asked CJ.

"We had an unusual case I was working. It's still open, but I'm not sure if they'll make me go back or not. Right now, my assignment is to help with this case."

"What was so unusual about the case in Hamilton?"

"Someone shot four head of cattle during a thunderstorm. They cut out the loins and left the rest to rot. Nobody paid attention to the shots because of the noise from the lightning."

"That's strange," said David. "Any luck in finding the shooter?"

"No witnesses, but I got casts from the tires. It was a mismatched set. I also recovered a shell casing and two of the bullets."

"What caliber?" asked David.

".308."

"Another .308?" asked CJ.

"Where are the bullets and casing now?" asked David.

"In an evidence locker. The rounds were pretty messed up, and the lab in Austin couldn't match them to anything on file."

"When are you going for more of your things?"

"I thought I'd go on my first day off, but that's not for several days."

David had a gleam in his eye. He wasn't asking these questions to hear himself talk. This was one .308 too many. It wasn't much of a lead, but he'd follow up on it.

"That reminds me," said Tommy. "Did they ever find the bullet that killed Judge Kraft?"

David shook his head. "The lab boys looked for a full day with a metal detector. They never found the bullet."

Tommy shrugged. "That means they weren't looking in the right spot."

David raised his chin. "Do you think you can do better?"

"Can't do any worse. I'll bring my metal detector back with me. I bought it myself and I'll venture it's more advanced than what the crime scene investigators used."

CHAPTER FOURTEEN

Two days of rain ended when high pressure settled over the heart of Texas. Sunshine brightened CJ's mood almost as much as the prospect of her and Maria interviewing Alejandro Vega again. CJ took one look at Maria's compact car and suggested they take her SUV instead.

"If you get any bigger," said Maria, "you'll have to ride in the bed of a pickup."

CJ scowled and tossed her the keys. "You drive."

Holding the top strap of the seatbelt away from her did little to make the trip more comfortable. "David received a report on Alejandro. He has enough family to fill a bus in Mexico. Over half of what he earns ends up south of the border. His mother is a widow and isn't in good health."

Maria gave an almost imperceptible nod. "Anything else?"

"An extra-large money transfer went to Mexico the week before the murder. I had a hard time talking David into letting us conduct this interview. If we don't get something out of Alejandro today, David and Blake Cruz will take over."

The muscles in Maria's cheeks flexed. "Will Mrs. Kraft be there?"

"She's meeting us at the barn. I told her we need to talk to Alejandro again."

"Did you ask her where Alejandro's extra money came from?"

CJ's hand slipped off the seat belt, and it drew tight. She shifted in her seat, trying to get comfortable. "She didn't know, but said he's frugal. It could be money he's saved over the years."

Maria's lack of response wasn't out of character. She wasn't prone to small talk when the subject involved work, but that didn't apply to her newfound romantic interest. Jabbering on about Tommy was a different story.

"Where's Tommy working today?"

"We might run into him. We drove to Hamilton last night and picked up his metal detector. He's itching to find the bullet that killed Judge Kraft."

CJ rubbed her chin. "David didn't mention anything about that."

"Tommy didn't want to tell him he was searching until he found it."

"Just as well. David would spend the day helping him and wouldn't get anything else done."

They passed the university campus, its foliage ablaze with the last colors of fall. CJ thought of the number of times she'd walked the campus and driven down its streets. Memories flooded in, including one she wished she could forget. A gang member killed a university officer during a routine traffic stop. It was the worst night of her life as a supervisor. A campus street was also the place where she'd chased a reckless speeder. A truck ran a stop sign, clipped her patrol car, and she crashed into a tree. That event took the life of their unborn daughter. A shiver ran over her arms as she looked at the buildings and students. They seemed distant, a part of the past, not the future.

"Last of finals today," said Maria. "Things will be dead until after the new year."

It was CJ's turn to be quiet. They rode in silence as she pondered again her decision to return to work or become a full-time mom.

As if awakened from a foggy dream, CJ realized they'd reached their destination when Maria put the SUV in park and turned off the engine. Chris Kraft, dressed like a ranch hand, came toward them. Her chin tilted up and her lips pursed.

"Good morning," said CJ as she slid out of her vehicle.

"Morning." Chris looked at Maria. "I need to have a word alone with CJ."

Maria asked, "Is Alejandro in the barn?"

"Yes."

That was all it took for Maria to clear out.

Chris took off her baseball cap and brushed a lock of blond hair from her face. "What kind of girl is Nancy?"

CJ stiffened. "Why would you ask a question like that?"

"Answer the question."

"She's a loving mother, a hard worker, a brilliant student, and a young woman who's overcoming one of the worst child-hoods you can imagine. Despite everything she's been through, she has a bright future." CJ realized she was speaking through clenched teeth, but did nothing to stop it. "Again, why do you ask?"

"Did you know she and Kevin have been calling and sending text messages to each other?"

"She told me they ran into each other's grocery carts before Kevin went back to college. I knew they exchanged numbers."

Chris looked away for a few seconds and brought her gaze back to CJ. "I'll not beat around the bush. I don't want Kevin involved with your house guest. He's at a vulnerable time and

I don't want him making a mistake he'll regret for the rest of his life. I expect your cooperation in making sure this irresponsible fling stops."

It took everything in CJ not to lash out. How dare Chris tell either her or Nancy what to do. Especially since the words came from a serial adulteress who needed to clean the mess out of her own nest before she worried about anyone else. The hypocrisy longed to be put into words that would cut and sting, but CJ would not give her the pleasure of a rash response.

Chris didn't wait around for a reply. With ponytail bouncing from side-to-side, and shapely hips swinging, she made for her truck and left flinging mud.

It took several long minutes for CJ to bring her emotions under control enough to go to the barn and meet with Maria and Alejandro. Even after practicing her deep breathing exercises, she was in no mood for deception of any kind.

With clear skies and no wind, the day had warmed since she left home, but not enough to go without a jacket. She grabbed a coat from the back seat of the SUV. Since none of her coats were big enough to meet in the middle, she'd been forced to borrow one of David's. The sleeves had to be rolled up, but at least it kept her warm. Besides, she'd determined at the end of the seventh month that fashion and late-term pregnancy didn't co-exist. Put on what was serviceable and throw style to the wind.

Maria and Alejandro weren't in the barn, so she kept walking down the barn's middle aisle and came out at the far end in bright sunshine. She found the two of them standing by a corral, each with one boot on the bottom rail and the other on the ground.

Alejandro turned to face her. "*Buenos dias, Señora.*"

CJ nodded, turned to Maria, and spoke in a firm tone. "Ask him why he lied to us about his family in Mexico."

Maria didn't have a chance. Alejandro's eyes widened and his nostrils flared.

CJ took a step forward. "Next, ask him why he's been pretending he can't understand English."

This time, he looked at his boots.

Maria gave him her own hard look through squinted eyes. She reached in a pocket and pulled out a set of handcuffs. "Want to take him in for questioning?"

"We will if he doesn't cooperate."

The two women said nothing. In a negotiation like this, the first one to talk lost the game of hide-and-seek-the-truth. It proved to be Alejandro.

"What you want to know?"

His spoken English might come out slow and with poor grammar, but he understood what was being said.

"You send most of your money back to Mexico. Right?" asked CJ.

He nodded.

"Your mother is sick?"

"She needed operation."

"Did she have it yet?"

Again, he nodded.

CJ was getting close. The next questions and answers would either unlock an important door, or he'd shut down. "You sent her twenty-thousand dollars the week before Thanksgiving?"

"*Sí*."

"Did Mrs. Kraft or the judge give you extra money for the surgery?"

"No."

Maria had been quiet long enough. She tore into Alejandro with short, snappy sentences in Spanish. The tone of derision and threats gave the rolled r's of her speech even more menace. She turned away from the man who wouldn't look up. "I told him he'd better not lie; the next one would earn him a trip to jail."

"Who gave you the money?"

"I don't know the name. I see a white Chevy pickup truck. He tells to me—"

The words stopped. CJ had to get them going again. "What did he tell you? Did he threaten you?"

"No me."

"That means he threatened your family."

Alejandro's voice didn't rise above a whisper. "He know about Mama. He know where family live in Mexico. People back in Mexico kill for cheap. He bad man."

"Tell us what he wanted and leave nothing out."

"He want to know about Judge Kraft. When he leave in morning and come home at night."

"His schedule?" asked CJ.

"*Sí.*"

"Did he ask you about Thanksgiving Day?"

"*Sí.*"

"And he offered you money if you told him?"

"Money for Mama's operation. Mama no live with no operation."

Maria broke in again, speaking Spanish. After another tongue lashing, she said, "I told him he should have gone to the judge or Mrs. Kraft for the money."

CJ needed more. "What did this man look like?"

Maria took over. "It might be best if he told me in Spanish. I don't think his English is good enough to describe someone."

CJ listened as the two went back and forth with Maria taking notes. When the talking stopped, Maria said, "All Alejandro saw was the truck deliver the cash. He never got a good look at the guy driving it, and all prior communication was by phone."

That was all the information CJ needed. She nodded to Maria, and the detective spoke again in Spanish. Alejandro put his hands behind his back.

CJ pulled out her phone and called David. He answered on the third ring.

"Where are you?" she asked.

"Passing the hospital, on my way to the crime scene. Tommy called and asked me to come as soon as I could. He sounded excited."

"Stop by the Kraft's horse barn and pick up Alejandro on your way. You'll need to take him in and get a formal statement about his role in Judge Kraft's murder."

CJ heard David's vehicle speed up through her phone's speaker. "ETA of three minutes."

It only took David two-and-a-half minutes to arrive. "Have you read him his rights?" he asked.

"Maria did," said CJ. "But that was after he told us about being approached by a man calling himself John Buck."

David shook his head. "Cute. The masculine version of Jane Doe."

"He paid Alejandro for information about Judge Kraft's routine. The money went to Mexico to pay for a life-saving surgery for Alejandro's mother."

David nodded and waited for more.

"Before Alejandro left the ranch around noon on Thanksgiving, Chris checked the horses. She told him to enjoy his afternoon off and the only time she'd be away from the ranch was to take a walk with her husband. John Buck called Alejandro after Chris left."

"How long after she left?"

"Only a few minutes."

"That means this Buck character was in the neighborhood watching, waiting for his chance."

David's gaze shifted to Alejandro standing by his SUV as

CJ continued. "Alejandro told him about the afternoon walk the judge and Chris were planning. That gave the guy plenty of time to set up in the house at the end of the street."

David took a step toward Alejandro.

"One more thing," said CJ. "Alejandro was supposed to get paid twenty-thousand dollars for information. He got the first ten grand the week before and was supposed to get the other half after he gave Buck the information he wanted.."

"Was he foolish enough to think he'd get the other half?"

"Of course not. He had money saved and only needed ten grand more for the surgery, so he asked for twenty. He's been around horse traders long enough to know how to play the game."

CJ put her hand on David's arm. "Don't be too hard on him. John Buck knew about Alejandro's family and used it as leverage."

David's phone rang, putting an end to the conversation. The call didn't last long. "Tommy thinks he's found the bullet that killed Judge Kraft, but he can't reach it."

Maria ran to the driver's side of CJ's SUV. "Let's go."

CJ looked at David. "I think my driver will leave me standing here if I don't get in."

INSTEAD OF PARKING on the road, Tommy had backed his truck into the yard of a home in the first stages of construction. He stood in the bed of his truck, reaching up into a tree with his metal detector. Thick earphones covered his ears.

David and Maria trotted ahead while CJ took her time. By the time she arrived, David had climbed into the bed of the truck while Tommy and Maria stood nearby, looking up at a place where a large branch split off from the trunk.

Tommy pointed to the house where the shot originated. "It's on a straight line."

David closed one eye, raised a finger and used it as a reference.

Tommy kept talking. "Put on these headphones and take the detector."

David did as instructed.

Tommy flipped a switch and David jerked the headphones away.

"Sorry," said Tommy. "Keep the sweep away from the metal on the truck."

David leaned the sweep against the trunk of the tree and put on the headphones again.

"Keep the sweep close to the tree and work your way up. When you get to the branch that goes to the left, follow it."

David eyes widened. He moved the detector back and forth several times. "There's metal embedded in the branch."

Tommy turned off the detector. "It's there, but I'm at least six inches shorter than you."

David studied the distance to the branch from the bed of the truck. "If I put one foot on the top of the tailgate and the other on the top of the side, I should be able to get it." The trunk of the tree acted as a brace for his hand, giving him the height needed to complete surgery on the tree.

"I can see where it entered." David pulled out his camera and snapped a picture. "We'd better get distant pictures of this, too." He looked down. "Maria, look in the console of my truck and get an evidence bag."

With the preliminaries completed, David took out a pocket knife and gouged a hole in the branch, taking care to keep the blade far enough away not to scar the bullet. It took several minutes before he climbed down empty handed.

"Isn't it there?" asked CJ.

"It's there, all right. I need to put on a glove."

Tommy pulled a pair from his coat pocket and handed them to David.

"Thanks. I only need one."

It only took a few seconds before David held the prize in the palm of his hand. He examined it like a jeweler might a diamond and showed it to the others. "It's pretty beat up, but there might be enough to get a match if we can find the rifle it came from."

Maria looked to be busting with pride. Tommy had found a key piece of evidence. "How did you know to look up in a tree?"

He climbed down from the truck bed and received a hug. "We know the shot went all the way through the body. It came at a slight downward trajectory. That means it hit concrete and ricocheted. The team searched the ground, but it's not natural to look up. The bullet still had enough energy to embed in the tree."

David added, "It went between two pieces of thick bark. I couldn't see where it entered until I got close."

The bullet went into an evidence bag, and the group huddled together. David cast his gaze at Tommy. "Do you have time to run CJ home?"

"No problem."

"Good. I need Maria to come with me and help me interview Alejandro. CJ will tell you about the progress she and Maria made today."

CJ pulled her shoulders back, which only made her bump stick out all the more. "Wait a minute, buster. Don't I have a say in who interviews him?"

"You've been on your feet too long. It's time for you to stop playing cop and take care of yourself."

She bit back the words on the tip of her tongue and resigned herself to compliance, even though she longed to complete the job she started.

On the way home, she explained all that had transpired to Tommy. He listened and said, "I thought the case had stalled and was destined for the unsolved file. What you and Maria did today will get things going again."

"Don't forget your contribution," said CJ. "That's the first piece of solid evidence we've gathered since day one."

"All we need is the gun." He turned to her. "And the guy who fired the shot."

"You're on your own for that. I've done all I can do until after I drop this load."

"Does that mean you'll be going back to work?"

The baby gave her a kick. "We'll see."

CHAPTER FIFTEEN

Nancy looked up from her bowl of sugar-coated corn flakes. "What time is your doctor's appointment?"

CJ lowered herself into a chair at the breakfast table. "Ten-fifteen. Didn't you say you're working at the vet clinic today?"

Red, curly hair bobbed when Nancy nodded. "One of his assistants wanted the day off to go to Austin and Christmas shop."

"I did mine online this year."

Nancy's eyes sparkled with mischief. "What did you get me?"

Before she could answer, David turned the corner and said, "A bucket of coal and a spoon for a shovel."

The teen held up her hands. "As long as the bucket and shovel are solid silver or gold, I'll take it."

Instead of sitting down, David moved to the refrigerator and considered his options for breakfast. "Do you want a hot breakfast?"

"Oatmeal and toast are what I'm supposed to eat," said CJ.

It wasn't David's idea of breakfast. "I'll fix it for you and leave early. I haven't checked in at the Black Kettle all week."

CJ thanked him and turned to Nancy. "Any results on your finals?"

The answer came as she lifted a spoon of cereal and milk. "Same as last time."

"Keep it up and you'll be in vet school right on schedule."

Nancy shook her head. "I'm upping my game and taking an extra class with a lab next semester. If I keep going at that pace and go summers, I'll finish a year early."

"Aren't you afraid you'll burn out?"

"The only classes that give me trouble are the ones I'm not interested in, like political science and sociology. With only a couple more required courses, I should breeze through my bachelor's degree."

"Weren't you talking about a double major?" asked David.

Nancy nodded. "Chemistry and math."

David poured the oatmeal into the pan of boiling water and put it on simmer. "Why do you want to finish in three years?"

She didn't return his gaze. "Here comes the interrogation."

David leaned against the counter. "You're not only smart, you're strategic. There's always a reason behind your decisions. I'm wondering why the sudden desire to get to A&M."

Nancy shoveled in hurried bites of cereal to avoid saying anything more.

CJ knew the answer. "I heard you talking to Kevin last night. How is he?"

"He'd be better if his mom would let us see each other."

"She hasn't relented?"

"We have a plan."

CJ shifted in her chair. "What does that mean?"

Nancy finished her cereal and spoke as she took her bowl

to the sink. "So far, he's negotiated phone calls to me, as long as we don't text each other. Of course, there's no dating on the horizon, but we're taking what we can get and working on the next compromise."

David checked the oatmeal. "It sounds like negotiations for an international treaty."

"Similar," said Nancy. "Patience and persistence will win the day."

Once Nancy was out of sight and the door to her bedroom closed, CJ looked at David. "Chris Kraft doesn't have a chance. Nancy will be dating Kevin by spring break and Chris will think it's her idea."

The toaster produced browned bread as David poured oatmeal into a bowl. The delivery of hot cereal, along with toast, earned him a kiss on the cheek. He asked, "What time is your appointment?"

"Ten-fifteen. It's my last weekly appointment before Christmas."

"Bea's driving you?"

"Uh-huh."

"And she'll look after Davey during the appointment?"

"Before, during, and after." She lifted her spoon and blew to cool the first bite.

David left the room, returned with a jacket, and bent down for another kiss. "Be careful."

CJ waved him off. "I'm going to a doctor's office, not a drug bust."

———

BEA STARGATE CAME through the back door humming The Twelve Days of Christmas. She wore a red sweater with a neck-to-waist felt Christmas tree appliqued on the front, complete with dangling ornaments and blinking lights. The only thing brighter was her smile.

"Reporting for duty," said Bea with a firm salute. "Where's that young 'un?"

"Not up yet," said CJ.

The words had no more left her mouth when little Davey rounded the corner. Like a homing pigeon, he headed straight for Bea and gave her left leg a monster hug, with grunts and growls included.

Instead of kneeling, Bea sat on the floor and filled her arms with the toddler. After the hug, Bea looked up at Nancy. "Has he eaten yet?"

CJ answered. "David made extra oatmeal. It should still be warm."

Nancy made quick work of scooping the oatmeal into a bowl, adding pureed peaches, and putting little Davey in his high chair.

"You have things to do." said Bea. "Get to work and let me shovel in his breakfast."

"Thanks, Bea. There'll be a line of dogs and cats waiting at the clinic. Doc Steele says business picks up around Christmas because there are so many new things for them to chew."

"That reminds me," said Bea. "I'm gettin' Billy Paul a puppy for Christmas."

Nancy's eyes lit up. "What kind?

"Something small and yappy."

"I thought Billy Paul would want a lab, or Irish setter."

Bea shook her head, but not a single hair moved. "He's been talking about an indoor dog for the last six months. He wants one that will warn him when someone's driving up to the house."

Nancy gathered her purse and kissed her son on the top of his head. "Gotta go. Thanks for all the help."

Bea spooned in oatmeal and peaches until the bowl emptied. While Davey was busy eating, CJ fixed a sippy cup of milk. Bea gave it to Davey and turned her attention to her hostess. "Anything new on the murder of Judge Kraft that you can talk about?"

"Some. Noah Epstein is out of jail with all charges dropped."

Bea's reaction told CJ this was old news. As usual, Bea knew more about things going on in town than she did. "The city council met last night. There was a motion to fire the chief, but they tabled the final decision until after the new year."

"Why put it off?"

The cup slipped from Davey's grip, but he made a fast recovery.

"Hold on to that cow-juice, little man," said Bea. She then answered the question. "I hear they want to give him a chance to resign. That, and it's bad luck to fire someone before Christmas."

Davey lost interest in the milk and banged the cup on the plastic table that pinned him in. Bea unclipped the top and took Davey down. His legs churned before his feet hit the ground. He made for the living room and a basket of toys.

"Any other progress?"

"Only one more thing," said CJ. "The rifling on the bullet that David dug out of a tree matched others that killed several head of cattle on a ranch near Hico."

Bea's eyes opened wide. "That sounds important."

"It is, but without the rifle, it doesn't get us much closer."

"Sooner or later, everything will come together."

"If I was the shooter," said CJ, "I'd be hiding out in Mexico."

While Bea played with Davey, CJ excused herself to shower and get ready for what she hoped would be her last weekly appointment. She didn't know why, but the gut feeling that their son would be born on either Christmas Eve or Christmas Day couldn't be denied. Thoughts of a healthy baby left no room for concerns over finding Judge Kraft's killer.

On her way out of the living room, she took note that it bristled with Christmas greenery and decorations. A trove of presents sat beneath a tree that sparkled and blinked. In her bedroom, a new crib, along with a changing table and all the supplies, awaited the child. She ran her hand over the mattress, where their special gift would soon lie.

After dressing, CJ puttered around the house while Bea played with Davey. She double-checked the bag Nancy packed for Davey and slipped on her coat. "You two ready, Bea?" She draped a wool scarf around her neck and waited at the back door. Bea finally corralled her young charge after he escaped to make another lap around the living room.

CJ's eyebrows lifted in surprise at the sight of Bea's ATV parked in the driveway. "I assume we're taking my car today?"

Bea grinned and explained, "I took mine to the Mercedes dealer for routine maintenance today, so I brought my hunting buggy instead. I hope it's all right if we take your ride."

"No problem. I'll let you drive." She handed Bea the keys. "It's awkward for me to drive with this child in the way."

The rocking motion of the car worked its magic on Davey who was asleep before they hit the main highway to town. With no toddler to distract them, Bea gushed about this Christmas being the best ever. She went into detail concerning the living nativity she and Billy Paul were planning. "We're setting it up on the far side of the river, and the entire community's invited to come on the five days leading up to Christmas. There'll be exotic animals, actors in period costumes, and free food. If a free meal doesn't attract a crowd, nothing will."

"Sounds fun. Nancy said you're going to have an airplane towing the banner of Santa's sleigh. Should be quite a sight."

Bea's eyes twinkled with excitement. "Don't forget the spotlights on Santa. One at the house and one in town."

"Santa," said Davey from the back seat.

Bea looked in the rearview mirror. "I thought you were asleep."

The magic word worked like a key to wind up the toddler. Conversation about Santa and reindeer filled the car for the rest of the trip to the professional building adjacent to the hospital.

Bea let CJ and Davey off at the front door and went to park the car.

"Lord have mercy," said Bea after sliding glass doors whooshed shut behind her. "I thought the wind was gonna' blow the hair right off my head."

They passed through the lobby and walked down a hall to an office that was one of many in the warren of halls. CJ checked in while Bea took a seat with Davey. Ten minutes later, she sat shivering in a thin gown, waiting for the doctor.

As usual, the stethoscope was cold, the examination quick but thorough, and there were no surprises.

"As things stand, you're right on schedule," said Dr Norquist. "My only concern is he's a large baby."

"What do you mean?"

She patted her on the arm. "The baby's fine. It's you I'm thinking about. You're not due until the first week in January. Because of your blood pressure problems, we may not have the luxury of allowing this young man to decide to arrive on his own. We may need to induce labor between Christmas and New Year's Day."

"I understand inducing doesn't always work. What happens then?"

"I don't think it will come to it, but if you haven't delivered by your due date, we're looking at a possible cesarean section. In the meantime, continue to watch your sodium intake, stay off your feet, elevate them as much as possible, and avoid high-stress situations. Your blood pressure is still borderline, but I'm confident it will go back to normal once you deliver."

It took self-control, but CJ didn't tell the doctor not to plan on a C-section, or even inducing labor. This would be a Christmas baby. She was sure of it.

After dressing, she checked out, confirmed the next visit, and went to the waiting room to gather Bea and Davey.

Bea looked up with smiling blue eyes. "Everything must be like it should be. You look happy as a kitten with new drapes to shred."

"Right on schedule," said CJ. She didn't say whose schedule.

As they approached the main entrance, Bea held out a hand in front of CJ. "Wait here with Davey, and I'll go get your ride. No need in you two getting out in this wind. One thing we don't want is Davey getting an ear ache with Christmas right around the corner."

CJ didn't argue, and it wasn't long before Bea wheeled the Lexus SUV under the covered driveway. Taking Davey by the hand, CJ headed for the door. A bearded young man came running from outside, having parked his vehicle behind Bea under the awning. The doors parted and a blast of wind took CJ's scarf and sent it flying. Distracted by the man when he raised his arm to catch it, CJ loosened her grip on Davey and he walked on by himself.

One half of the glass door exploded into a thousand shards. The man screamed and fell to the floor. Davey's wail filled the air. Working only on instinct, CJ grabbed the collar of his coat and pulled him away from the doorway. She turned him around to check for injuries. Blood trickled down his forehead and dripped from his nose. A shard of glass was embedded in his forehead. Without thinking, she pulled it out and watched blood make a stream down his face. The man on the floor had his right hand over a limp left arm with blood oozing from between his fingers.

"Crawl this way!" shouted CJ.

It was after she issued the command that reality set in. Someone was shooting and they might not be finished.

CHAPTER SIXTEEN

CJ's first responsibility was to get Davey out of harm's way and get him help. He screamed with mouth wide open as blood stained his coat, pants, and shoes. Scooping him up, she ran down the hall to the office she'd just left. Waiting patients greeted her with wide eyes as she threw open the door and took long strides to the reception desk.

"He needs to see a doctor... Now!" said CJ in her best cop voice.

Davey had his head buried in her coat so the receptionist couldn't see him. "Do you have an appointment?" she asked.

Before CJ could answer, Bea flew through the door. "Let me have him; you need to contact David, or somebody."

Davey went to Bea's waiting arms.

CJ's gaze bore into the receptionist. "Get this child treatment, now."

The woman bristled in defiance until she saw the stream of blood coming down the toddler's face.

CJ pulled out her phone and punched in 911. The dispatcher didn't have time to go through her normal script before CJ spoke. "This is CJ Harper, the assistant chief of

134

police at ACU. There's an active shooter at the medical professional building behind the hospital. Shots fired. At least two injuries. I'll keep the line open."

Gasps came from those in the waiting room. A woman wearing scrubs arrived and told Bea to follow her. CJ held up a hand to form a stop sign. "Put everyone in rooms with doors that lock. Shelter in place until the police tell you it's safe to come out."

The receptionist stood to leave.

"Not you," said CJ. "You have an emergency plan for sheltering in place. Call whoever is in charge and tell them what I said and to implement the plan." She dug in her purse to retrieve her pistol. "After you make the call, find a doctor. There's a gunshot victim in the lobby."

DAVID'S modest office at the local highway patrol looked like someone was packing to move. Boxes of files littered the floor and his desk. One by one, he scoured through court transcripts, searching for clues to Judge Kraft's killer. The name of the shooter might be somewhere in the hundreds of people who'd appeared before the judge in court. "Too many suspects," he whispered. Weldon Kraft was a no-nonsense judge who leaned toward stiff sentences.

David groaned as he wrote yet another name on a yellow legal pad and slipped the reviewed file into a box.

His hand reached for another file when a highway patrolman raced past his door, shouting, "Active shooter at the professional building by the hospital." He glanced at the circular clock and leapt to his feet so fast his rolling office chair slammed against the wall. "CJ's check-up. She's there."

The only reason he grabbed his coat was because it held his portable radio. He turned it on as he sprinted from the building to his SUV. It crackled with the broadcasts of responding officers.

He jerked open the door to his unmarked SUV and threw his coat into the passenger seat. The engine fired and he willed the vehicle to gain traction as he raced toward the exit. He brought his vehicle under control after it slid sideways coming out of the parking lot and floored the accelerator once again. Sirens screamed as he trailed another highway patrolman to the scene. Even though the clinic wasn't far, it seemed to be on the other side of the moon as the two of them wove their way through traffic.

By the time he arrived, a city patrol car and a deputy sheriff had the two exits to the parking lot blocked. A third police car from the city sat fifty yards away from the entrance. The highway patrolman and David passed the policeman at the entrance and made for the car closest to the building.

A broadcast from a dispatcher came through David's radio. "ACU 02 reports she has eyes on the building entrance and there's no sign of the shooter inside."

His heart skipped a beat. In his mind's eye, he could see his very pregnant wife with pistol in hand and nothing between her and a person with a gun. He keyed his radio and gave his call sign. When dispatch got back to him, he said, "Tell ACU 02 to get behind a locked door."

The dispatcher came back after several long seconds. "02 said she'll wait where she is until you come get her."

"Hard-headed woman," David muttered.

The dispatcher called out David's badge number again. "02 reports the shot came from the parking lot. She wants you to clear the lot before coming in."

More police arrived, including a highway patrol lieutenant. He assumed command and directed everyone to put on body armor before they checked the cars in the lot.

David took the time to heed the warning and put on his tactical vest and helmet. He also grabbed his assault rifle from the back of his SUV while he was there.

His phone rang. Instead of CJ, the voice of Texas Ranger Captain Crow filled the air. A wailing siren accompanied his words. "Talk to me."

"I'm on scene. CJ's inside with eyes on the entrance and front lobby. She said the shot came from the parking lot. I'm expecting a call from her."

David hung up. As soon as he did, his phone rang again.

"Who were you talking to?"

His wife's snippy voice sounded wonderful to him. "Captain Crow. It sounded like he's on his way."

"Is the parking lot being cleared?"

David felt his heart beating as if he'd sprinted a mile. "Officers are clearing it now."

CJ spoke in clear, calm sentences. "Davey caught some glass in his forehead. It's not too bad, but he's one scared little boy. Bea is with him."

"I heard there's a second victim."

"A guy was coming in as I came out. He took the shot. His arm looked terrible. A doctor helped him to a treatment room. The lobby's clear."

More panic drained away the longer CJ talked. David looked around the parking lot. Officers laced their way through parked cars, checking for any sign of the shooter. "Give us some more time to clear the lot and we'll be coming in. Is there any chance the shooter came inside?"

"It's unlikely."

"Where will you be when we come in?"

"I made a false barricade out of chairs. Look to the left of it. I'll be behind a wall, watching you in a concave mirror."

"Good thinking. You'll have a lot of company soon."

The world slowed. Perhaps it was because David was

eager to get into the building. Or was it CJ's voice that told him she was no longer in imminent danger? Adrenaline was still high, but his breathing and heart rate were closer to normal.

With the parking lot cleared, David led a group of three state troopers and a city officer into the building. Glass crunched under their feet as they passed through the retractable doors. One of them was missing half of its pane of glass. The rest looked like a spider web of fractures. CJ's wool scarf lay amid the shards.

"Over here," shouted CJ. "I'm coming out."

She walked with empty hands held toward the ceiling. Muzzles of weapons shifted away from her. She pointed. "Bea is in the first office. I called her while you were clearing the lot. She said she saw a white Chevy truck leave in a hurry after the shot."

"What direction?"

CJ shook her head. "She didn't know. She pulled the injured man out of the doorway and came looking for Davey."

More officers arrived. One-by-one they searched the offices and every square inch of the building. The long, laborious task of taking names of frightened patients and staff began. David and CJ went to examine the door and the wall next to it.

David leaned over to inspect a gash in the wall. "The glass and the guy's arm slowed it down, but here's where it entered." A water fountain sat in an alcove on the other side of the wall. There was an entry hole in the metal fountain, but no exit. A puddle had formed on the floor beneath it. "Forensics won't have to search for this one."

CJ grabbed David's arm, her eyes wide with alarm. "How could I forget? I need to check on Bea and Davey."

She turned and took long strides across the foyer. David trotted to catch with her. "I'm sure they're fine."

CJ burst through the office door and headed for the desk. "Where's the little boy I brought in?"

With no questions asked, the woman pointed to the door separating the waiting room from the examination rooms. "Second on the right."

Davey played with Bea's car keys as she bounced him on her knees. The lad pointed to his head and said, "Owee."

CJ took the chair next to Bea. "That's right. Davey has an owee, but it's getting better."

"Three stitches near his hairline," said Bea. "He didn't like the needle, but then who does?"

David asked, "Have you called Nancy?"

"I didn't think it would do any good. She might get in an accident trying to get here, and they wouldn't let her in yet, anyway."

Neither of them found fault with her logic or actions. David said, "This place will be a mess for the rest of the day. I'll get you out of here as soon as you give me a statement."

He pulled out his phone and put it on record.

Bea continued to bounce Davey. "I went to get CJ's SUV after her appointment, so she and Davey didn't get in the wind. A man parked behind me. I was getting out when he ran up to the door. As he went in, the doors spread apart and a gust of wind took CJ's scarf and sent it a' flying. She took a step back, and the man tried to catch it in mid-air as the doors were coming back together." Bea looked up with wide eyes. "Now that I think about it, that shot went right over Davey's head."

"And the truck?" asked David.

"I spun around when I realized what was going on. The shooter parked the truck several rows back. Like I told CJ, it's a Chevy half-ton, all white. Not a new model, but not that old, either. The shooter wore a cowboy hat and a red bandanna over his face. He must have had the truck running because he took off like a cat with its tail on fire."

"You didn't see which way the truck turned out of the parking lot?"

Bea shook her head with vigor. "The driver wasn't waiting around, and I had to get to Davey and CJ."

David verified that was all Bea could offer and turned off the recording app. "Come with me. You and Davey can stop by Doc Steele's on your way home and fill Nancy in."

"What about CJ?"

"Half the cops in the county are here," said CJ. "I won't have any trouble finding a ride."

David and CJ escorted Bea and Davey out of the building and were walking back in when a black SUV pulled up. Out stepped Captain Crow. With no preliminaries he said, "Find an office where the three of us can talk in private."

CHAPTER SEVENTEEN

The receptionist pointed to the door leading to the examination rooms when the trio approached her. No words necessary this time.

CJ led the way to the room Bea and Davey had just vacated. The door clicked shut behind them, and David pointed to a chair for her. He drew a second chair to face her and put her swollen feet in it.

"I want to hear every detail," said Captain Crow. "Let's start with you, CJ."

She breezed through the preliminaries of her purpose for being at the clinic, and other non-essentials. Her narrative slowed when she described Bea leaving to bring their vehicle to the building's entrance.

CJ closed her eyes and spoke as she visualized the man parking his car behind Bea in the driveway, him jogging to the door, the wind snatching her scarf, and sending it flying. She opened her eyes and explained how she took a step back, out of the man's way.

Captain Crow asked, "Did you know the man?"

CJ shook her head. "I still don't."

"And the toddler broke away from you?"

"He was excited about Aunt Bea taking us for hot chocolate and Christmas cookies on the way home. He didn't run ahead as much as I shied away out of reflex when I saw the man's arm coming at me. You know kids; they don't pay much attention."

She explained the glass shattering and her jerking Davey out of the doorway. Next, she told them how she removed the shard of glass from his forehead and saw the man writhing on the floor.

"What about the man? Did you try to move him?"

"I had my hands full with Davey. My only thought was to get him help and out of harm's way."

The Ranger remained expressionless. "Go on."

"I came back here to my doctor's office. Bea Stargate came in and took Davey from me before they could get him back to a room."

"And then?"

She closed her eyes again. "I think I hollered at the receptionist. She was frozen and she needed to make sure the building implemented their shelter-in-place protocols. That's when I called 911 and retrieved my pistol from my purse."

Captain Crow nodded. "You have your gun in hand. Are you still talking to the 911 dispatcher?"

"I stayed on the line and went to the lobby to make sure the shooter didn't come in."

He looked through squinted eyes. "Did you stack those chairs as a barricade?"

David answered for her. "It was a ruse. She made it look like a barricade but knew the chairs wouldn't stop anything. She stayed behind a wall and looked at the lobby in the reflection of a convex mirror."

That earned her a "Huh," which she interpreted as approval.

"I waited there until David arrived with the cavalry."

CJ's grimace brought an immediate reaction from David. "What's wrong?"

She took in a deep, cleansing breath and spoke on the exhale. "Having a contraction. Nothing serious." She ran her fingertips over the mound that had taken the place of her trim midsection. "Play your recording of Aunt Bea's account for Captain Crow and tell him about the bullet."

David took out his phone, and Bea's voice filled the room. The Ranger listened while staring at the floor. He waited until the recording stopped before he said, "At least we have some pieces to add to the puzzle. We know for sure the shooter drives a white Chevy half-ton, and I believe he meant to kill CJ. I'll check out the injured guy, but I don't think he was the target."

Captain Crow's gaze fixed on David. "What about the bullet?"

"It's embedded in a water fountain on the other side of the entryway wall. I estimated the trajectory. It appeared flat. Based on what Bea Stargate said, combined with the entry and exit holes of the wall, I believe the shooter rested a rifle on the hood of the truck, took the shot and didn't wait around to see the results."

The Ranger pulled a hand down his face. "Any other conclusions?"

David swallowed. "You're right. The shooter intended to hit CJ. I also think it's the same person tied to Judge Kraft's murder. Whoever it is, they're not a real professional, but they're motivated."

The reality of David's and Captain Crow's words hit CJ like a club. For a few quiet seconds, she thought about challenging them, but it was no use. If the man hadn't bolted through the door and tried to catch her scarf, she wouldn't have taken a step back. Davey was short enough that the bullet passed over his head. The man with a mangled arm was an unlucky victim of a shot meant for her.

The memory of the person watching her in the white pickup at Judge Kraft's funeral flashed through her mind. It must be the same guy that came to the judge's funeral. What she didn't know was, why would someone want her dead?

Her mind blazed with questions. She almost missed Captain Crow ask David, "How's the security at your place?"

"Good, but not what it's going to be."

"Do you have room for a couple of state troopers to stay with you?"

"Sure. We already have a game warden living in the travel trailer."

"You need someone else in the house."

CJ broke into the conversation they'd left her out of. "I'd like Maria Vasquez to come. Nancy and Davey can go to Bea's until you catch this guy."

No objections came from either man. Captain Crow looked at David. "Has anything caught your eye in the court cases you're reviewing?"

"A lot of possible suspects, but none that made me tingle."

"Nothing else is going to happen here today," said Captain Crow with certainty. "Take the troopers you need and search your house, barn, and anywhere you think a marksman could shoot from. I don't want another ambush. I'll have the boxes of files in your office transferred to your home. Find something that makes you tingle and call me the minute it happens."

"I'll help him," said CJ. "It's better than watching television or looking at my fat feet."

Captain Crow scowled. "I'd be wasting my breath if I told you no. You two work together and get something for us to follow up on." His attention turned to David. "In case I

JUSTICE ON A MIDNIGHT CLEAR

haven't made myself clear, your only responsibilities are reviewing files, finding suspects, and keeping your wife alive."

CJ wondered about the order of importance, but said nothing.

A knock on the door preceded Dr. Norquist coming in. She gave a stern look to CJ, but it was nothing compared to the glare she gave Captain Crow and David.

She held the door open. "If you two are finished endangering my patient, I'll examine her again."

David and Captain Crow beat a quick and silent retreat.

The exam took less time than the lecture. It took all of CJ's skills of persuasion to assure her obstetrician that she'd restrict her activities to a bare minimum. She omitted any talk about her home becoming an armed fortress.

To further appease the frowning physician, CJ volunteered to stay still and quiet for at least an hour before she went home. Again, this was a bit of subterfuge. David and the troopers needed time to search their home, outbuildings, and land. She wouldn't be able to leave for an hour or more, even if she wanted to.

When a nurse's aide brought her a blanket and pillow, she used the exam table as a makeshift bed. A flick of the switch by the young woman took care of the glaring overhead light. Once she was alone, CJ used relaxation techniques to calm her soul. A light knock on the door brought her out of a half-awake, half-asleep dream.

Maria Vasquez peered around the door, spilling light into the room. "How can you be sleeping?"

"I've been practicing," said CJ through a yawn. "What time is it?"

"A little after one."

The ebbing of adrenaline combined with the relaxation techniques did the trick. She'd slept at least an hour. "Turn the light on, Maria."

A nurse came in as CJ swung her legs off the table. "I need to get your blood pressure. Dr. Norquist said you can go home if it's not too high."

CJ passed the test and she and Maria were soon heading away from the clinic. The trip through town seemed surrealistic when compared with what had occurred less than three hours prior. It was business as usual for everyone else.

CJ noticed hanging clothes and a gym bag in Maria's back seat. "I guess David called you and asked you to babysit me."

"Not exactly," said Maria. "There wasn't any asking. Captain Crow called President Cummings and told her you requested me. Your mother-in-law seems to have a very high opinion of you." Maria grinned. "I suppose making sure you give her a grandson had something to do with it."

"How did she sound?"

"Insistent."

"I hope it didn't upset her too much. Does she know we think the shooter was trying for me?"

Maria slowed for a stop light. "She knows. That's why she didn't ask."

"I hope this doesn't interfere with any plans you might have had."

Once coming to a full stop, Maria stared at her. "You may not realize it, but you're giving me the best Christmas present I could ask for. They assigned Tommy and me to protect you. That means we'll be close to each other throughout the holidays."

"I hadn't thought of it that way."

Maria's phone came to life. A man's voice came through her car's speakers. "There's a white Chevy truck headed your way, westbound. Didn't get a good look at the driver."

"Turning right. I'll go two blocks, turn left and then cut back over."

CJ put her hand on the dash as Maria made a quick right turn. "Who was that?"

"A city cop. He's been two blocks ahead of us looking for anything suspicious ever since we left the clinic."

"Good grief," said CJ.

"There's another one following us," said Maria. "Both are in unmarked cars."

CJ leaned forward enough to see a car turning at the intersection. "This seems like overkill."

"Not a wonderful choice of words," said Maria.

The rest of the trip to their farm went without incident. Maria backed into the carport in the spot nearest the mudroom door. David opened the door and walked her inside. He'd discarded the helmet but still wore the tactical vest.

Something was missing, but CJ didn't know what it was until David deposited her on the couch. Then she asked, "Where's Sandy?"

"On patrol with Tommy. There's nothing that dog likes better than to be outside looking for intruders."

CJ nodded, but her home felt out of balance. The blinds were closed and someone had drawn the drapes. Nancy and Davey were conspicuous by their absence. David assumed a demeanor of full army mode. With greenery on the mantle and blinking lights on the tree, her home had taken on the vibe of a well-decorated bunker.

"You just missed Bea, Nancy, and Davey."

"How's little Davey?"

"Fussy. The shot must have worn off. Nancy fixed him a bottle, but he pushed it away."

"Tired, hungry, and hurting," said CJ.

David nodded. "What about you? Need something to eat?"

Maria came into the living room before CJ could answer.

"I put my things in the first bedroom. Is that where you want me?"

"Perfect," said David. "That puts you on the south end of the house, close to the door by the carport. We'll have someone at all times in the middle, guarding the front and back doors. CJ will be in the master bedroom at the north end of the house."

"I hope you don't intend to keep me locked in the bedroom," said CJ.

"Only at night. Make sure you don't leave the blinds or drapes open."

With great effort, she held back a snarky comment. The desire to criticize clued her in to her need to elevate her blood-sugar level. "Is there any casserole left from last night?"

David ran a hand over her shoulder and stepped into the kitchen. Maria followed and their muted voices drifted in from the east side of the house.

CJ hollered from the couch. "When will the boxes of files arrive?"

David walked back into the living room, lifted her feet, and placed them on his lap. "Maria's heating the casserole in the microwave. Belinda's bringing the boxes of files this afternoon."

"Is she staying, too?"

"I requested her."

"Wasn't she a Marine?"

David rose and placed her feet on a throw pillow. He moved to the front window and nudged the edge of the curtain aside. He spoke as he watched the field in front of their home. "Don't use past tense with a Marine. They take offense to it."

CJ sort of enjoyed all the attention people were giving her, but wondered how long until it wore thin. Still, there was work to be done after the files arrived. "What will I be looking for in the court transcripts?"

"Anything that strikes you as odd. We're going on the theory that there's a link between Judge Kraft and someone shooting at you. I think we'll know it when we see it."

Maria delivered lunch with a glass of water and a paper napkin. She looked at David. "Where's Tommy?"

"He's between here and the river. The land is mostly open on the other three sides. If it was me trying to get to CJ, I'd stay in cover and follow the river. Do you want to go see him?"

"He knows I'm here." The corner of her mouth turned up. "I'll let him wait a while."

CJ couldn't help but smile. Maria was learning how to play a game she'd never played before.

CHAPTER EIGHTEEN

"What do you mean we can't come for Christmas?"

"It's hard to explain on the phone, Mom," said CJ. "Things are a little tense around here."

"Things are always tense in the last week before a baby comes. All the more reason for me being there to help you."

She grimaced as the words leaked out. "It's not the baby."

"If it's not the baby, then what is it?"

"Well, uh. It's..."

"Catherine Jo, you have a college education. Use some of those words you learned and tell me what's going on."

It was never a good sign when her mother used both of her given names. How do you tell your mom someone tried to kill you a few hours ago?

CJ took the coward's way out and handed the phone to David. He looked at the device as if it were a venomous snake. "Uh... hello, Grace. It's David. There was an incident this morning when CJ went for her doctor's appointment."

"An incident?" Grace's voice stiffened with concern. "Was she in an accident? Is she hurt?"

His voice lifted half an octave. "She and the baby are fine.

It wasn't an accident." He searched for soft words but couldn't find any.

"Quit stalling, David."

Words spilled out like a knocked-over glass of milk. "Someone took a shot at CJ when she was leaving the clinic."

"Good Lord!"

"She's all right. We have her safe at home and I'm not leaving the farm. Two other officers will be here day and night and a third is on the way."

"Are you sure they were shooting at her?"

"There's little doubt."

"Who and why?"

"That's what we're trying to find out."

"She's still in danger, and don't try to tell me she isn't."

"We're not taking any chances."

A few seconds of silence passed before Grace spoke in a calmer voice. "Where are Nancy and little Davey?"

CJ held out her hand and received the phone back from David. "They're staying at Bea and Billy Paul's. Little Davey had to get stitches in his forehead."

"Because of the shooting?"

"Yes."

"Was anyone else hurt?"

"One other."

"Serious?"

"I haven't heard the latest update on his condition."

The next question took CJ by surprise. "Who's cooking for you?"

"Huh?"

"You heard me," said Grace with impatience salting her words.

"Uh... We haven't discussed it."

"LeRoy and I will be there tonight. With a house full of armed guards, you'll need someone to cook and clean."

David tilted his head and raised his eyebrows. It was his way of saying Grace had thought of something he'd missed. They needed the extra help.

Her mother added a post script. "We'll bring our pistols."

CJ remembered the time her mother retrieved a .22 revolver and dispatched a rattlesnake on the family farm. It was one of those childhood memories embedded in CJ's mind and the reason she became proficient with firearms.

The call ended with the understanding that mother and daughter would have a long talk when she arrived about not calling after an emergency. CJ put the phone down and massaged her temples. She looked up when David said, "This is good news. Having two more people inside means I can deploy more resources outside."

"You sound like a general positioning his troops."

"Same tactics." He rose and spoke to Maria. "There's too much land for Tommy to cover by himself. I'll take the land from here to the river until the boxes of files arrive. You can relieve me then until midnight. Make sure you wear warm clothes."

The afternoon progressed with Maria making frequent trips to the bedrooms to peek out windows and then beat a path back to the living room. Routine gave way to boredom. CJ whiled away the time in silence, trying in vain to find a common thread between her and Judge Kraft. She only knew the judge by reputation, but she was a witness for the prosecution in a couple of cases he presided over. Neither of them was for serious felony offenses, and the defendants didn't seem surprised or upset by the outcome of their trial. It had to be something else. There must be some other invisible strand that pulled their lives together.

Headlights swept across the windows. With the winter solstice upon them, darkness settled in early.

"David texted. That's the officer with the files." Maria passed through the living room on her way to the mudroom.

CJ took stock of the latest addition to the body guards as Belinda toted box after box into the living room. She walked with broad shoulders pulled back. The close-cropped red hair accentuated green eyes that could comfort, or spark with anger, as the occasion dictated.

"How are the kids?" asked CJ on Belinda's second trip in.

"Teeth are falling out right and left. If the tooth fairy doesn't break the bank, Santa will, for sure." She stopped and looked down. "You had a close call today. How are you feeling?"

"Not bad for a beached whale."

"How long are you planning on staying home with the baby?"

The baby gave her a good kick as she opened her mouth to answer.

Belinda chuckled. "I saw that. He's expressing his opinion." She looked away. "If I could, I'd take off this uniform tomorrow."

"What's stopping you?"

She started with the pinkie finger and worked her way to the thumb. "A steady salary, health insurance, life insurance, retirement benefits, braces for the kids." She ran out of fingers but kept talking. "Then there's the car payments, mortgage, birthdays, Christmas, and a thousand other things that nibble away at us." She heaved a sigh. "Serves me right for marrying for love and not money."

CJ grinned. "Charley does all right, doesn't he?"

She dismissed the conversation with a wave of her hand. "Don't pay any attention to me. We're fine. I always get crabby around the holidays. You know what it's like having to work when everyone else is with family."

CJ realized this was the first year in over a decade she

hadn't been on duty or on call over the holidays. The idea of answering the cry of her child instead of the ringing of her phone in the middle of the night appealed to her.

"I'd better finish up," said Belinda. "It's been a wild day and Charley's coming down with his annual Christmas flu. I need to get home and make sure the kids don't open their presents."

"I thought they assigned you to stay here."

Belinda shook her head. "That was the original plan. Between the overtime worked today, people getting sick, and the Director's emphasis on cutting down on DWI's and traffic fatalities from now until after the new year, we're stretched to the breaking point. I worked last night, and they called me back in when things kicked off at the clinic." She paused. "Even if they'd okayed it, as tired as I am, I wouldn't do you any good."

CJ knew what it was like to be at the end of physical and mental endurance. No need to add guilt to Belinda's woes. "I have two people coming to take your place. They'll both be armed and they work for free."

"Must be family," said Belinda.

"My mom and her friend." CJ shifted in an effort to get comfortable. "Does David know you're leaving?"

Belinda gave her red hair a firm nod. "He scared the Christmas out of me when I drove onto the property. I thought he was a bush walking toward me."

It didn't surprise CJ. "He's a different animal when he reverts to sniper training."

"He sure fooled me, and that takes some doing."

Those were the last words Belinda said as she walked down the hall and out the mudroom door.

Maria came in with yet another box. "This is the last one. Belinda said to tell you Merry Christmas. I thought she was staying."

"Change of plans." CJ wondered how many other changes there would be before the shooter was in jail and they could get on with their lives.

CJ's phone chirped to inform her she'd received a text message. She pulled it off the coffee table and read: *Coming in. Have Maria ready.*

"David wants you to spell him. Belinda not staying messed up his schedule."

Maria didn't need prodding. She jogged down the hall and was back in the living room, dressed in winter gear by the time David came through the mudroom door.

His scowl informed the two women he wasn't happy. "Who left the door to the mudroom unlocked?"

Maria hung her head. "My hands were full carrying the last box." She looked up. "Sorry."

David's huff of exasperation was enough to get his point across.

CJ changed the subject. "Speaking of boxes, show me where to start."

He peeled off a coat and threw it across the back of a recliner. "Let's put you in the bedroom. I'll bring you a box."

CJ didn't make a move from the couch. "Help me to my recliner. I want to be up when Mom and Leroy get here."

"The bedroom will be safer. You'll also be closer to the bathroom."

Maria spoke up before the two rams could butt heads. "Where do you want me?"

"Outside," snapped David. He took in a deep breath. "My turn to apologize. Stay off the road but work from the house to the gate. Call if anyone drives slow past the property, pulls off the main road, or comes toward the house. Make a trip or two past the house, like you're going on the back road to Bea and Billy Paul's. Move slow and stay out of sight as much as possible. I'll relieve you in about thirty minutes."

"What about Tommy and Sandy?" asked CJ.

"What about them?"

"They need a break."

David ran his hand down his face.

Maria said, "I'll stay on the south side of the road when you relieve Tommy. Don't rush to change places with me at midnight. I enjoy being outside in the dark."

"Good idea," said David. He looked at the boxes and then at CJ. "You may be on your own tonight, reading files."

"You go play Rambo. I'll be fine."

That earned her a kiss and a rub on her belly. He cast his gaze to Maria. "Send me a text if you need anything or see something unusual." He followed her to the door and locked it behind her.

David looked through the boxes, rearranged them into an order that must have made sense to him and brought one to CJ. He then pointed at the boxes. "The ones on the right I've already looked at. The rest need review. I used a legal pad to rate the cases in terms of likelihood someone would have a good reason to kill Judge Kraft."

"Don't they need to be gone over again because of what happened today?"

"Let's move forward before we backtrack. Besides, I would have noticed if your name appeared in any of the paperwork." He then walked to his office and came back with a yellow legal pad and two pens. After one more kiss on her cheek, he grabbed his coat and disappeared like a ghost into the night.

It wasn't long before a thump sounded against the doggie door, which meant it was locked. Another security measure as Sandy's pet portal was large enough for a small person to squeeze through. CJ sighed. Even the dog had lost her freedom.

Before she could get up to let her in, Sandy appeared

beside her, giving kisses to her hand. Tommy announced his presence by saying, "David gave me his key to the back door."

CJ looked up from giving Sandy's ears a much-appreciated rub. "That's good. I'm a little slow on getting up these days." Sandy gave a shake from head to tail and jogged toward the kitchen.

Tommy turned to follow her. "I guess she's ready to eat now."

The sound of dry dog food hitting her bowl reached CJ. She hollered from her chair. "Give her an extra half-scoop. She'll be out in the cold all night."

It wasn't long before Tommy entered the living room, toting a steaming mug. "You look pretty good for someone who was shot at this morning."

"Thanks," said CJ. "You look pretty good yourself. Nothing like a long kiss from a pretty lady to warm you up."

The full smile gave his face a youthful appearance with two deep dimples. "The wind is dying and the clouds are moving out. There will be frost come morning."

Tommy then settled in David's leather recliner and took a tentative sip of coffee while CJ opened the first file. Instead of reading, she asked, "See any deer?"

"Not until I was coming in. Wind always makes them skittish." He looked around the living room. "Someday I want to have a home and land just like this."

The logs in the fireplace shifted, causing sparks to fly against the metal screen. "It didn't come quick or easy," said CJ. "I'm thankful for every inch of the three hundred acres and this beautiful home. Every so often I pinch myself when I look around and see how blessed we are."

Tommy took another sip from the mug and rested it on his thigh. "Do you have homework?"

CJ held up the file. "Court transcripts. I'll be looking for someone who had a big enough grudge against Judge Kraft to kill him."

"What about someone with a grudge against either you or David?"

"David?"

"Sure. What better way to get to David than to harm you and your child?"

The shiver jerked CJ's shoulders. "I hadn't given that angle any thought."

Tommy's coffee cup approached his lips. "You can bet David has." He swallowed and added, "Don't forget about the ranch outside of Hico."

"That's right," said CJ. "They shot the cattle with the same gun that killed the judge."

CJ tried to focus on the transcript, but her thoughts locked on to Tommy's theory of how someone might be trying to get to David by harming her. It startled her when Tommy asked if he could make himself a sandwich.

She nodded and told him anything he could find to eat was fair game.

Sandy lay curled in a ball on her bed by the fireplace. With eyes closed, but ears erect, CJ knew Sandy would soon want out. The unusual activity in the house and in the fields made her wary. It wasn't long before she rose, stretched, and moved to receive more ear rubs and instructions.

"Go find Maria. Keep her and Daddy safe tonight."

"Tommy," shouted CJ. "Sandy's coming your way. Please let her out to patrol with Maria."

CJ focused on a file that concerned a lawsuit between a rancher and an insurance company that didn't want to pay a claim. The file became the first in a stack that didn't rate a second look.

Tommy returned to David's chair with another cup of

coffee. "I'm supposed to wait inside until someone relieves me."

"Take a nap if you want to. My mom and her boyfriend are coming sometime this evening."

"Do they know you might be in danger?"

CJ nodded. "They're bringing their pistols. I'm not sure about LeRoy, but I know Mom can hit what she aims at."

Tommy leaned back in the recliner. "Will you be all right if I rest my eyes?"

CJ reached under pillows and pulled out her pistol. "The doors are all locked and I have plenty to keep me busy."

Less than five minutes later Tommy's breathing became slow and steady. Before CJ started reading the next file, she paused to write on the top of the legal pad the words:

PEOPLE WITH A GRUDGE AGAINST:
1. JUDGE KRAFT
2. ME
3. DAVID
She then added a fourth column:
LIVESTOCK SHOOTER.

CHAPTER NINETEEN

Two hours into a fruitless review of files, CJ's phone came to life with a text message from Maria. Your mom's here.

The alert brought Tommy out of his slumber. He lowered his feet, stood, and stretched. "How long have I been out?"

"A couple of hours. My mom and LeRoy are driving in now. I'll need you to open the mudroom door for them."

CJ heard her mother's voice, presumably introducing herself and her long-term boyfriend, LeRoy to Tommy. A few seconds later, Grace came from the direction of the guest rooms and headed straight for the couch. With a frown wrinkling her forehead and concern in her gaze, she bent down to kiss her only daughter.

"Pleasant trip?" asked CJ.

"Long," said her mother with a single, clipped word. "Why aren't you in bed?"

"Speaking of beds," said CJ as a way of ducking the question, "you have your choice of Nancy's bed or the queen bed in the room across the hall from Davey's. LeRoy, you can take

160

whichever is left over. Maria is staying in the other room. That leaves little Davey's room empty."

"You didn't answer me. What are all these files and why aren't you in bed?"

CJ realized afresh some things never changed with her mother. Dodging questions hadn't worked when she was growing up, either.

LeRoy excused himself from the fray by saying he needed to get their bags.

How was it that her mother could pin her to the wall with so little effort? Better to tell the whole truth and not try to sidestep the inevitable. "These are trial transcripts from cases Judge Kraft presided over. As for my being in bed, I wanted to be awake when you arrived. Besides, I'm in the same position here as I'd be in bed."

"Have you eaten supper?"

"Not yet, but I had a very late lunch."

Grace moved to CJ's feet, lifted the fleece throw, and made a quick exam. The corners of her mother's mouth turned downward. "What did the doctor say about this?"

"The same thing she's been saying for the last month. No salty foods, rest, and no stress. I blew the last one this morning."

"It's to bed with you, young lady. I'll bring you a light supper."

CJ didn't argue, but said, "Can you bring this box of files or get LeRoy to?"

Grace rose to her full height and placed hands on her hips. "Rest means rest."

It did no good to argue, at least not tonight. Perhaps her mom was right. It had been a day to remember... or perhaps one she should try to forget.

She swung her feet down from the couch, stuffed them into slides and extended her hands for her mother to help her from the couch. Rising with a groan, she padded her way to the bedroom.

Minutes later all vestiges of constricting clothing were replaced with a loose-fitting gown. As usual, her mom was right. She needed to unwind from the day, and the cool sheets were an improvement over the couch and the fleece throw.

Her light supper consisted of unsalted scrambled eggs, whole wheat toast, and canned peach slices. The dreaded mother-daughter tête-à-tête concerning reticence about sharing important information didn't materialize. After eating, she was left with nothing to do but think, read a book, or watch something fluffy on television. She chose the latter and fell asleep to the sounds of Christmas carols in a Hallmark movie.

Sleep came too deep and too fast. Instead of waking refreshed, CJ thrashed herself awake from a dream she'd prayed would never haunt her again. It was a repeat of the watershed event that changed her life the night she shot and killed a man. A simple traffic stop when she wore the uniform of a state trooper turned into a fight for her life. The drug-addled hulk named Bigalou Murphy wanted nothing more than to violate her before he killed her. She'd prevailed, which earned her celebrity status and selection as a Texas Ranger. She declined the latter and did her best to ignore the former.

The nightmare lay dormant for years, only to resurface on this cold December night. Her scream brought her out of a mental fog. It also brought David into the bedroom with pistol drawn and flashlight sweeping the room like a miniature beacon. He cleared the closet and bathroom before he came to her. "Did you hear something?"

"Nightmare." A shiver chased away the remnants of the bad dream. "Sorry."

Grace entered the room with pistol in hand, but pointed at the carpet. "I heard a scream."

"Sorry," said CJ. "Just a bad dream. Go back to bed."

"We'll talk in the morning," said Grace. It sounded like an ultimatum.

David waited until Grace was well away from their room. "Are you sure you're okay?"

She shrugged. "It was the same dream I had after I killed Big Murphy."

David eased into bed and pulled her against him. His arms around her brought more comfort than words could. After a couple of long minutes, she asked, "What time is it?"

"A little after four in the morning."

"Have you been outside all night?"

"Tommy relieved me not more than ten minutes ago."

CJ reached for David's face and stroked the stubble on his cheek. "Your face is still cool."

"Um."

"Are you going to sleep?"

His chest expanded. "Not in here." He paused. "Not unless you need me to. It makes better tactical sense for me to be in the center of the house where I can monitor all three doors."

"I'd love for you to stay, but do what you think is best." She looked at the open door that led to the rest of the home. "Could you bring me the box of files I was working on? There's no way I can go back to sleep after that dream."

He slid from the bed. "If your mom asks, I didn't bring them to you."

"Coward."

"Tommy told me she laid the law down to you about resting. I don't want to get any residual wrath." He moved to the door. "Do you want coffee?"

"Might as well," she said as she swung her feet off the bed and rearranged the pillows so she could sit rather than lay.

"That dream was so real, like watching a movie. I don't want to chance a double-feature."

David had placed the box of files in the spot he'd vacated when she came out of the bathroom. He returned with coffee before she had time to slip off her robe and climb back into bed.

"Could you get my bed jacket out of the closet for me?"

"Do you mean that thing that looks like the top half of a robe?"

"Yeah."

As he helped her slip the bed jacket on, she asked, "Why do you think I dreamed about Big Murphy?"

He lifted his shoulders and let them fall.

"Do you think his brother is still alive?"

"Which one?"

"Tig. The one that's still missing."

David drew the covers over her expanded midsection. "We've talked about this before. I don't know where Tig is."

"Do you think he's alive?"

"No."

The brevity of the answer caught CJ off guard. Up to now, David had remained noncommittal, but in the early hours of this December day, he spoke with authority.

"Why don't you think so?"

David pulled his hands down his face before he answered. "You talk about knowing something deep down, even though you can't prove it. Right?"

She answered with a nod.

"I know deep down that Tig Murphy will never be heard from again." He added, "I can't prove it, but I know it."

He rubbed the place his son rested, gave her a tender kiss, and left.

The next hour and a half passed in pre-dawn silence. She made good progress in processing the transcripts, but nothing stood out. The more she read, the more she was thankful she didn't take her brother's advice and apply to law school after she graduated college.

The tap on the door came at 5:45 a.m.

"Come in."

The door swung open and her mother, wearing a full-length winter robe and house shoes, came in. It always amazed CJ that even though her mother didn't have her height, she appeared tall. Perhaps it was her erect posture and the way she carried herself with quiet confidence.

"I see you didn't go back to sleep."

"Not after the nightmare."

"Do you want another cup of coffee?"

"Thanks, but not yet."

Grace pulled a chair from under the window and put it next to the bed. She put her cup of coffee on a coaster and settled in. CJ knew there would be no escape from what was to come, but perhaps she could soften the lecture.

"Mom, I can't tell you how much we appreciate you coming."

Her mother nodded but didn't otherwise respond. Instead, she went on the offensive. "Explain to me why you didn't call and tell me someone tried to kill you."

CJ's chin rested on her chest and she dry washed her hands like she did as a girl when caught red-handed doing something she shouldn't. She looked up. "I don't have a clever excuse. I guess I didn't want you to worry."

Her mother leaned forward. "You are days away from being a mother. That precious child you're carrying will watch every move you make and listen to every word. He'll use you and David as examples of how to live, and he'll copy much more than you think he will. Do you want him to grow up hiding important things from you?"

CJ swallowed hard. "No."

Her mother continued on. "I realize you're a married adult and you'll soon add a son to your family. You'll say and do things that are none of my business, but that doesn't apply to everything. When it concerns health and safety, your well-being will always be my business."

All CJ could do was say, "I'm sorry, Mom. It wasn't right that I didn't call you and keep you informed."

Her mother leaned back. "I hold David equally responsible. I've already spoken to him, and he knows how I feel about this. He was very apologetic."

Before CJ could apologize again, her mother moved on. "What's done can't be undone, so let's agree we need to stay in touch more often and not get so tied up in our own little worlds that we abandon each other. Can you commit to that?"

"Yes." She took in a deep breath. "Mom, there's something that I want to talk to you about. I'm having second thoughts about going back to work."

Her mother gave her head a slight sideways turn and a single nod. "What does David say?"

"He says I should do whatever makes me happy, but I know deep down he wants me to be a full-time mom. David enjoyed having his mom at home when he was young, and I always liked that you were there every day when I got home from school. Of course when Dad died, everything changed."

Grace nodded and said, "It will be a sacrifice for you to give up the career you've dreamed of since you were young."

"I think that's one reason I didn't give much thought to leaving ACU at first. But the closer the time comes to actually holding our baby, I don't think I want someone else raising him. I want us to be the ones who shape our children."

"I understand, honey. And I know the right path for you will come clear. You'll know which way to go when it's time."

CJ added, "Of course, besides raising our son, there's

always plenty to do here. There're crops to plant, and we could increase our small herd. I've been thinking about expanding the garden in the spring. The quality of the food in the grocery stores keeps going down. A greenhouse where I could raise fresh vegetables all year would be a blessing."

"Sounds like you've put plenty of thought into this. Are there any other things you've been thinking about doing differently?"

CJ couldn't help but chuckle. "I missed out on so much free education from you when I was growing up. I want that to change."

"What do you mean?"

"The joke in this house is that I can't make steam without burning it. Nancy says I use the smoke alarm instead of a timer. I play it off, but those words hurt. It's time I learned how to cook and I want you to teach me."

"That would be easier if I lived close by."

"I've been thinking about that, too." CJ realized her words were coming out faster and with a sense of excitement. "If there's one thing I learned from you, it's that there's a solution to almost any problem if you look hard enough."

Her mother leaned forward again, listening with renewed intensity. "Tell me."

"We could video chat several times a week in our kitchens. You could walk me through each step of learning to cook."

Grace's head bobbed. "That's wonderful. I show you each step and answer all your questions. We could plan out the next meal in advance and list the ingredients you'll need." Her voice became more animated as fresh ideas came to her and she expressed them. The words came to a sudden stop as she looked up. "We'll do it, and we can start today. It won't hurt you to sit in the kitchen and watch."

"What about now? It's about time for breakfast." asked CJ.

That's all it took for her mother to rise from the chair. "Let me help you with your robe and we'll find something simple to start with. Do you have oatmeal?"

"When I make it, they call it wallpaper paste."

"Not after today," said Grace with confidence. Then she looked at the file box on the bed and shook her head.

CJ spoke as she pulled back the covers. "Don't worry, Mom. Those transcripts are like reading the most boring novel you could imagine. I haven't come across anything yet that didn't lower my blood pressure."

"I hope it stays that way."

CHAPTER TWENTY

CJ scraped the bottom of her bowl of oatmeal, spooning up the last speck of what she considered the perfect breakfast cereal. She looked down at the notes she'd taken and gave her head a firm nod. "I can do this, Mom."

"The secret to cooking is to add layers of flavor. You like your oatmeal with butter, brown sugar, and chopped pecans. Some people like to add fruit, either fresh, dried, or canned. Others add milk. Give people options of how they want to dress it up. The only way you can ruin it is to burn it or not cook it long enough."

CJ stretched and announced, "I'm going back to bed and read through some more transcripts."

"Before you go, do you know when Maria will come in?"

"David said at ten. She and Tommy are rotating shorter shifts than David's working. She'll need something hot and to get some sleep." CJ gave her mom a kiss on the cheek. "Mom, you might start a fashion trend by wearing a pistol while cooking."

"I feel silly, but not as much as if I needed it and it was in my suitcase."

A sense of safety and wellbeing descended on CJ. She doubted anyone would make a foolish attempt to get to her at home, but she couldn't deny the events of the preceding day.

After a quick shower, CJ dressed and prepared to read boring court transcripts. She had little doubt that a nap or two would sneak their way into the schedule. She fluffed the pillows, straightened the bedspread, and readied a throw to cover the lower half of her body. Grabbing the next file in the box, she renewed her task, even though she was losing hope it would reap results.

After two hours of disappointing reading, she moved to the couch. "Where's LeRoy?" asked CJ.

"In the barn," said her mother who was sneaking a peek out the living room curtains. "David sent a text asking LeRoy to make sure Tommy didn't oversleep. He needs to eat and relieve Maria before long."

Voices came from the direction of the back door. Grace had her hand on her pistol as she went to check. CJ followed in time to see her mother turn the dead bolt.

"It's LeRoy and Tommy. I need to cook and you need to either sit down or find a place to get horizontal."

LeRoy came in first, rubbing his hands together. "The frost is burning off, but it's still chilly." He shifted his attention to CJ. "Look who's up and looking fresh as a spring day. How are you feeling?"

"Do you want the sanitized version or the truth?"

"Either."

Grace shot her a look that said the sanitized version would be her preference.

The relationship between Grace and LeRoy had been going on for over three years. In that time CJ had grown past the silly comparisons of the widower to her long-departed father and had learned to appreciate the man for his qualities, of which there were many. He was solid and dependable, a good companion to her mother, and one she could see as being her stepfather someday. His children, all grown and doing well, were raising their own families in two other states and one foreign country.

"I'm ready to have this baby," said CJ after considering other things to say.

"I thought you were having it yesterday. Your mother called and told me I had ten minutes to pick her up or she was leaving without me. It's a good thing I already had a go-bag ready."

Tommy retrieved a cup of coffee and perched on a barstool overlooking the kitchen. CJ asked, "Did you see anything last night?"

"The moon is on the rise and there wasn't a cloud. I can't tell you how many deer I saw. Other than that, a raccoon and a family of opossums. I heard a coyote, but he was on the other side of the river."

"Were you cold?"

He shrugged. "It was chilly, but I'm used to it."

CJ's phone announcing an incoming call interrupted further talk. The screen read Bob Harper. Her father-in-law started the conversation in a way she expected. "How's everything at the bunker this morning?"

"Safe and warm."

"What's the secret password to get past the armed guards?"

"You've been talking to David. Are you coming to visit?"

"Your stepmother is ready to climb over barbed wire and crawl through a mine field to see you. Are you receiving visitors today?"

"Sure. The more cars and people that are here, the less likely anyone will set foot on the property."

CJ's mother spoke up from the kitchen. "Tell them to come for lunch. We're having chicken and dumplings."

"I heard that," said Bob. "We'll be there around noon."

With the call completed, CJ placed the phone on the table. She looked up and found her mother's gaze locked on her.

"You can go to the couch, a recliner, or bed. Take your choice."

"Recliner," said CJ. "I'll need the box of court transcripts if someone could get them off my bed, please."

LeRoy was the first to respond. "No problem."

She padded her way to the recliner, elevated her feet and pored through a file concerning a messy divorce. After reading it, she concluded they should award the husband a medal for putting up with his wife as long as he did. Despite all the heartache the wife caused him, he still requested she receive a generous property settlement. Judge Kraft, however, divided the property and funds as equal as he could. The woman threw a screaming fit worthy of reality television and earned herself ten days in jail for contempt of court. CJ added her name to the list of suspects.

Maria came in from the cold, downed something to eat, and went to her room.

The morning ended when Alice sent a text saying they were crossing the cattle guard at the front of the property. CJ slipped a file back into the box, which completed Judge Kraft's cases from the previous six years. Although there were several names on the yellow tablet, she'd seen nothing that set off any lights or bells. Perhaps she'd have better luck with year seven.

Unlike her mother and LeRoy, Bob and Alice didn't come packing pistols on their hips. CJ doubted if Alice owned one, and Bob's sixteen years in prison for a crime he didn't commit made him content to avoid firearms altogether.

Alice sat in the recliner next to CJ while Bob settled on the love seat not far away. Alice began the conversation by saying, "I was in my office at the university when I received the news you were involved in a shooting at the clinic. It was the longest hour of my life while I waited for word from Bob."

Bob added, "Alice is big on delegating. I sent six texts to David before he responded. I understand he couldn't talk for long, but it took him almost an hour to text me you and the baby were unharmed."

The conversation didn't surprise CJ. She'd noticed through the years that one commonality of traumatic events was people's desire to tell where they were and how they responded.

CJ's thoughts focused on what Bob said about Alice tasking him to do something for her. He'd used the word delegating. That was CJ's hardest thing to do when she shifted from being an officer to a supervisor. Her world would soon go back to not being able to delegate. Another change.

Before the conversation could continue, they heard LeRoy call out from the kitchen. "Lunch is ready. Come and get it."

Conversation flowed between the two sets of parents, which suited CJ fine. She'd been up a long time and had read transcripts until the words ran together. The comfort of a savory bowl of chicken and dumplings had a sedative effect. She didn't realize she'd yawned.

"Time for bed," said Grace. She was already standing with a hand out to help her up.

"Sorry. I've been awake since way before dawn." CJ looked at LeRoy. "Would you mind carrying the next box of files back to the bedroom for me? It's marked 7."

Grace gave out a huff, but CJ cut her mother off with an upraised hand before she could issue a complaint. "Don't say it. I won't read another word until after a long nap." She looked around the table. "Sorry to be such a poor hostess, but Mom puts some sort of sedative in her dumplings."

All but LeRoy remained at the table. He placed the box on David's side of the bed and left after wishing her a peaceful sleep. She remembered the door clicking shut, but nothing else.

A SLIVER of light from a tiny gap in the bedroom curtains greeted CJ as she wiggled her toes and rubbed her stomach. She'd traded the nightmare of last night for a half-awake, half-asleep memory of her and David snorkeling in the azure waters of Cozumel. The vacation he'd surprised her with would always be an extra special memory. Besides the black coral necklace he bought her, she returned with the child she carried.

She spent the next several minutes reliving the trip and wondering what vacations would look like from now on. Her musings gave way to a grim reality when she looked to her right. Instead of her handsome husband lying beside her, she saw box seven in his place.

"Back to the salt mine," she whispered as she resettled pillows to support her back and turned on her reading lamp. She pulled the box closer to her and grabbed the first file. After clearing her lungs with a cough, she glanced at the folder's tab. Typed on a white label, it read *Texas v Murphy*.

She gasped, and the baby reacted by giving her a firm punch.

"It can't be," she said out loud. She had to force herself to turn back the file's cover. She looked at the style of the papers. Her eyes focused on *The State of Texas v Sidney Murphy*.

She chided herself for cowering away from words on a

piece of paper. Judge Kraft had been the presiding judge over the trial of Sid Murphy, the brother of Big, the man she killed. There was also a third brother. Tig Murphy had been behind a drug operation in Riverview earlier in the year. CJ became involved in the case when an ACU student died and drugs were discovered on campus. A warrant was issued for Tig Murphy, but the Rangers and David believed someone dispensed a less expensive, but more permanent, form of justice.

The desire to know overcame her shock at seeing the name Murphy. With finger gliding down the pages, she soon had a mental image of the trial. The prosecution sought a twenty-five-year sentence for aggravated robbery with a deadly weapon. The defense proposed five years for simple robbery. A jury set punishment at fifteen years, aggravated. The deadly weapon turned out to be not one, but two knives. A witness gave testimony that Sid said the man wasn't emptying the cash register fast enough and sliced the man's arm. It was a deep cut that left permanent damage.

Questions exploded in CJ's mind. Was Sid still in prison? Was he back in Riverview County? How much time would he have to serve on that sentence before he was eligible for parole? Wait. The charge of aggravated robbery with a deadly weapon meant he'd have to serve more time than normal before considered for early release.

She grabbed her phone and checked the time. David should be inside, taking his break.

Carrying the file, she threw the bedroom door open so hard it hit the stopper and bounced back. Blocking it with her arm, she walked as fast as she dared and didn't stop until she entered the living room. The eyes of all four prospective grandparents looked up at her.

"Where's David?"

Grace was on her feet. "What's wrong?"

CJ waved the file at her. "Nothing's wrong with me. Where's David?"

As her mother pointed, the sound of a bedroom door opening down the hall caught her attention. David came with pistol in hand, looking in all directions.

CJ extended the file to him. "I found something. Read this."

He took it, opened the cover, and read only enough to make him nod in agreement that this could be important. "I'll be in my office."

With four sets of questioning eyes staring at her, CJ pulled her hair away from her face and sat in her recliner. "It's the first file I opened after my nap. It may be what we've been looking for."

"You've been asleep all this time?" asked her mother.

LeRoy patted Grace on the leg and gave her a look that said it was time to listen.

"I think I found something that will help identify Judge Kraft's killer, and it could be the same person who took a shot at me. David will do some checking. He'll keep us posted."

CHAPTER TWENTY-ONE

David kept his head down when CJ came into his office. He had the look of a homeless man rather than a clean-cut state trooper. Hat hair, followed by bed-head, were two of the primary culprits to his disheveled look. The two-day growth of beard gave him a rugged look she liked, but he'd need a shower before they shared a bed.

A few minutes into his deliberative reading, he asked, "Did you notice where this trial took place?"

"It was in Riverview, wasn't it?"

His answer was a one-word reply. "Hamilton."

"Why Hamilton?"

He kept his head down. "Sometimes a judge has to recuse themselves and they bring in a replacement. I'll need to dig deeper to find out the reason."

She fidgeted in her chair. "You don't think it's a coincidence, do you? I sure don't. I wonder how much time Sid served. Have you gotten to the witness statements yet?"

David raised his eyes, but not his head. "Let me finish, then we'll talk."

She huffed. "Hurry. This could be the break we're looking for."

He looked up and pointed to the door. "Would you check on our guests? I promise I won't do anything until I've read this and taken some notes."

"Are you kicking me out?"

"I'm asking you to give me time to study the transcript. I don't want you telling me what it says."

The bruise to her ego stung, but only enough for her to stick her tongue out at him. She pushed up from the chair and shuffled back to the living room. Once there, she said, "He kicked me out."

"Good," said her mother. "Your face is pink. That means your blood pressure must be sky high. You need to get back in bed and turn on the television." Grace turned to LeRoy. "Get that box of files away from her so she can rest."

"Mom," said CJ, drawing the word out into an extra syllable. She thought about defending her right to do what she wanted in her own home, then reconsidered. It didn't seem worth the hard feelings it might cause. Instead, it was time to negotiate. "David wants to talk to me about what I found in the transcript he's reading. I'll go to bed after that."

Her mother's wordless scowl communicated both parties had reached a compromise, albeit grudgingly.

David's father asked, "Can you give us a hint about what you found?"

"I recognized the name of someone who might have a grudge against me and Judge Kraft." She threw in the next statement in to mollify her mother. "David will have to follow up to see if there's anything to it."

"Can you tell us the name?" asked Alice.

"Let me talk to David first."

The response had no more left her mouth than the door

to David's office swung open. His gaze went to CJ, and he beckoned her with a crooked finger.

David passed the file to her as soon as she entered the office. He circled his desk while she sat on the edge of her seat and asked, "What do you think?"

"All the pieces fit, except one. They released Sid Murphy from prison this morning."

The words flattened CJ's emotional high. "Are you sure?"

It was a foolish question that he didn't answer. Instead, he rubbed his temples. "He's a nasty piece of work and he'd be the first one I'd go looking for, but no one can be at two places at the same time."

CJ looked toward the door. "Mom is on a rampage about me getting excited. She's having LeRoy take the file folders out of our bedroom. I may have to sneak them out of the living room when she isn't looking."

David's response came with conviction. "You've already done more than you should. It's time to listen to your mom and stop being a cop."

CJ huffed. "This is ruining Christmas for everyone. You, Maria and Tommy are outside most of the day and night."

He raised a hand with palm facing her. "There's nothing I can do about it." Then, he rubbed sleep deprived eyes. "I need to rest a little longer and you need to get in bed and stay there." He added, "Without searching through any more files."

"What about Captain Crow? He told you to review everything in the boxes."

David stood. "I can't keep watch and read at the same time. If Captain Crow doesn't understand that, he can come read the files himself."

CJ knew David's fatigue played into his last statement. She stood and blocked his path. Her hand cupped his whisker-stubbled face and he patted her midsection. They managed an awkward hug. As they separated, she said, "Go shower, shave, and get in bed. I'll wake you in two hours."

"One hour," he said.

"Three," she countered.

A modest grin parted his lips. "Two hours it is."

David spoke as he walked through the living room. "CJ will explain everything."

Four sets of eyes followed CJ until she eased down in her recliner and elevated her feet. She held up the file and waved it. "We thought we had our man, but it turns out he was in prison until this morning."

Heads nodded. Alice repeated her question about the identity of the mystery man.

"This file contains the transcript of a criminal case Judge Kraft presided over many years ago. The defendant was Sid Murphy."

Bob's eyebrows shot up. "He must be kin to Big and Tig."

"Sid is the third and last of the Murphy brothers."

"Holy smoke," said Bob. "No wonder you thought you had something."

"Everything fit," said CJ, "until David discovered Sid couldn't have committed either crime. Now we're back to square one."

Grace gave CJ a stare.

"Don't say it, Mom. David's in full agreement with you and I promise not to read any more files today. It's time we celebrated Christmas."

"And speaking of," said Alice. "Bob and I are on our way to Bea and Billy Paul's. I understand people from all around are flocking to the living nativity and the other festivities. They even brought in a pair of camels. Billy Paul and Bea are giving tours of their home, and I have reports they pulled out all the stops on decorating. I can't wait to see it."

Bob stood. "That's my cue to warm up the car." He looked

at Grace and LeRoy as they sat close together on the couch. "I have an idea. Why don't Alice and I come by tomorrow and give you two a break so you can see what everyone is raving about?"

Alice nodded with vigor. "What a lovely idea. You must go."

LeRoy and Grace traded glances, and both nodded.

"Perfect," said Alice. "We'll be here in the early afternoon and you can stay as long as you like."

CJ stuck out her bottom lip. "What about me?" She knew she sounded like a spoiled child, but missing out on seeing Bea's Christmas extravaganza seemed like a prison sentence. Even the back porch swing was declared off limits.

Grace stood before her with a hand extended. She said nothing, nor did she need to. The message was obvious. There would be no viewing of lights, decorations, camels, living nativity, or Santa's sleigh in the night sky without the apprehension of Judge Kraft's killer.

Something had to be done to escape her prison, but CJ couldn't imagine what it would be. She lowered her feet, scooted to the edge of the chair, and rose without her mother's help.

Grace hooked her arm in CJ's and walked her to the master bedroom.

"Take a nap with your husband and be thankful."

It was excellent advice, and it wasn't long before David, with a little residual shaving cream under his ear lobe, slid between the sheets. He took in a deep breath, let it out ease out and didn't move for an hour and forty-five minutes.

CJ remained still, but her thoughts jumped from one thing to the next, starting with the activity taking place a quick drive down the private gravel road between their home and Bea's. She also thought of Maria and Tommy on opposite sides of the pasture and on different shifts. What a crummy way to spend their first Christmas together. David relegated himself to the role of full-time bodyguard. She'd lost the doting husband and expectant father. Something had to give.

The beeping of David's cell phone at the end of the allotted time brought his eyes wide open. He rose without stretching and went to the closet to dress for another long night in the cold.

CJ retrieved a mug of coffee for him. She returned as he was putting on thick socks. "I had plenty of time to think while you were sleeping."

"Oh?"

"I want to go to Bea and Billy Paul's before Christmas."

He spoke without looking up. "That's not going to happen."

She expected this to be his immediate response. The situation called for a strategy to overcome his objections. She placed the mug on his nightstand. "Here's your coffee. It's how you like it. Extra strong."

He looked up at her. "Bribery won't work."

She sat beside him and tickled his ear. "We could go early in the morning, before anyone else arrives. Maria and Tommy could come, too. I know Bea and Billy Paul would like to have us come for breakfast."

"Out of the question," said David. "That would leave this place unguarded. I don't have time to recon the living nativity, let alone their home and grounds."

The firmness in his voice meant there would be no compromise. She huffed in pretend frustration. In reality, she expected him to nix her suggestions, but he didn't need to know this. She stood and crossed her arms. "If I can't go early in the day, I want to go at night. Christmas Eve."

"No way."

CJ straightened her posture and then crossed her arms. "You're the military genius in the family. If you don't like my ideas, come up with a plan of your own. I don't care how you do it, but I'm going to see the living nativity and Bea's home in all its Christmas glory before Christmas Day."

David stood and put on his tactical vest, complete with metal plates in the front and back. It bristled with extra clips of ammunition. His gaze locked on to her. "The only way you're leaving this house before the baby comes is if the person who took a shot at you is in custody." He paused. "Or dead."

Her arms remained crossed as he gave her a peck on the cheek.

The closing of the door reverberated through her emotions like the clang of a cell door. The negotiations had not gone as planned. Without an arrest of some unknown person, she'd remain in her home until the baby came.

A contraction brought her attention away from schemes, so she settled on the bed, took a deep cleansing breath, and practiced her breathing.

David came back in as she was visualizing white, fluffy clouds and massaging her stomach. He took quick steps toward her. "Is it the real thing?"

"Another Braxton-Hicks contraction. Don't worry." She took his hand. "Mom's here. She'll know when it's time."

She hadn't noticed it, but David had returned with a package. "What's that?" she asked.

"An early Christmas present. I'll open it for you."

"When did it arrive? I didn't hear a delivery van."

"Maria stopped the van before it made it to the house. She made sure it's a legitimate delivery." David chuckled. "She said the driver might need a stiff drink when he gets off work."

CJ could see the scene play out in her head and smiled as David placed three identical items on the bed.

"White undershirts?" asked CJ.

"Not just any undershirts," said David. "These are long-sleeve maternity undershirts with a special cloth holster sewn in." He pulled one out of its plastic bag. "Everything is cloth with a special pocket under the left arm where you carry a slim-line pistol."

"The smallest pistol I have is my .38 Chief's Special. It's only five shots, but it's too bulky for this."

"Where is it?"

"You know where it is. Right beside me in the biometric gun safe on my nightstand."

"And your Glock?"

"In the gun safe in the closet. I didn't like the idea of having a pistol under my pillow that doesn't have a safety."

"That means you're walking around the house with no way to defend yourself." David's eyes took on a look of mischief. "That should be enough clues for you to guess what this evening's delivery will be."

"What did you buy now?"

He patted her leg. "You know it's against the rules to ask that question between Thanksgiving and Christmas." He made for the door. "I need to get outside. Maria's overdue for her break."

CJ decided now would be a good time to shower. If she shampooed her hair today, she wouldn't need to again until the morning of the twenty-fourth. She believed with every fiber of her being that the baby would come on either Christmas Eve or Christmas Day.

The knock on her bedroom door came after she slipped on her new undershirt. Her mother walked in and nodded her approval. "I like it. It's a little late in the game to be receiving maternity undershirts, but you won't get your figure back for a while and it has nice long sleeves."

It was then CJ realized that if she kept her left arm down,

the extra material for the built-in holster didn't show. She changed the subject. "Can you help me dry my hair?"

Her mother grabbed a hand full of the brown mane that fell halfway down her back. "You should have cut some of this off. It's only going to get in your way with the baby. You're not seventeen anymore."

"I think it will be okay. I can always cut it later if it's too much hassle. David loves for me to wear it down."

She stroked it. "It's lovely, but practicality will win out. Besides, David will love you with long hair or short. You landed a trophy when you caught him."

CJ swallowed the lump in her throat. "Thanks, Mom. And speaking of landing a good man... what are your intentions?"

Her mother stopped stroking. "My intentions with LeRoy are to have supper with him and whomever wants to join us. After that, we'll do the dishes. Then, we'll watch some television and I'll go to bed in my bedroom and sometime later, he'll go to bed in his."

CJ followed her mother to the bathroom. "In other words, it's none of my business."

"I'll let you know if it is."

David had moved a small, backless chair into the over-sized bathroom. CJ spoke as she perched on the edge. "I told David I wanted to see the living nativity at Bea's house before Christmas. I don't think my chances are very good at pulling that off."

Her mother had the hair dryer in one hand and a brush in the other. "I hope he told you no."

"He did, and in no uncertain terms. It's going to take a Christmas miracle for me to break out of this jail before the baby comes."

The hair dryer came on and all talk ceased, but that didn't mean CJ's thoughts of how to get to Bea's celebration didn't continue to swirl.

CHAPTER TWENTY-TWO

eRoy and Maria ferried supper dishes to the kitchen counter. CJ's head turned when Maria's phone vibrated.

"Yes?" said Maria.

Muted, garbled words seeped out from the phone as it pressed against her ear.

"Have him come to the back door."

More garbled words.

"I know. We'll make up for it on New Year's Eve."

She lowered the phone and moved to a window. While parting the blinds, she said, "CJ, your Christmas present will be here any minute. Tommy wants you in your bedroom until the delivery guy leaves."

CJ huffed as she pushed up from the table. "This is ridiculous."

She went down the hall to her bedroom door, where she opened, and then closed it. What she didn't do was go into her bedroom. She tiptoed back down the hall and made sure she remained hidden from the kitchen and breakfast nook. As long as someone didn't go into the living room, she'd get by with the deception.

A knock sounded on the back door.

"Put it on the table," said Maria.

A familiar voice answered. "Is CJ here? I'd like to show it to her."

"You need to leave," said Maria.

CJ rounded the corner. "Tony? Is that you?"

A silver-haired, elderly man came into view. He wore a red Santa hat trimmed in white. "Merry Christmas. David told me to expect tight security. He wasn't kidding. Can't blame him after the close call."

"I'm still in one piece and I'm dying to see what David bought this time."

"Bad choice of words," said LeRoy.

Everyone looked at LeRoy as he grinned, and the mood lightened. He didn't crack many jokes, which made this one even more funny.

Tony set a bag on the table and unloaded it. CJ made introductions and added, "Tony owns the gun store in town."

"David and Billy Paul are my best customers."

She moved to the table and sat in front of a group of three boxes, two of them ammunition. She pushed her eyebrows together. "I can use the box of .223 Remington rifle shells, but I don't own a .410 shotgun."

"Open the other box," said Tony.

She did and beheld what might be the smallest pistol she'd ever seen, other than a derringer. "What is this thing? It looks like a toy."

"This," said Tony, "is a Heizer Defense PAP 1." He looked at questioning faces. "Don't ask me what all that means." He went on at a good clip. "It's a single shot that comes with a barrel that shoots the .223 Remington. There's an interchangeable barrel that can handle a .410 shotgun shell. David wanted both so you could choose."

Tony took the slim line pistol in his hand and pushed a

lever. The barrel sprung open like a breach-loading shotgun. He handed it to CJ for her to examine.

"It's light," she said.

"Twenty-three ounces."

"Length?"

"Six and three-eighths inches."

"The shells must be as long as the barrel."

"Almost," said Tony with a look of satisfaction.

CJ closed the breach, raised her left arm, and slipped the weapon into the built-in cloth holster of her undershirt. Her mother took in a deep breath, but didn't put words to her thoughts. CJ lowered her arm and stood for inspection.

"I can't see it," said LeRoy. "Turn around."

CJ turned in a circle, and Maria asked. "How does it feel?"

"Better than any back-up gun I've ever carried. It wouldn't take the place of the sixteen-shot Glock I've carried for years, but it's sure comfortable."

"There're instructions on how to change out the barrels, as well as proper cleaning and maintenance," said Tony.

"What barrel is on it now?" asked CJ.

"The .223."

"Put the shotgun barrel on it. I want to try it out."

Maria pulled out her phone. "I'll let David and Tommy know you're going to make some noise."

After retrieving ear protection, CJ stood at the front door overlooking the front yard and the west pasture. The cattle were nowhere in sight. Leroy propped up a large piece of cardboard about ten yards from the porch. The tiny gun erupted when CJ squeezed the trigger and ventilated the target with five round balls of .00 buckshot.

"How was it?" asked Maria.

"Kicks like a mule with a toothache." She looked at Tony. "The shots spread out more than I expected. Only two balls would have hit center mass. Let's try the other barrel."

The rifle round made a distinct sound, more of a crack than the boom of the shotgun shell.

"Which did you like best?" asked Tony.

"Both," said CJ as she took off her ear muffs. "If the bad guy was within ten feet, I'd like to be using the .410. Anything farther away than that, I'd prefer the .223."

CJ went to the table, exchanged the barrels, and slipped in a shotgun shell. She then tucked the pistol into the special pouch under her arm. "Since I'm staying indoors, the shotgun makes more sense."

Her mother looked at her. "Are you planning on carrying that in the house?"

CJ pointed to the bulge under her mother's apron. "Everyone here is armed but me. Darn right I'm going to carry it. I might even sleep with it."

For the first time today, CJ got her way. She thanked Tony, and he walked into the night after wishing everyone a merry Christmas and a prosperous new year.

The evening wound down as Maria left to catch some sleep and Grace went to her room to read. CJ and LeRoy watched a television documentary on people decorating their homes for Christmas to absurd levels.

CJ wasn't tired but, after two hours in her chair she decided her bed would be more comfortable. She wished LeRoy a good night as he prepared to keep watch until her mother relieved him at four in the morning.

Once in bed, sleep came to CJ toward the end of an old black and white movie about a gangster that controlled his far-flung empire of illegal activities from his prison cell. Because she now slept on either her back or her right side, the tiny gun didn't bother her at all.

CJ AWAKENED BEFORE DAWN, as she did almost every day. She longed to follow her normal pattern of taking her first cup of coffee to the back porch swing and watch first light awaken the world with another day. Instead, she sat at the table in the breakfast nook, watching her mother putter around the kitchen.

"You're not very talkative this morning," said her mother.

"Nothing much to say. Another day of staying cooped up inside. I'd pay good money to go on the back porch."

Out of the blue, her mother asked, "Have you decided for sure if you're going to work at the university after the baby comes?"

CJ looked into her mug of coffee, wishing an answer would appear. "I thought I had the answer. Then, David and I were first on the scene of Judge Kraft's murder. There's something about involvement from the very beginning that keeps pulling me in." Her words came out slowly as she struggled to explain her feelings. "I didn't want to get involved in the investigation. I'd already decided to trade in my badge for a tractor. But after seeing the judge's body, it's like I have to see it through."

Her mother moved to the island that separated the kitchen from the breakfast nook. She stood motionless, listening to the explanation. "You've always been one to finish what you start, but this is different."

"I know, but it's driving me crazy that I can't complete this last case."

Her mother came to the table with a coffee pot in hand. She topped off CJ's mug. "Are you saying that once they solve this case, you have no desire to continue with your job?"

"I'll always have the desire, but there's something much stronger inside me now. It sounds so old-fashioned, but I want to be the best mother I can." She paused. "I guess I'm frustrated with everything. David's been staying in touch with the Rangers and they've hit a wall. The longer things go, the less chance they have of discovering the killer and the person who tried to kill me."

Grace sat by her and took her hand. "Things will soon change."

"I know, but I can't stop thinking about it." She looked away, searching for words. Then they came to her. "David and I are playing defense. That's not how you win. We have to go on offense and take the initiative against whoever did this."

"But, how?"

"That's the question of the day, isn't it?"

A text message interrupted the mother-daughter session. "Tommy relieved David. He'll come in tired and hungry."

Grace moved to heat the griddle and a skillet, the first for pancakes and the second for eggs. Pre-cooked bacon and sausage stayed warm in the oven.

David shucked off his coat and tactical vest as soon as he entered. He eased into a chair and settled in for breakfast. While waiting for his two fried eggs, he patted CJ's hand.

"Your fingers are like icicles," she said.

"Another frosty morning."

"Anything new?"

He released her hand and wrapped it around his mug of coffee. "We have a family of skunks that moved in close to the property line between us and the road. Otherwise, I had plenty of time to think."

"About what?"

"The case." He leaned back and ran a hand through his hair. "Do you remember how we concluded the person who shot Judge Kraft wasn't a true professional hit man?"

CJ nodded. "He left a dent in the aluminum window sill when the rifle bucked up and slammed down."

David rose to pour more coffee. "Also, a pro would have

waited until you were outside the clinic. Instead, he got impatient and shot through a thick glass door."

She couldn't deny the logic, but didn't know what to do with the information. "How does that get us any closer to the shooter?"

He shrugged. "You never know how a scrap of seemingly unimportant information will help. If nothing else, it should eliminate some people."

Grace delivered his meal and accompanied it with a pointed question. "Won't the discussion of murder and mayhem during a meal give you indigestion?"

David took the hint and ate with a minimum of words. He placed his dishes in the sink and scuttled off to the bedroom. CJ went to her chair in the living room, raised her feet, and wished she could at least open the blinds. The day dragged with her trying to picture a competent, but not overly skilled, hunter.

Bob and Alice arrived after lunch to give Grace and LeRoy the opportunity to spend the afternoon and evening with Bea and Billy Paul.

Alice came equipped with her lap top and a satchel stuffed with end-of-year university spreadsheets. She stayed in the breakfast nook writing reports while CJ and Bob parked in the living room's matching recliners.

"Anything exciting happen last night?" asked Bob.

"David found a new family of skunks near the property line by the road."

Bob chuckled. "They may have their eye on the new home we're building. Do you know how to get rid of skunks?"

"Not really, but you might ask Nancy. If she doesn't know, I'm sure the vet can give you some ideas."

Bob nodded and then snapped his finger. "I bet Tommy knows. I'll ask him when he comes in."

CJ glanced at the curtains. "I never knew how not being

able to see outside affected a person. I can't imagine how you kept your sanity all those years in prison."

"There were times I thought about ending it all, but then I'd think of David." Bob shivered. "Enough about me. What have you been doing to keep from going stir-crazy?"

"Who says I'm not? I've watched more movies in the last month than I've seen in my entire life. I fell asleep last night watching a 1930s gangster flick about a bad guy who controlled his mob from his prison cell."

Bob scratched his chin. "That reminds me of an embezzler on the same prison farm as me. They released his cell mate on parole and he hooked up with the guy's wife. There the husband sat, stuck in prison, getting reports back from the street about his wife and the man he thought was a friend. They were living it up. Not only did the former cell mate get the wife, they were spending the money the embezzler stole from a big construction company. I always wondered which one made him the maddest, losing the wife or the money."

"What did he do?"

"Hired a hit man, but that backfired, too. They tacked on another thirty years to his sentence."

CJ loved talking to David's dad, but she'd been up far too long. "I'm going to try and get a nap. Holler if you need anything. Maria is in her room and she's a light sleeper."

"Security seems looser. I don't see anyone with a gun hovering over you."

CJ pulled back her unzipped vest and lifted her left arm.

Bob craned his neck. "That's a cute little thing. I haven't seen that one."

"Cute and deadly," said CJ. "An early Christmas present from David."

"I should have known."

CJ shuffled off to bed and an early-afternoon nap. She was

almost asleep when the baby kicked. Her eyes cracked to let in light. Then, they flew open as a revelation hit her. She pushed herself up in bed and grabbed her phone. Who to call first? David? No. She'd need to think about this for a while. It wouldn't do to cry wolf again and be wrong twice about Sid Murphy.

With phone in hand, she scrolled through her directory until she found the name of a man she hadn't spoken to for quite some time. She punched the number and waited. An artificial intelligence voice came on the line.

"You've reached the Records Department of the Institutional Division of the Texas Department of Criminal Justice in Huntsville, Texas. If you know your party's extension, please enter the number now."

CJ punched the numbers and waited with fingers crossed.

CHAPTER TWENTY-THREE

After three rings, an impatient voice came on the line. "Records department."

CJ couldn't help but smile. "Juan? Is that you?"

"Yeah. Who's calling?"

"It's CJ."

The sound of a chair creaking preceded a complete change in tone. They'd been study partners in college over a decade ago, and she could still see the round face and toothy grin.

"I was wondering if you were going to call this Christmas."

CJ crossed her fingers as she prepared to stretch the truth. "How could I forget? You helped me pass statistics class."

"You forgot to call last year."

She kept her fingers crossed. "I thought it was your turn."

He laughed. "You can uncross your fingers now. How are you?"

"Nine-months pregnant and miserable."

"We had our third in September. My wife sent me to the doctor in August to make sure there wouldn't be any more."

His voice took on a more serious tone. "I read that someone took a shot at you. Does it have anything to do with that judge getting killed?"

"It might. I need information about an inmate that was released two days ago. He couldn't have done it, but I'm wondering if someone he was close to is responsible."

"What's the name?"

"Sid Murphy. The first name is Sidney, but he goes by Sid."

"Murphy? Wasn't that the name of the guy that put the scar on your face before you put him down?"

"That was Bigalou, Sid's brother and another alumnus of your system."

Clicks from a keyboard sounded as Juan looked up the name.

"There he is. I'm looking at the family history page. It lists another brother besides Big. Tiger Murphy."

"That's Tig," said CJ. "He seems to have fallen off the face of the earth. There's a warrant out for his arrest, but the Rangers have stopped looking for him."

"Do you think Tig is the one responsible?"

"Not Tig, but I have a theory that Sid's involved. Don't you keep track of people who visit inmates?"

"Yeah. Let me check."

More clicks from the keyboard as CJ crossed her fingers and waited for the answer she hoped would bring the case to a quick conclusion.

Juan came back on the line. "Sid wasn't a very popular guy. Only two visitors on his list. The brother named Tig was one, but it looks like he never came. The second is a woman named Crystal Key."

"Do you have an address?"

"It's on a farm to market road in Hamilton. I'll text you

the exact address." He added. "Her visits started three years ago, and she came as often as allowed. That's a long drive from Hamilton County to the Ellis 1 unit." More clicks. "Interesting. Sidney Murphy paroled to Crystal Key. You might call Warden Henderson and see if he remembers her."

CJ's mind was running at full throttle by the time she wished Juan a Merry Christmas and hung up. Too many pieces fit together for this to be a coincidence. Her first thought was to tell David, but she hesitated. What if she was jumping to conclusions again? It would be after the sun went down before he came in for his next break. He insisted on establishing an outside perimeter and maintaining strict vigilance. With her mother and LeRoy away, that left two less armed people inside the home. She looked at the phone, swallowed, and found the number for Captain Crow. Her finger hovered over the call icon for a full three seconds before she punched it.

Captain Crow answered after only one ring. "I hope you're calling to tell me you had the baby. I need David working on those files."

CJ took in a deep breath. "I may have a hot lead on Judge Kraft's killer and it could be the same person who took a shot at me."

"I need a name."

"Before I tell you, I need to ask a favor."

"Why does this not surprise me?" His voice dripped with sarcasm. "What kind of favor are we talking about?"

"Don't get your boxers in a tangle, it's a little-bitty favor. No one here knows what I've found, and I want to keep it that way. That includes David, at least for now."

He let out a huff. "Quit stalling and tell me who this mystery person is."

She rolled her eyes, even though he couldn't see it. "All right, but this information didn't come from me."

"This goes against my better judgment, but I won't tell David you told me for at least a day. That will give you time to come clean."

"Two days."

"One, and tell me, before I hang up."

"You'll be glad you didn't and I'll be nice and give you the short version. Check out a woman from Hamilton County by the name of Crystal Key. She's been a regular visitor to Sid Murphy at the Ellis I unit for three years. He paroled out to her the day after someone took a shot at me. I have a hunch he wrapped her around his finger and sweet-talked her into doing the dirty work for him."

The phone went quiet for several seconds. "David sent me a report about the links between Judge Kraft, you, and Sid. If you're right, this could be a two-for-one arrest. Anything else?"

"David concluded that the shooter isn't a professional, but has enough skill to use a rifle. That fits with someone living on a country road in Hamilton County."

"I can't argue with that. There's good hunting out there."

"My friend at the records office suggested I call Warden Henderson at the Ellis I prison farm and ask if he knows anything else about Sid or Crystal Key. I'm leaving that up to you."

"Why didn't you want David to make the call?"

"Marital and family harmony," said CJ. "I'm under strict instructions from my mother and David not to touch anything dealing with this case, or even think about it. I didn't follow up so both of us would have one less thing to hide from David."

"Hold on a minute," said the Ranger captain. "We know the rifle used to kill Judge Kraft was the same one used to slaughter several head of cattle on a ranch near Hico."

"And Hico is in Hamilton County," said CJ.

"Isn't that where the game warden that's helping guard you moved from?"

"His name is Tommy. If you're looking for someone who knows Hamilton County like his face in the mirror, he's your man. There's a better than even chance he either knows Crystal Key, or knows of her."

"I may have to steal him from you for a day or two."

"Steal away. If there's any shooting to be done, I'd rather it take place in Hamilton County than in my bedroom."

"I'll keep you posted," said Captain Crow.

"No, you won't. Tell David, and I'll act surprised. Remember, you heard nothing from me."

It was the first time she'd ever heard Captain Crow chuckle.

———

BOB AND ALICE TAG-TEAMED, making supper while CJ perched on a bar stool, taking copious notes of the ingredients and the process. Alice used portions of almost every fresh vegetable she could find to make a salad while David's father whipped up a main course of chicken Alfredo.

"You two make it look so effortless."

"We all have our strengths and weaknesses," said Alice. "I'd have made a lousy policewoman."

CJ glanced at the clock on the microwave. "Mom and LeRoy should be back from their tour of the living nativity and Bea and Billy Paul's home any time now."

Maria came from the south wing of the home. Dark circles under her eyes gave evidence that the six-hours-on and six-off schedule was taking its toll. She covered her mouth as she yawned and plopped down at the table.

"I've seen you look better," said CJ.

Maria didn't respond except to give a tight-lipped grunt.

"What's wrong? Too much time in the great outdoors?"

Maria placed her hands flat on the table. "I guess you haven't heard. They're taking Tommy for a couple of days. He said it had to do with unfinished business in Hamilton County."

"When is he leaving?" asked Bob.

"First thing tomorrow morning. David knows about it and told him to stay on patrol until midnight."

"I wonder what's going on?" asked CJ. Deception didn't come natural to her, but this was one of those rare occasions she justified it.

Alice filled the silence. "Won't David need a replacement to keep watch outside?"

Bob gave his opinion. "One outside lookout isn't enough. I could go out and keep watch, but all I can do is call someone if I see anything unusual."

Alice tented her hands on her hips. "I think you need to leave the bodyguard business to professionals."

"LeRoy and I could spell each other," countered Bob. "That would put us up to full strength."

Alice moved to the refrigerator and retrieved a bottle of Italian Dressing. "CJ, how many officers are covering the campus tonight?"

"We always cut back once the winter break begins. There should be four, unless someone called in sick."

"Is it unusual for there to only be three officers on duty late at night?" asked Alice.

"Not during the winter break."

Maria spoke up. "Lieutenant Grimes is the supervisor tonight."

"Call him and put him on speaker phone," said Alice.

CJ watched as the mini-drama played out in front of her. The phone rang and the veteran lieutenant answered with a measure of concern in his voice. "Is everything all right, Maria?"

"We're a man short after midnight. Can you help?"

Before he could respond, Alice broke into the conversation. "Lieutenant Grimes, this is Alice Cummings-Harper. Maria and CJ tell me you might spare an officer tonight. Is that possible?"

"No problem," came the immediate reply. "We might as well be patrolling a graveyard. No one's called in sick and even if they did, two of us can handle an empty campus two days before Christmas."

It was CJ's turn. "This is the expectant mother. Pick an officer that doesn't mind being in the woods all night. Tell them to dress warm and bring their rifle and body armor. Have them wear camo or black instead of their uniform. David has night vision binoculars for them to use."

"What about tomorrow?" asked the lieutenant.

Alice took over again. "Let me talk to David and get back to you on that."

When the call ended, CJ asked Maria to send a text to David to let him know a replacement would arrive before midnight.

He replied with a single word. "Good."

Maria was peeking out the window of the breakfast nook when headlights raked the back yard. "It's Grace and LeRoy," she said as she moved to unlock the door.

There wasn't time for CJ to ask her mother about the Christmas decorations before Grace gushed high praise of what they'd experienced. "I've seen nothing like it. Bea pulled out all the stops in the living nativity. There were church choirs taking turns singing carols and Christmas hymns. Loads of adults and children came dressed in period costumes, and the animals were amazing. Donkey rides for the small children and rides on camels for the teens. We munched on fresh-popped caramel popcorn and drank hot apple cider."

"Then we toured Bea and Billy Paul's home," said LeRoy. "Imagine the Christmas display window in the fanciest department store in the world. Now multiply it by a thousand and you're still not there. Each room of their home had its own Christmas theme."

"I liked the Hawaiian luau Christmas by the pool," said Grace.

Alice piped up. "I couldn't believe the *It's a Wonderful Life* room. Where did she find a man that looked and sounded like George Bailey?"

CJ held up her hands. "No more. You're spoiling it for me. I want to experience everything fresh tomorrow night."

Her words fell on deaf ears. The four eldest kept rattling on about their favorite things that were taking place not more than a few miles down the gravel road. CJ nudged her head toward the living room as she and Maria exchanged glances. It was a signal for them to leave the elders to rave.

Once settled in recliners, CJ said, "Can you believe every one of them is on the downhill side of fifty and they're still nuts about Christmas?"

Maria stared at the logs in the fireplace. "And here we are without our men. David acts like he's on a tour of duty with the army and Tommy won't be here for Christmas Eve."

CJ realized how bummed-out Maria was. As far as she knew, this was Maria's first serious romance. What made it worse was she'd recommended Captain Crow enlist Tommy to help in the search for Crystal Key. All she could say was, "I'm sorry, Maria. It's my fault he's leaving."

"Don't say that," snapped Maria. "You didn't kill the judge or fire the shot at the clinic."

CJ wanted to say more, but words wouldn't help what was wrong with Maria. She'd have to deal with disappointment in her own way and get used to it if she was going to carry a badge.

Both of them watched in silence as the flames in the fireplace licked. CJ asked, "Are you hungry?"

"A little."

"Let's get you fed. You need to rest before you relieve Tommy." She paused. "Who knows, he might be home for Christmas."

"Not likely," said Maria.

CHAPTER TWENTY-FOUR

CJ peeked at the soundless television as it bounced light around the living room. LeRoy sat on the couch, watching dialog come and go beneath the images. A fleece throw covering her made her realize she'd fallen asleep. "What time is it?" she asked in a half-asleep voice.

"Eleven twenty-five," said LeRoy. "Your mom covered you before she went to bed."

"Did Bob and Alice leave?"

"About nine-thirty, but they came back. You missed the excitement. As they were leaving, they saw a car parked on the road that runs in front of the property. It took off in a big hurry when they saw the headlights coming their way."

"Did they get a description?"

"Bob thinks it was a Ford Mustang because of the sequential turn signal lights. Other than that, they didn't get close enough to even make out the color. It put David on edge when Bob reported it to him."

"You said Alice and Bob came back?"

"We're back," said Bob as he walked in from the kitchen carrying a mug of coffee. "Your mother is in her room. Alice is getting settled in Nancy's room and LeRoy and I will take turns catching naps in here."

Maria made her not-so-grand appearance by walking through the living room on her way to the kitchen. Her only word was, "Coffee."

CJ's mind tried to put together whether the threat was real or not. Cars parked on the side of the road away from the city were not unheard of. There could be a hundred reasons someone would need to stop. One had to do with underage drinking. That theory would fit as to the reason the car took off in a hurry. If Bob noticed sequential tail lights, that would also fit with a teen driver. Besides, the vehicle they were most concerned about was a white Chevy half-ton truck, not a Mustang.

She turned to her father-in-law. "David shouldn't have made you come back. I'm guessing it was teenagers out doing what they do."

Bob dismissed her with a wave of his hand. "Don't think a thing about it. Better safe than sorry."

Maria came back in. "Jacoby is crossing the cattle guard. He'll be here any minute."

CJ nodded her approval. "Jacoby grew up hunting and fishing in the swamps of Louisiana. He would have been my first choice."

"I thought I was your first choice," said Maria with a pretend pout.

The knock on the mudroom door didn't give CJ a chance to respond.

Maria hustled down the hall to let the ACU patrolman in. After exchanging muffled words, they entered the living room. The latest member of the security detail came dressed in full camo, including face paint. He had a baby face buried under smears of green and black. His black, curly hair poked out from the edges of a floppy camo hat he took off when he entered the room.

CJ took care of introductions and asked Jacoby if he wanted a cup of coffee while waiting for David to arrive. He agreed to the offer. Everyone but LeRoy moved to the kitchen.

Bob's phone announced a text message, and he went to the back door. David breezed in, took one look at Jacoby, and nodded his approval. "Let's go. I'll show you where to patrol and what to do."

Jacoby put his coffee on the bar and the two left with no parting words.

Maria slipped a knit cap over her head and said, "Guess I better go on too. Don't want the boss hollering at me again."

Bob puttered around the kitchen, wiping down a pristine counter then turned off the lights in the kitchen and breakfast nook. He opened the blinds enough so he and CJ could see the back yard and the barn. Security lights lit the area so they had no trouble in seeing Tommy cross the road from the field and disappear into the barn, his new place of residence.

Bob had turned around when CJ noticed a movement coming from the field that separated the river and the barn. She followed the dark figure as it worked toward the barn's door. She opened her mouth to sound a warning, but the night-stalker turned and faced her. Maria was sneaking in to see Tommy one last time. Instead of her going in, he came out, and they disappeared into the night, holding hands and carrying rifles. CJ closed the blinds and kept one more Christmas secret from David.

DAVID SLEPT on his back in long underwear. CJ didn't think he moved a muscle in three and a half hours. He lay beside her with his hands laced together, resting on his stomach. He didn't normally sleep with his pistol under his pillow, but he'd made an exception since the last shooting.

Because he was now living on a strict schedule, it didn't surprise her when David slipped out of bed at four in the morning, showered, shaved, and readied himself to be back on patrol before first light. The sound of glass breaking caused him to bolt from the bathroom with shaving cream on half his face.

"Get in the closet," he said as he slipped his tactical vest on.

"Mom must have dropped a glass," said CJ, but she humored him and moved from the bed to the walk-in closet. She did, however, have the tiny pistol in her hand by the time he returned.

"It's me," said David as he came back into the bedroom. "All clear. You can come out."

CJ did and chuckled at the sight of him. "You may start a fashion trend by wearing a towel and a tactical vest."

He ignored the comment. "You were right. We're down one more glass from the set we received as a wedding present."

"Good," said CJ. "I never liked those glasses. They reminded me of the jelly jars we used when I was growing up. I think I'll switch to acrylic for everyday use."

It wasn't long before CJ and David joined Grace. Tommy came in looking fresh and ready for a full day's work in his game warden uniform. It reminded CJ of how little sleep she'd gotten by on when love was new to her and David.

The two men concentrated on eating their waffles as CJ looked on and Grace played cook and server. To break the quiet, CJ asked, "Do you think you'll have any trouble getting a search warrant?"

Tommy shook his head. "Her parents picked a prophetic

name for Crystal Key. Her troubles began with her use of crystal meth. She's no stranger to law enforcement in the area. The place she lives is between nowhere and nothing. It wouldn't surprise me a bit if she killed those cattle. I know she kills her legal quota of deer every year, and rumor has it she's not averse to taking a few more out of season."

"What does she look like?" asked CJ.

"Mid-thirties. Long, black hair and dark skin. Decent figure that she shows off in tight jeans. She'd be real pretty if she hadn't done so many drugs. Her face is scarred with pock marks." He stabbed a bite of waffle.

David spoke through a bite of sausage. "Typical of meth users."

Tommy took another bite of waffle. "Another thing about Crystal. She has the deepest voice I ever heard from a woman. Sounds just like a man."

CJ snapped her fingers. "That's it. Alejandro said a man called him wanting information on Judge Kraft's movements."

"Who?" asked Tommy.

"Alejandro Vega," said CJ. "He's the horse trainer for the judge's wife. He needed money for family medical expenses in Mexico and traded information for ten grand. That's how Crystal knew where Judge Kraft would be on Thanksgiving."

David put down his fork. "That fits. Sid Murphy orchestrated everything and told Crystal what to do. She took out the judge and tried to do the same to CJ. Sid tried to settle old scores while he had the perfect alibi of being in prison."

The room went quiet. It became apparent to CJ how important today's raid would be.

Grace broke the silence after her gaze settled on David. "Why would using drugs cause pock marks?"

CJ answered while David continued eating. "Crystal methamphetamine can cause severe itching, especially the face and arms. They pick at their skin until they cause scabs, sores, and scars."

"How sad," said Grace.

"Anyway," said Tommy. "Blake and I will meet with a judge this morning and get him to approve the warrant to search Crystal's home and property for the rifle, her cell phone, computer, freezers—"

Grace interrupted. "Freezers?"

"We think she shot and butchered three head of cattle on a ranch south of Hico."

David looked at CJ. "Remember what Dad craved after all that time behind bars? Steak, twice-a-day for a week."

Tommy picked up where he left off. "If we find any weapons in the house, that'll be enough for us to arrest Sid Murphy. He can't be near firearms."

"Two birds for the price of one," whispered CJ.

David swallowed the last bite. "I'll relieve Maria early today." He looked at Tommy. "Can you stay long enough to tell her good bye?"

"I'd like to, but I can't be late."

Tommy checked the blinds before opening the door while David locked it behind him.

CJ knew David would leave soon, but she had to broach a touchy subject one more time. "Honey," she began. "If they arrest Crystal Key and Sid today, I want to see the living nativity and Bea's house this evening."

He took in a deep breath. "You're not going anywhere if you don't spend the entire day with your feet up."

She beckoned him to come close with fluttering eyelashes. After delivering a kiss, she said, "This is going to be a Christmas to remember."

CHAPTER TWENTY-FIVE

CJ exited her bedroom wearing a fresh, long-sleeve T-shirt and her most comfortable black maternity slacks. She considered wearing one of David's sweatshirts, but realized she wouldn't be able to get to her tiny pistol if she needed it. She laced her arms into the down vest and left it unzipped, as she'd done all week.

Thoughts of their son's birth flooded in. His grand appearance would be tomorrow, Christmas Day. Convinced of the accuracy of her prediction, she experienced a lightness in her steps. The only sound coming from the living room was the soft crackle of logs in the fireplace. Her mother looked up from reading a book. "You should have called me. I would have helped dry your hair."

CJ shooed away the offer with a flip of her hand. "I feel better today than I have all month. I checked my blood pressure, and it's down to near normal."

"That's good. Now sit down before it spikes again."

CJ walked to the front window and peeked around the curtain. She spoke as she took a long look at the front pasture. "Not a cloud in the sky and the temperature is going to be in the high fifties this afternoon. I can't wait to go to Bea's tonight."

Grace closed the book. "I hope you're not getting ahead of yourself. There's no guarantee of arrests."

"Think positive, Mom. After all, it's Christmas and you're about to be a grandmother again."

Grace responded with a smile. "I have to admit, I'd love to go back to Bea and Billy Paul's for another tour. I'm praying everything will work out so you can see what they've done."

"Don't forget the living nativity," said CJ. "I haven't seen one in years. It always helps to remember the reason for the season."

CJ sighed. "It's going to be a long day. Waiting for word on the raid may have me pulling out my freshly washed hair."

Grace rose from the couch. "Come with me to the kitchen. It's time you learned to make Christmas cookies. Where's your notebook?"

"In the last drawer, next to the refrigerator. I'll sit on a barstool and take notes."

Being with her mother, talking about the triumphs and tragedies that accompany life, made the morning pass quicker than expected. Before CJ knew it, leftovers appeared on the counter to reheat for lunch.

Maria came in carrying her cell phone, dressed in pajamas and a robe. "Tommy sent me a text. They have the search warrant and the team is waiting on one more state trooper before they drive to Crystal's."

It was as if time swallowed a slowdown pill. Lunch came and went with little conversation. CJ and Maria went to the living room with cell phones at the ready.

"I wish I was there," said Maria.

"This is one time I'm glad I'm not." CJ let out a sigh. "It doesn't make the waiting any easier though." She raised her legs by pulling back on a handle on the side of the recliner. "Do you know if Tommy sent David a text?"

Maria shook her head. She'd gone into her quiet mode. A half-hour passed in silence until they traded notes about the officer who'd relieved Jacoby at five forty-five that morning.

LeRoy passed through on his way to eat lunch. Grace walked him back to his room and gave him strict instructions to go back to sleep. He escaped the kitchen with warm cookies wrapped in a paper napkin.

Finally, Maria's phone signaled a call. She put it on speaker and said, "Are you all right?"

"Everyone's fine, but things aren't going as planned. Flames are shooting from the roof of Crystal's house."

CJ couldn't keep quiet. "Any sign of Sid or Crystal?"

"Not yet. The fire department is just now arriving. Being this far out of town, it takes a while for the nearest volunteer fire department to respond. The white Chevy truck that belongs to Crystal is in the driveway. I found Sid's release papers in the seat." He paused and coughed. "I need to get out of this smoke. Hold on."

Both CJ and Maria moved to the edge of their seats and waited.

"There's another fire truck coming," said Tommy. "I can't talk long, but I wanted you to know what else we found in the truck. It's a .308 rifle with scope. I'll call back with more information when I can."

The phone went silent.

CJ grabbed her phone and sent a long text message to David, giving him details of Tommy's phone call.

He responded with, *Keep me informed.*

"That's all he said?" asked Maria.

CJ eased back in the chair and raised her feet again. "He's processing the information and coming up with various scenarios."

"Like what?"

CJ rubbed her stomach as a contraction began. "It could be a ploy? Sid and Crystal might have planned to burn the home so they could run away and start fresh somewhere else. Or, is the fire an accident and they're on foot? It might be a double suicide. Did Sid and Crystal get trapped inside? Perhaps they were so wired on drugs they didn't know or care."

The contraction intensified, so she hurried to say, "The next phone call will be important." She held up crossed fingers for luck and breathed until the pain passed.

Maria's body tensed as she watched CJ, but didn't say a word.

"As I was about to say, I'm not wishing anyone dead, but this house seems smaller today than it did several days ago."

"You have many more of those contractions and you won't have to worry about how small the house is. You'll be at the hospital."

Hours passed, but still no word. Instead of a call coming to either CJ or Maria, a knock on the back door sounded. Muffled words from the kitchen preceded David's entrance into the living room carrying a glass of iced tea. He all but fell in his recliner and took a long drink.

"You're looking rather relaxed. You must have heard from Blake and you think it's safe now."

David pulled off a camo hat and placed it on his lap. "The fire crews found two bodies in the remains of the house."

The baby kicked. Maria noticed the movement and raised her eyebrows. CJ stayed on topic. "Sid and Crystal?"

"Blake believes it's them. Both bodies were burned beyond recognition, but Crystal wore a distinctive belt buckle. They found it on one body. She owned only one vehicle, and it's the white half-ton they found in the driveway."

"And Sid?" asked CJ.

"The two bodies were side by side, their hands interlocked."

"When will Tommy be able to come home?" asked Maria.

"Sometime late tonight."

He then looked at CJ. "They found simple wedding rings on both bodies with identical inscriptions of yesterday's date and SM & CM FOREVER."

CJ didn't realize she'd been holding her breath until she relaxed and it came out in a rush.

Maria stood. "Is it all right if I go home?"

"Sure," said David. "Thanks for helping. Next time you might want to keep your mind on the job at hand. Sneaking off to meet the latest love interest could get you both killed."

Maria threw her head back and rolled her eyes. "I should have known you'd catch us."

David covered his smile with his hand. "I expected it. If I were in Tommy's shoes, I would have asked CJ to do the same thing."

"It wasn't Tommy's idea." said Maria. She winked at CJ and shuffled toward her bedroom.

Grace walked behind the couch and made for the curtains. With quick pulls, they parted, exposing a pastoral scene of cattle grazing in the afternoon sun. The flood of light chased away the cloud of trepidation that had settled on the home.

CJ looked at David and pointed toward their bedroom. "Change clothes. You're taking me to Bea and Billy Paul's."

David shook his head. "I need an hour in bed before I go anywhere."

"Forty-five minutes and I'll have a double expresso waiting for you."

"It's a deal."

To appease her mother, CJ put her feet up on the coffee table while sitting on the couch. "Mom, you and LeRoy go on to Bea and Billy Paul's. David's changing and we'll be an hour behind you."

It took no convincing. Grace went to her bedroom and came back with her coat in hand. "We don't mind waiting. Let's all ride together."

"That won't work. If David isn't on scheduled time off, he's supposed to drive his work vehicle. Besides, I might go into labor tonight. If I do, he'll want to get me to the hospital in a hurry. Flashing lights and a siren come in handy."

Grace tilted her head. "Are you having contractions?"

"Nothing regular."

LeRoy entered the living room with his jacket already on. "Did I hear something about having a baby?"

CJ rubbed her belly. "Not yet. I have to see Bea's Christmas extravaganza first. Did I tell you I let her know we're coming?"

Both Grace and LeRoy shook their heads.

CJ kept rubbing the protruding mound. "I didn't realize the living nativity and having her home open to the public ends at sunset. They wanted all the participants and attendees to get home at a decent hour and enjoy Christmas Eve with their families. She said they're having a few special friends after everyone else leaves to watch the banner of Santa's sleigh being pulled by an airplane."

"That's going to be quite a sight," said LeRoy. "There's no moon, so it's going to be dark as a cave when the searchlight hits the banner."

Grace asked, "If all the townspeople are back home, how are they going to see it?"

"There's a second searchlight in town. It's mounted on the roof of the old Sterling Building, which is the only five-story building in Riverview. The plane will pull the banner in circles around the city."

"What time can we expect to see Santa?" asked LeRoy.

"Seven forty-five for Bea and Billy Paul's house. The plane will make a couple of practice runs and be over the city at eight. They planned it so the children could get a look before they're shooed off to bed."

Grace came over and gave CJ a kiss on the cheek. "We'll run along." She stood and gave an exaggerated wag of her finger. "Plan on doing a lot of sitting and looking tonight. The one thing you don't want to do is wear yourself out before you go into labor."

CJ nodded, more for her mother's sake than in agreement. She longed for fresh air, conversations, and decorations. Most of all, she wanted to stand in front of the nativity.

The closing of the door behind LeRoy and her mother brought a new revelation. The home was empty except for her, David, and Sandy. How long had it been since it was only the original three? Their family unit gained two when Nancy and little Davey burst onto the scene. Soon, they would add another.

Sandy lay on her bed by the fireplace with head down, eyes closed, snoring. She'd earned her keep after long days and nights on patrol and received her reward of leftover chicken and dumplings. CJ doubted Sandy would follow them to Bea and Billy Paul's tonight, but then again, she might.

After forty-five minutes, she went to check on David. She opened the bedroom door to find him stretched out on the bed, sound asleep.

"Hey!" she shouted. "What are you doing?"

He cracked open his left eye.

"Trying to finish a nap."

"You're supposed to be changing clothes. If we don't hurry, we'll miss the living nativity."

"That's the plan."

CJ bent over and shook him. "What do you mean?"

"There's no way we can park close. That means a lot of walking. If you go to that, you'll be on your feet for a full hour. What would that do to your feet and ankles?"

"I thought we agreed that if—"

David didn't allow her to finish. "I agreed that if they captured Sid and Crystal, we'd go to Bea and Billy Paul's house." He glanced at the clock. "This is for your own good and for the health of our son."

"But..." She ran out of persuasion and could tell by his tone that David had run out of patience.

"I'm going to sleep fifteen more minutes and then we'll leave."

CJ didn't mean to slam the bedroom door as loud as she did, but didn't go back to apologize. She stewed in anger for ten minutes and felt sorry for herself for another five. By the time David arrived, she was ninety-five percent over being mad at him. It was always that last five percent that gave her trouble.

CHAPTER TWENTY-SIX

"I still don't understand how you can snatch an hour's sleep and wake refreshed." That last five percent of anger ebbed away when she looked out the SUV's window and beheld a starry night. After all, this was the time of year when joy and forgiveness reigned supreme. Unkind thoughts vanished altogether when she caught sight of the glow and blink of lights from Casa Stargate.

"Wow," said David.

It may have been an understatement, but CJ couldn't think of anything more to say but, "Double-wow." From a distance, the multi-story home shimmered with an untold number of white lights. Yard decorations depicted various scenes from Christmas movies, while the deck around the swimming pool paid homage to Christmas in Hawaii.

David parked as close as he could, but it was still a hike to get to the pool's entrance. Coming through the gate, a puppy met them with high-pitched, excited yaps.

"Good boy," said Billy Paul. "You did your job, Door Bell." He snapped his finger. "Sit. Be nice. That's our neighbors,

David and CJ." The dog responded with silence and settled on his haunches.

CJ gave her friend and neighbor a sideways glance. "Door Bell? Is that his name?"

Billy Paul had abandoned his John Deere baseball cap for something that belonged on one of Santa's elves. He hooked his thumbs in the bib of his overalls. "I always try to name my dogs something that describes 'em. Bea bought me this pup for Christmas after I told her I wanted a dog that would let me know when someone's driving up to the house. After being around heavy equipment most of my life, my hearing isn't as keen as it once was. He's my early warning system."

"I don't recognize the breed," said David.

Billy Paul rocked back and forth on the soles and heels of his boots. "He's what you might call a cross between a second-chancer and a lucky-to-be-aliver. He's a pound puppy that got returned after the family that adopted him discovered their daughter was allergic to dogs."

"Looks to be terrier," said David.

"Nancy says there're more breeds in him than she could name. Don't matter to me as long as he lets me know company's coming."

CJ bent forward as far as she could and received doggy kisses on her outstretched hand. "He's friendly."

Billy Paul gave a shoulder shrug. "Only if he likes you. A few people here tonight earned a growl. I don't blame him; I'd like to growl at one or two myself."

"Not tonight," said CJ. "It's Christmas Eve."

"You're right," said Billy Paul. "Goodwill toward all men."

Nancy came toward them with Kevin Kraft in tow. CJ hoped her eyebrows didn't shoot up too much when she saw them together. What would Kevin's mother think?

When she saw CJ's face, she said, "Don't worry. Kevin's mom's here. She's been nice to me and Davey. I told you she'd warm up to the idea. In fact, she's inside taking care of Davey."

David looked at Kevin. "Would you go get your mom?"

"Is it bad news?"

"Not bad, but both of you will want to hear what I have to say."

Kevin nodded and returned a short time later with his mother and little Davey. She wore black wool pants and a red sweater with a gold Christmas broach pinned on it.

Billy Paul excused himself when Chris joined the mini-gathering. She wrapped her arms around her midsection in a gesture of self-protection.

"Has anyone contacted you today from law enforcement?" asked David.

Chris shook her head.

David nodded. "I spoke with Captain Crow a little while ago. He wanted me to tell you that nothing is official yet, but we believe your husband's killer and the person who planned his death died today in a house fire. They're the same two responsible for trying to kill CJ."

Chris stood motionless until her chin quivered. "How sure are you?"

"Almost one-hundred percent. Dental records and DNA will make it official, but they will only confirm what we know to be true." He paused. "Do you want details?"

She took in a deep breath, let it out, and shook her head. "Not tonight. It's enough to know the person won't harm anyone else."

Kevin spoke up. "I want to know."

Chris held out her hands and little Davey launched himself from Kevin's arms to Chris's. "Nancy, why don't we girls go in and let the men talk by themselves."

"Good idea," said CJ, as another contraction caused her to wince.

Once inside, Bea met her with a sideways hug and blue eyes that seemed to always see more than other people could. "You're going to have a Christmas baby," she said, as if she could feel it herself. "Let's sit you down."

"It will pass," said CJ, but she took Bea up on the offer of a chair in the massive living room. Spellbound by the scene in front of her, the contraction passed and left CJ in a winter wonderland of decorations. Nancy, Chris, and Davey had split off to get drinks and snacks with a promise to bring her hot apple cider and a small plate of holiday treats.

"You've outdone yourself," said CJ. "I wish I could have seen the living nativity, but David had our home guarded like I was the Crown Jewels."

Bea patted her leg. "You're worth more than those old rocks." A smile of mischief crossed her face. "All the people are gone, but the animals are all still on the hillside across the river. The keys are in my four-wheeler if you and David want to go look at Bethlehem and the nativity."

"Not David," said CJ, with alarm in her voice. "He's worse than my mother about me being on my feet."

CJ looked around and guessed the intimate gathering had swelled to well over a hundred people. She tilted her head. "I heard this was a small gathering. How many are here?"

Bea shrugged. "I told Billy Paul I wanted to invite people who might need cheering up on Christmas Eve. People like Chris Kraft who lost their someone special." Her eyes came alive with delight. "Billy Paul and I invited people as we saw them in town, or heard about them from someone else. Now that they're all here, there must be almost two hundred people. I had no idea we knew that many people who'd lost loved ones and are alone for their first Christmas."

"It's wonderful. People are moving from room to room. That's what I want to do; take my time and soak in all the sights and sounds of people celebrating Christmas."

"It's still a couple of hours before Santa flies by on his way to town. He'll come out of the east, make a couple of laps over the living nativity with the spotlight shining on him, and head to town." She rose from the couch. "It wouldn't have been Christmas without seeing you and David."

"Thanks so much for taking in Nancy and little Davey."

"Best Christmas ever. Billy Paul took Davey to help him feed and water the camels and donkeys every day. There's nothing like watching an old child and a young one during the holidays."

CJ spent the next hour and a half moving from one room of the mansion to the next, taking her time talking to people she knew, and some she didn't. Nancy caught up with her in the sunroom, a miniature version of Santa's workshop.

"There you are," said Nancy. "Any more contractions?"

"A few."

She didn't want to tell her they were coming with increased regularity. Not yet, at least. She had one more thing she wanted to do to complete her Christmas wish list.

"Bea left the keys in her farm buggy," said CJ. "I want you to drive me up to the living nativity before everyone goes outside to watch Santa's sleigh being pulled across the sky. I've been thinking a lot about Mary and what it must have been like for her to give birth to Jesus among farm animals. It's almost as if I have to go on this pilgrimage and experience it. We won't take long and we'll be back before anyone misses us."

Nancy wore the smile of a co-conspirator. "I'll tell Kevin. He'll cover for us. Are you ready?"

"Grab my coat for me. I'll meet you on the front porch."

Once outside, CJ looked into a sky without clouds. The stars would have been even more stunning if there hadn't been so many Christmas lights to dim the view. "I'll be able to see the heavens better from the nativity. Just like Mary did."

A car started. CJ watched it make its way across the bridge over the river and across more than a mile of treeless river bottom land. It rose to the crest of the hill, where headlights gave outlines of the replica of Bethlehem and the nativity scene off to one side. Everything vanished when the car's tail lights topped the rise and disappeared.

The front door opened and Nancy handed CJ her long winter coat. She slipped it on and shoved her hands in her pockets to pull it over as much of her baby as it would cover. They followed the same route she had just watched the car take, with the pretend town of ancient Bethlehem rising in front of them. Nancy drove without headlights, which gave an added dimension of going back in time.

"With everyone gone, we can drive through the buildings," said Nancy over the engine noise.

CJ pointed. "Pull behind the first building. I'd rather walk."

The copious lights coming from Casa Stargate shone with intensity enough to see the faux-stone homes and the replica of the inn that had denied Mary and Joseph lodging. CJ breathed deeply and smiled at the smells of hay and animals as they passed corrals housing donkeys and camels. This was no sanitized depiction of the humble birth of the baby who would change the world. How she'd longed to experience this moment.

On they walked. They neared the place CJ wanted to see. Was it an accurate representation? It didn't matter. A chill ran through her body all the same. The three sides and roof constructed of weathered, rustic wood with gaps between the boards wouldn't provide much protection. Still, there was hay for Mary's bed and the manger was a small feed trough.

For long minutes, Nancy and CJ stood in reverential silence until Nancy whispered, "It's so different at night without people. So real. It's like we're waiting for Mary to arrive on the donkey she rode all day."

A contraction hit CJ that doubled her over and made her yelp in pain. When she looked up, a figure in black had his right arm wrapped around Nancy's throat. Bending her backward, it only took a few surrealistic seconds for Nancy's body to go limp. She fell in a crumpled heap on the ground.

Before CJ could do anything but scream, the man produced a knife that looked to be at least a foot long. He pointed the tip toward her belly. "Take off your coat, Catherine Jo Harper."

"Who are you?"

"Don't play dumb. You and your husband killed my brothers. It's time for payback."

CJ swallowed a huge lump of fear that tasted like a rotten egg. "Sid Murphy."

CHAPTER TWENTY-SEVEN

With the tip of the knife only inches away from her unborn son, CJ had no choice but to take off her coat and let it fall to the ground.

"Now the vest," said Sid, as he pushed the knife even closer.

She complied, first by taking out her right arm and then allowing the vest to fall, on its own, from her left shoulder. There she stood, wearing nothing more substantial than her white T-shirt and dark maternity pants. She didn't know if it was the chilly night air or if it was time for another contraction, but she couldn't stand straight.

Sid laughed. "Might as well lie down. I've been waiting years for this night, no need to rush."

CJ spoke as she eased onto the bed of hay. "Did you have to kill her?"

"Put your hands in front of you and don't say anything until I tell you to."

She complied. Before she could think of a way to prevent it, a thick, plastic zip tie had her hands secured.

Nancy moved and groaned. Sid abandoned CJ for the

moment, but not before issuing a stern warning. "I don't need to kill her, but I will if you run. It would be a shame if Nancy's little boy doesn't have a mommy." He pulled out another zip tie from the back pocket of his jeans.

"How do you know her name?" asked CJ as she settled on Mary's makeshift bed and asked for a concession. "Do you mind if I use my coat as a pillow?"

"Not before I check it."

She leaned back against a bale of hay instead of lying flat and concentrated on her breathing as she watched Sid motion with the knife for Nancy to stay down. He then secured Nancy's hands and her ankles. "No talking or I'll shut you up for good." He added, "Do you understand?"

With stalks of hay sticking from her curly red hair, Nancy nodded.

The contraction passed and CJ watched as Sid stood and looked at the manger separating her and Nancy. He picked it up and threw it away from the structure. "No salvation for you tonight, CJ Harper." He stepped toward her. "I could have killed your young friend, but I released the choke hold as soon as she passed out. Her staying alive depends on you not doing something stupid."

"I can't do anything stupid or otherwise." said CJ. "I'm in labor."

A malevolent chuckle came forth. "This is better than I thought." He picked up her coat and vest. Searching both, he found her cell phone, but nothing else. Next, he walked to where Nancy lay and searched her. Unlike CJ, Nancy's coat pockets contained a treasure trove of objects, most meant to entertain or pacify Davey.

"Thanks for the cookies," said Sid. "Why do you have surgical scissors?"

"I'm a vet's assistant. I always carry an extra pair."

A smile parted Sid's lips. "I like animals, too." His smile

left as quick as it came. "It's people like CJ and David Harper that should die, not dogs and cats."

CJ tried for the first time to take mental notes of Sid's features. Despite the dark night, the glow from Casa Stargate cast enough light to make out details. She guessed him to be about the same height as her, six-foot even. He wore a black knit cap, but it only covered the crown of his head. Below it, his head, face, and neck were smooth. She concluded he shaved from the neck up. His jeans and jacket looked new and crisp. Instead of cowboy boots, he wore black boots built for work, with thick soles and black laces. He had a thick frame. She guessed he'd spent a considerable amount of time lifting weights in prison. This didn't bode well. He could break Nancy's neck like a twig if they weren't careful.

After a quick analysis of her situation, CJ went into hostage negotiations mode and tried to establish a rapport. She began with, "I'm confused, Sid. How did you know I'd be here?"

"Your question needs to be more specific. Do you mean here at the living nativity, here at the home of Billy Paul Stargate, or here in Riverview?"

"All of them," said CJ. "Start with Riverview."

Sid put the knife he'd been holding in a scabbard under his jacket.

As he did, CJ asked, "No pistol?"

"I might have one, and then again, I might not. Let's get back to your other questions." Standing between her and the lights coming from Bea and Billy Paul's home caused his face to look like a black pool silhouetted by a ring of white. "Anyone can find where you live. While I was in prison, I talked one of the college instructors into showing me how to use the maps program on her phone. Between that and the prison library, I found an aerial view of your farm. I verified everything on Crystal's phone after they released me."

"Did you do the same thing with Judge Kraft's home?"

"No need. By then I'd already talked Crystal into taking care of him. I put the word out in prison and learned the judge's wife had a Mexican working with her horses. It took time and money to find out more, but it was worth every penny. The horse trainer traded cash for information. It was almost too easy." He shifted his weight and the lights from the distant home shone in CJ's left eye, making it even more difficult to see his face.

Sid took a step closer, pointed his finger and shouted, "You shouldn't have stopped my brother that day!"

Nancy interrupted his tirade, "Can I sit up like CJ?"

His gaze shifted to her, his countenance relaxing. "Sure, Red. Make yourself comfortable."

Nancy scooted on her backside until she had a bale of hay behind her. Her movements told CJ that the zip ties had very little slack in them, not near enough for Nancy to get away, even if she could rise to her feet.

Sid focused on CJ again. "None of this would've happened if you hadn't stopped Big on some trumped-up speeding charge. He was minding his own business, going to visit some friends."

CJ tried to interrupt, but Sid held up a hand and pulled open his coat to expose the knife. "It's not your turn." He lowered his hand and continued with his version of events that took place years ago. "My brother was tough and smart. There's no way he'd let a man, let alone a woman, get the best of him. After you killed him, you planted a gun at the scene."

Nancy spoke up. "That's not how it happened."

Sid shifted his gaze to his left and his voice took on an icy tone. "Were you there?"

"Neither were you," said Nancy.

Sid's hat moved up and down. "Tell me, little Miss Vet's Assistant, what are the odds of this woman overcoming a man that weighed twice as much as her? We're supposed to believe she escaped the grasp of one man, knocked him unconscious, and drew her pistol before Big could get to his. Then she claimed to put two shots dead center in my brother's chest when she was bleeding and had a concussion." Words came faster and with more venom. "To top it off, a news crew just *happened* to be on hand to film her becoming a national celebrity. How did they get there?"

He let the question sink in before he continued. "The next day they declared her a hero and the governor chose her to be a Texas Ranger. It was all a set up by the governor because he was behind in the polls in an election year. Don't kid yourself, Red. She executed my brother and tonight she's going to pay for it."

CJ's mind flooded with memories of the night. The events didn't unfold as Sid imagined, but there were enough elements of truth in his version to make it plausible for someone with a twisted mind. Her thoughts of that fateful night melted away as the next contraction hit her. She struggled to keep from crying out, holding it back so as not to give Sid the satisfaction of seeing her in pain.

Nancy made a noise by shifting and said, "Enough ancient history. I want to hear what caused you to hate Judge Kraft enough to have him killed."

Sid took two steps to stand in front of Nancy.

CJ tried to pace her breathing while he continued with his story.

"They said aggravated robbery with a deadly weapon. Judge Kraft should have dropped the weapons charge. He caused me to serve twice the time in prison that I should have. Every year I watched men make parole who did things ten times worse than I did. It's all because Judge Kraft tacked on those three little words: *With Deadly Weapon.*" He let out a snort. "I might carry a knife, but I never carry a gun. A knife is a tool. A pistol is a weapon."

CJ caught the last sentence as the contraction faded.

Nancy shook her head. "I understand you were mad, but that doesn't seem like enough to kill a judge who was only doing his job. There must be more to it."

Sid raised a hand and scratched his chin. "You're a smart kid." He pointed at CJ. "You don't know what it's like behind bars when someone kills your brother. They still had me locked up when her husband killed my other brother. If Judge Kraft wasn't trying to make a name for himself, I'd have received probation and been around to protect both my brothers from people like David and CJ Harper."

"You have quite the imagination," said CJ.

Sid returned to stand in front of her. "That's rich coming from the hired killer herself. Both you and your husband. That sniper training he got in the army comes in handy, doesn't it?"

She didn't respond, so Sid continued on. "They took him off the case because they needed him to get rid of Tig. The prosecution tried to railroad Tig into prison and it backfired. The Rangers had your husband do their dirty work for them." Sid threw out his chest in a show of superiority. "Are the Rangers looking for Tig?"

CJ shook her head.

He kicked her foot. "I didn't catch what you said. You'll have to speak up."

"No," said CJ. "They stopped looking for Tig."

"Then where's my brother?"

"I don't know," said CJ.

"That's right. Nobody knows but the one who killed him —your husband."

"David had nothing to do with it. You don't have any evidence that says otherwise."

Sid threw his head back and roared out a laugh. "You don't get it, do you? I don't need evidence. I know who killed my brother. Murphy men create our own justice. We always have. It's a lot simpler, faster, and efficient. You and your husband have already been to trial. I found you both guilty of killing one brother each. The only thing that remains to be seen is who dies first. Will it be you or that baby you're about to have... or both?"

"Why the baby?" asked Nancy.

"Well, Red, I figure there's nothing worse that I could do to David Harper than what I'm about to do to his wife and baby."

Sid used his left hand to pull open his coat, exposing the knife. CJ's blood ran cold. She hadn't noticed it before, but the handle of a pistol shoved in his waistband caught the light.

Sid saw her gaze land on the pistol. "Yeah, I made an exception to not carrying a weapon tonight. Just in case I needed it. But I've decided I won't shoot you. That'd be too quick." He ran his fingers up the leather sheath until his right hand closed around the knife's handle.

The drone of an approaching airplane caught Sid's attention. He took a step into the pasture, out from under the patchwork planks of the roof. The massive searchlight flicked on in the front yard of Casa Stargate and raked across the sky.

CJ gazed across the open expanse separating her from David by more than a mile. She looked between the planks above her searching for the plane, but another contraction began and she had to concentrate on controlling the pain.

Through the hardest contraction yet, she heard Sid burst out laughing. "This works out better than I ever dreamed it could." He closed the distance between them. "Are you havin' a boy or a girl?"

Nancy spoke for CJ. "A boy."

BRUCE HAMMACK

Sid kept staring down at CJ. Despite the chilly night air, sweat stung her eyes, and she couldn't help but let out a yelp of pain.

Sid spoke with glee. "With that big spotlight, your husband will see his wife and son die, and there's nothing he can do to stop it."

The contraction intensified. Warm liquid soaked her pants and the straw under her.

CHAPTER TWENTY-EIGHT

The airplane towing Santa made a wide circle around Casa Stargate, with the searchlight keeping Santa's sleigh in its bright beam. It passed overhead as the contractions came with greater frequency and ferocity. Sid stood in the pasture, smiling at the sight, but glancing back at her every few seconds.

Nancy used the time to inch closer. She didn't get far before Sid froze her in place with a shake of his head and a hard stare. As he looked up at the sky, she whispered. "I've been timing your contractions. You have very little time before the baby arrives. Do you have a plan?"

CJ spoke between breaths, "Not yet."

"No talking," shouted Sid.

The plane completed the second pass overhead and moved on to Riverview. Sid's focus returned to the grim task at hand. He took a couple of steps forward to where she lay. CJ fought off the pain. The success of his plan so far made Sid all the more dangerous. No matter how bad the pain, CJ knew their lives depended on her being alert. If he thought

233

he was losing control of the situation, he could change the rules at any moment.

"You never told me how you planned everything. If I'm going to die, I'd like to know how you outwitted everyone."

Sid crouched a couple of yards in front of her feet. "It's difficult getting a woman to fall in love with you when you're behind bars, but I did it." His words came at a normal pace, but had a braggadocio tone to them.

"I learned from the best," said Sid. "The man I studied under was a rapist who talked one of his victims into marrying him while he was still in prison. His prison bank account stayed full and he had a new car waiting for him when he got out. He also talked her into changing her will. If he hasn't taken her for every penny by now, he soon will."

"Sounds like you made him your hero," said Nancy.

"Not a hero, a role model." He turned back to CJ. "I knew Crystal before I went in. We had some good times back then, and her looks made up for that man-voice of hers. That was before she went off the deep end with drugs and destroyed her face."

The pain subsided, so CJ asked, "How long did you court her with letters before she came to see you in prison?"

"It took over a year. My mentor taught me what to write and how to be patient. After all, time was the one thing I had plenty of."

"Tell us how you talked her into shooting and butchering the cattle near Hico."

With the light shining on the side of his face, CJ saw an eyebrow go up.

"How did you figure that out?"

"Not me. Ballistics showed the rounds that killed Judge Kraft and the cattle came from the same rifle."

"I bet your husband had something to do with putting that together," said Sid.

CJ didn't deny it, but kept talking. "How did you get Crystal to butcher the cattle during a thunderstorm. That was a stroke of genius."

Sid lifted his chin. "When Crystal did that, I knew she'd do anything I asked. All it cost me was a promise to put a ring on her finger when I got out."

Another contraction came with unbearable intensity. Nancy drew his attention back to her. "Did you marry her?"

"We got the license the day she picked me up from prison and we married as soon as we could. It was just a piece of paper and a couple of cheap rings to me, but it meant the world to her. We went from the Justice of the Peace to the bank. Once she put me on the signature card, I had full access to her account."

"I bet she didn't have much," said Nancy, challenging him with the tone of her voice.

"You're wrong, Red. The thing I did that made her fall in love with me was help her get off drugs. That's not an easy thing to do when she's on the outside and all I can do is write letters, but it worked. Then, I taught her how to sell them without getting caught. Like my brothers, I made good money selling merchandise people wanted before I went to prison. I didn't realize then how much I didn't know about the drugs. Being taught by the best in the business was like getting a master's degree, all courtesy of the prison system."

CJ tried everything she could, but the pain overwhelmed her to the point she cried out. Sweat slid down her face, as did tears. She opened her eyes in time to see Sid cast his gaze at Nancy. "How much longer before the brat comes out?"

Nancy huffed through her nose. "How should I know? Even if I could examine her, I'm used to delivering lambs, calves, and horses."

Sid shrugged. "It doesn't matter. I have plenty of time."

Her body's need to push and move through the birthing

process grew stronger with each contraction. CJ clenched her teeth and made a silent commitment she wouldn't do anything to hasten the birth. She missed what Nancy asked, but heard Sid's response.

"I'll give you this much, Red. You ask good questions. All right, I'll tell you. Crystal sealed her fate when she botched killing the famous CJ Harper. All she had to do was wait until she stepped through the door of the clinic. She claimed she waited, but I knew she was lying. That's when I put together the plan to get rid of her and make the cops believe I'd died with her."

The contraction subsided enough for CJ to catch her breath. Sid acted like he wasn't paying attention to her, but she saw his eyes cut to her every few seconds. She lay still, praying that David, or a Christmas angel, would appear and save her baby boy.

Sid's voice cut through her prayers with renewed, harsh reality. "Look at her," he said. "She's praying." He stood tall and took a step toward her. "Sorry, no miracle for you or your kid this Christmas."

Nancy broke into his malevolent words. "You haven't finished telling me your story."

Sid took a step back. Once again, his voice softened. CJ recognized a pattern to his speech and actions. Whenever he focused on either her or David, he'd come unhinged. If the conversation turned to his skills or abilities, he became a different person. The key was to keep him talking about how clever he was. Nancy must have figured this out and was buying time with her questions.

And talk on he did. "The plan was simple. I told Crystal to get a man and woman to witness our marriage. After the ceremony, we sent them to Crystal's house, which is way out in the country. We had their drugs of choice waiting for them. The guy got wasted, but the girl took hers to share with her boyfriend and left. I took care of Crystal first and then the guy. They went in a new chest freezer I'd told Crystal to buy." He laughed. "She thought we were going to fill it with more late-night bargain beef. I took Crystal and the druggie out of the freezer last night and put them in bed together to thaw. This morning I used two gallons of gasoline to make sure the house burned to the ground. I knew that would make a quick identification impossible and give me enough time to take care of Mrs. David Harper."

He finished with a boast of self-praise. "I passed a line of cops and a game warden heading to Crystal's land. They didn't give me a second look."

"You left your release papers in Crystal's truck," said CJ. "I have to admit, that was pretty smart."

Sid's voice changed back to something sordid and evil. "Drop the flattery. You sealed your fate when you killed Big."

The cold-blooded recounting of two murders put to rest any of CJ's lingering thoughts about Sid's mental state. Standing over her was a full-blown psychopath, a man without a conscience. He had to be stopped, but how? She hadn't forgotten about the tiny pistol tucked under her arm, but his eyes darted like those of a bird, looking for a tasty worm in the grass. They never left her for more than a second or two.

CJ braced herself for another round of searing pain. She felt the urge to push, but again fought with all her might to relax until it passed. She remembered a statement she'd read from a book on natural childbirth. It said a midwife coached her patients to believe they could deliver their baby's head one hair at a time.

When the desire to push subsided, she looked up to see Sid glowering down on her. CJ fought to maintain her composure even though she couldn't imagine being in a more compromised position. She needed to buy more time.

A question came out of her of its own volition. "Did you come straight to Riverview after you killed Crystal and the guy?"

The question gave Sid another chance to brag about himself. "I came to Riverview twice. Once at night to see if I could get in your house and take care of both you and your husband. When that didn't work, I came back today.

"That explains the mustang parked in front of our property a couple of nights ago. I guess it belonged to the guy that witnessed your marriage. Your plan was foiled because You were seen."

He lifted his shoulders and let them fall. "It only delayed me. I came back, and here we are. I spent today in town and found out about all this." He raised an arm and made a sweeping gesture that included the mock town of Bethlehem and Casa Stargate. "When I heard the Stargates were opening their home tonight to people who'd lost a loved one this year, I took a chance and came." His laugh held no mirth. "Isn't it a coincidence that my wife died this week? I didn't have to lie about losing a spouse."

"Not funny," said Nancy.

He glared at her. "You're smart, but you need to work on your sense of humor."

Undaunted by the reprimand, Nancy asked, "How did you know CJ would be at Bea and Billy Paul's tonight?"

"I studied her for years. I knew she'd come if she wasn't in the hospital."

CJ tried again not to scream. It came out all the same. When she quieted, she heard Nancy's calm voice and Sid's answer, but words made no sense until she came out of her latest bout of searing pain.

Sid had her cell phone in hand. He pushed a button and then another to put it on speaker phone. It rang only twice before she heard David's voice. "Are you all right?"

"Hello, David. This is Sid Murphy. CJ's a little tied up now and can't come to the phone."

She knew it took every ounce of self-restraint in David not to react. He'd forced himself to go into sniper mode. Sid wasn't mistaken about David being a trained killer. He'd taken lives while wearing the uniform of the U.S. Army, but not as a state trooper.

"Where is she?" asked David in a calm voice.

"With me," said Sid with a cocky, prison hardened voice. "I'm keeping CJ and Nancy company. I thought you might like to see your wife on Christmas Eve. By the way, you're about to become a widower and lose another child. That will almost make up for killing my two brothers."

"You didn't answer my question. Where are you?"

CJ shouted, "Nativity."

Instead of exploding in anger, Sid looked down and smiled at her. "That's right, David. The three of us are at the nativity, over a mile away." He paused. "According to Nancy, your wife is in the last stages of labor."

Sid's voice changed to pure evil. "Get that huge spotlight on and shine it across the river bottom. You have thirty seconds. I want you to see what the Murphys do to killers."

CJ's back felt like it was on fire. The word *labor* didn't begin to describe the pain. Her sweat-soaked T-shirt and pants clung to her. She moaned, but fought off the urge to cry out again.

Nancy called out to Sid, but he ignored her, except to say, "No more questions, Red."

CJ looked up from her panting. The baby had dropped from the last time she ran her bound hands over the mound. The searchlight burned a hole in the sky but didn't move from its earth-to-heaven direction. Sid opened his coat and withdrew the knife. He shouted into the phone, "Put the spotlight on me!"

The beam moved, but at an agonizingly slow pace. David's voice came over the phone. "It's coming down, Sid. Be patient. We can't find the guy who knows how to operate this thing."

This was her chance. Despite the pain, CJ knew she had to get to the tiny gun nestled under her arm. With hands still bound, she eased them across her chest. They moved far enough to where she could feel the Velcro tab. She didn't have to fake the loud moans as they covered the scratching sound of the safety tab being torn apart. She felt the gun's handle and withdrew it in a single motion.

"Keep that spotlight coming down," said Sid, with his eyes skyward. He'd taken a step to the side and stood where the manger had been. "Keep it coming." The gleeful voice belonged to a demon and not a man. He raised the knife high, which caught the light on its silver blade and danced the reflection across the pasture.

CJ raised her little gun with the big punch, but a fresh spasm of pain caused her to close her eyes and jerk the trigger. The little gun roared. When her eyes opened again, the light blinded her. The scene hadn't changed. Sid was still a black silhouette against a white background.

"You missed!"

She lifted the gun again and tried to blink away the pain so she could take aim. Once again, she pulled the trigger, but this time, the tiny gun didn't jump in her hand. By the time her vision cleared, Sid's outline had disappeared. What sounded like a sonic boom reached her ears and caused her to flinch.

Pain like she'd never experienced before put all thoughts but giving birth out of her mind. She glanced to her right and saw Nancy rolling toward the light. The glint of the knife blade flashed as it pointed upward, caught between Nancy's feet. With hands free, Nancy made quick work of freeing her feet and coming to CJ. She eased the pistol out of shaking hands and set it to the side.

"You won't need that."

"What happened?"

"I don't know what happened, but Sid's dead and you're having a baby. I'm going to pull your pants off and check to see how far along you are."

CJ heard David's voice coming from her phone. "Hang on, honey. I'm on my way."

Nancy answered for her. "Hurry if you want to watch your son's birth. I'm looking at a full head of hair."

CHAPTER TWENTY-NINE

A turn of her head was all it took to bring a wide smile to CJ's face. David slept in a hospital recliner by her bed while her perfect baby boy clutched her little finger as he slept in her arms. Last night's events seemed long ago, and in a distant land. Gone was the indescribable pain, the desperation, the fear, all swept away by things marvelous and new. After all, it was Christmas Day, a time for renewed hope, and most of all, new life.

The door cracked open and CJ saw Nancy's smiling face. What a blessing she had been.

David sensed Nancy's presence long before he saw her. He pushed down the leg rest, shifted his gaze from his wife and child, and smiled. "Come in," he said in a quiet tone.

Kevin and his mother followed Nancy into the room. Nancy came to the bed, showing off two rows of white teeth. She shifted her gaze from CJ to the baby. "He looks a lot different today than he did last night."

Kevin's mother added, "He's gorgeous." Her gaze went to CJ. "I knew he'd be something special."

"Mom's an expert on genetics and breeding stock," said Kevin as a goad to his mother.

"That's not what I meant," said Chris.

The banter between mother and son held no hint of offense.

CJ held out her hand for Nancy. "I'll never be able to thank you enough for what you did."

"It's Kevin you need to thank." Her gaze shifted to David. "Have you told her?"

"Told me what?" CJ shifted her gaze to David.

He took in a deep breath. "You've rested enough to hear the details of last night. I let my guard down and didn't keep track of you, even after you hounded me about going to the nativity. We were searching the house and grounds when Captain Crow called. He told me something was fishy about the man they found at Crystal Key's house. They were going to check his identity by dental records, but the guy didn't have any teeth. So they called the prison. Because it was Christmas Eve, they had a hard time finding someone to look for dental records, but the assistant warden remembered Sid had a full set of shiny teeth. It turns out, he was a clean freak."

Kevin joined in. "When I found out they were searching for you, I told him you two took Aunt Bea's ride up to the living nativity."

"A minute or two later, Sid called me on your phone."

"He threw me his keys and told me to bring his big rifle case to the spotlight," said Kevin.

"His speed was a life saver, literally. If he hadn't run so fast to bring me the Barret .50 caliber, things would be different today."

"Keep going," said CJ.

"Billy Paul had the guy that operated the spotlight point it straight up and bring it down slow. I needed to find the range and make adjustments to the scope. If you remember, there wasn't any wind last night."

"Yes, there was," said Nancy. "At least there was on the hillside."

A look of surprise crossed David's face, but he continued. "I dialed in and prepared to shoot when you cut loose with that little pistol. It's a good thing you did because it caused Sid to shy away from you and step into the round I fired."

"We both would have missed him if he hadn't moved," said CJ.

"Whether it was the step he took or the wind that caused the round to drift, I'm saying it was a Christmas miracle," said Nancy.

Heads nodded as the baby squirmed and stretched. Chris cooed as she looked down at the not-so-tiny baby.

"Do you want to hold him?" asked CJ.

"Oh, yes. What's his name?"

"Christopher David Harper. We'll call him Chris. Every time I speak his name I want to think of Christmas."

David ran his hand over his son's head. "We already have a David and a Davey under our roof. And CJ's maiden name was David. He definitely needs to go by another name."

"Speaking of names," said Kevin's mother. "I'm going back to using my full name, Christine. It's time to step into the future."

Nancy turned to Christine. "That sounds so much more refined. It's a name that fits a successful businesswoman who raises champion horses."

CJ looked at Nancy. "Speaking of Davids, where's little Davey?"

"Aunt Bea and Billy Paul have him downstairs."

David added, "We'll be going home soon. The doctor said there's no reason to keep either of them overnight again. The grandparents are home waiting to spoil these two and open presents."

That was all the cue the three visitors needed to leave. Christine kissed the crown of the baby's head and handed him back to CJ.

David settled himself in the chair as the door shut and said, "I wonder what's keeping those discharge papers."

CJ smiled. "I guess hospitals aren't too different from law enforcement. Sometimes it's just hurry up and wait."

A knock on the door brought David to his feet again. "Good. Maybe that's the nurse."

He opened the door and stood back. In walked Captain Crow with his felt cowboy hat in hand. He nodded to David and moved to the side of CJ's bed. "I needed to come by and... Well, I guess I wanted to say... Merry Christmas."

David stepped toward the door. "I'll check to see how much longer it's going to be before we can leave."

CJ had never seen Captain Crow stumble over his words before. As the silence threatened to stretch, she saved him any additional mumbling and said, "His name is Christopher. We'll call him Chris."

The hardened Texas Ranger stared at the boy in the receiving blanket and blinked more times than normal. He cleared his throat. "I came to apologize. I should have paid more attention to the reports from you and David, and all the others. Everything was right in front of me and I didn't put it together. Sid Murphy was the worst of the three brothers, and the smartest."

He continued to roll his hat in his hands as he worked his way through the *mea culpa*. "I wanted to believe that he'd died in that house fire."

"We all did," said CJ. "I should have seen it, but with Christmas and the baby, I let my guard down. David did too, but I blame that on sleep deprivation."

"My fault again," said Captain Crow. "It was my responsibility to find enough troopers to keep you safe. I failed you."

CJ reached out her hand and placed it over Captain Crow's. "There's more responsibility on your shoulders than anyone should have. On the positive side, you taught me to take the initiative and get the job done. We found the help we needed, even if it took a little divine intervention. Everyone's safe and I'm looking forward to many years of peace and quiet on the farm."

"I hope you get it."

His words were genuine, but they came with a measure of doubt.

CJ cocked her head. "You don't sound convinced that I'm serious about staying home and teaching my son to grow crops and raise livestock."

He held up a hand to block her words. "No, I believe you will. You and David will have a BB gun in his hand before he loses his first tooth. It's just..."

"Just what?"

Captain Crow walked around the bed and looked out the window. "There's a lot of evil out there. You and David have a particular knack for recognizing it and dispensing justice." He turned around. "I can't explain it, but there are some people who are born to put things right in this crooked world. I know you'll spend years in peace, doing all the things you've been dreaming of, but one of these years, trouble will come your way again."

CJ shivered. "You sound like an Old Testament prophet."

He laughed. "More like a silly half-Cherokee who still believes in things I can't explain." He reached into his pocket and drew out something.

"Hold out your hand," he said in a firm voice.

She did, and he dropped a circular badge on it. "I have special permission from the governor to give you this. He still wants you to be a Ranger, but I told him you'd turn it down like you did last time. It may take years, but when that trouble comes again, pin this on. There'll be a spot for you alongside David helping the Rangers."

CJ swallowed hard and watched the man she admired leave the room. Her son kicked his legs. She kissed his forehead and said, "Not for a long time, Chris. I promise."

Ready for a new mystery series to challenge your whodunit skills? Turn the page to check out the Smiley and McBlythe Mysteries!

SMILEY AND MCBLYTHE MYSTERY SERIES

Hammack weaves a multi-layered whodunit...
Bookbub Reviewer

Blind and widowed, Steve Smiley struggles with the hand life has dealt him. When he hears his college roommate is dead, Steve's long-buried police detective intuition rises to the surface. It's no accident. It's murder. But he needs help, a partner, to prove it.

Heather McBlythe's domineering father never lets up. His underhand tactics cost her another job in law enforcement. She needs a place to hide for a few months, just until she comes into her inheritance. Smiley's unorthodox proposition sounds like just the ticket.

And so a unique partnership is born: a blind detective with a special gift for solving homicides and a straight-to-the-point Boston debutante-turned-detective.

Turn the page for a sneak peek of *Exercise Is Murder*.

EXERCISE IS MURDER EXCERPT

Three firm knocks sounded on the classroom door.

"Enter." The command came from the instructor.

Heather McBlythe looked up from her desk at Houston's Police Academy, a sprawling complex spread over seventy acres, butting up to the southwest corner of George Bush International Airport. She found the location of the airport to be a noisy aggravation at first, but decided it was a good setting for learning to deal with frequent interruptions and the resulting stress.

A loud creak from a squeaking hinge interrupted the chatter of the room's occupants. Into the classroom walked a disheveled man, feeling his way with a white cane. The sweeping motions, like the slow wag of a dog's tail, came with a light tap and scrape. He stopped briefly as the instructor announced, "This is retired homicide detective Steve Smiley. You can see on your syllabus that he'll be teaching SKILLS OF OBSERVATION AND DEDUCTION. They're all yours, Steve."

Who could imagine that a blind former cop would be teaching at the Academy, let alone a class dealing with observation? A snicker came from the back of the room. Instead of speaking, the retired detective adjusted his sunglasses and used his cane to orient himself to the room. He felt his way around the front without speaking, his steps slow and balking. Most of the recruits sat in silence, watching the man shuffle until he had explored the front of the classroom. A muffled conversation rose from the rear of the room. When the former detective came to the wall nearest Heather, he turned and followed it until she felt the cane touch her foot.

"What's your name, young lady?" Smiley asked.

She rose to her feet. "Heather McBlythe, sir."

"Thank you, McBlythe. Please be seated."

The cane scraped the vinyl composition tile floor in back-and-forth searches as he made his way along the first row of seats toward the door of the classroom. Along the way he slowed as the metal tip, the approximate size of two nickels glued together, came in contact with one foot after another. At the last row before reaching the door he turned and shuffled down an aisle until he reached the rear wall. He backtracked and turned to the occupant in the last seat.

"What's your name, son?"

"Hank Strother... Hank Strother, sir."

"Don't bother standing, Hank."

Some of her classmates stifled a laugh while others straightened their posture. Heather covered a grin with her hand. She'd heard enough in the last few days from the yokel in the back row. He needed to be thrown back to whatever backwater he came from.

The mysterious former detective traversed his way back to the front of the classroom. Once there he pointed down the center aisle. "Fourth seat. What's your name?"

"Mary Bannon, sir," she said after she had risen to her feet.

"Tell me, Bannon, what do you know about the death of former District Attorney Ned Logan?"

"Uh... nothing, sir."

"Nothing? You haven't heard about it on TV or read about it? Are you telling me a former assistant district attorney is dead and you and your fellow recruits haven't been discussing it?"

She spoke in a weak, warbling voice. "Well, yeah. I mean, yes, sir. I overheard some of—"

"So you do know something about it. Is that what you're saying? Why didn't you tell me the truth the first time I asked you?"

The serrated edge of his words cut through the air and left Mary Bannon a stuttering mess. Heather tilted her head. There was more to the curmudgeon than she'd originally thought. Time to pay attention.

"I... I thought you meant..."

"Meant what, Bannon?"

She tried to speak, but whatever it was didn't rise to the surface.

"Sit down."

A low rumble of bodies rose as recruits shifted in their seats and sat erect. The former detective brought silence by speaking in a voice that demanded to be heard. "First lesson of the day. Most people know something about important events even if it's pure hearsay. It's your job to push through their desire not to reveal what they know. You determine what's important, not them."

Heather jotted a quick line in her notebook. Steve Smiley continued, "One more. The man behind Recruit Heather McBlythe. Stand up."

The chair behind her scraped. "Sir, Troy Franks, sir."

"Front and center, Franks."

Troy Franks drew to within a few feet of the man who

253

commanded a bigger presence than his five-foot-ten-inch frame portrayed. Without asking, the former detective reached out and found Troy Franks' shoulder. His fingers slid down to Franks' hand and then retraced the path back to the shoulder. He didn't stop. He felt Franks' neck, ran fingers along the crown of his head and did the same to his face.

When he had withdrawn his hand, Smiley announced, "Six foot two inches, approximately one hundred ninety-five pounds, Caucasian male, age twenty-five, scars over both eyes. Prior military. Most likely Army Special Forces. Bandage on shoulder indicates a recent tattoo or, more probable, the modification or removal of a tattoo. I suspect recently divorced, or in the process. No wedding band. The tattoo might be a woman's name. I also noticed he's sitting directly behind Heather McBlythe."

Smiley issued a wide grin. "Someone put the clues together for me. Is Franks interested in getting to know Heather McBlythe much better?"

A chorus of affirmative answers erupted.

Steve Smiley patted Franks on the shoulder. "Well? How'd I do, Franks?"

"A little too good, sir. Thanks for ruining my chances."

"I saved you time and aggravation. She's not interested in you." Without turning his head he barked, "Are you, McBlythe?"

"Negative, sir." Heather cocked her head to one side. How did he know that?

"Have a seat, Franks. Okay, everyone, take out your notebooks and pens. Turn your chairs around and face the back wall." He waited until the noise died down before further instructions. "You have fifteen minutes to write down every observation and deduction you made of me. Whatever you do, don't turn around." He paused. "I'll know if you do."

Heather worked until Smiley said, "Time's up. Turn around."

Papers and chairs rustled.

"Look at your list and count how many things you observed about me by using sight. Write an 'S' at the top of the page and put the number."

He waited until the sound of pen to paper had ceased. "You should have at least twenty things recorded from sight alone. Less than twenty means you failed this exercise and you need to be more observant. A good habit to develop is start at the top of a person, their hair or the hat they're wearing, then work your way to the shoes or lack thereof. When I had my sight, I trained my mind to recall a minimum of forty distinct observations of every person I questioned." He lifted his chin and asked, "Did anyone get forty?"

Silence.

"Thirty-five?"

"Thirty-seven," said Heather.

"Not bad, McBlythe."

A mumbled "showoff" came from the back of the room.

Heather ignored the critic. Guys like him didn't last long.

Smiley continued, "Now add up every other characteristic you wrote down from sound, smell, taste, or touch. Put an OS at the top of your page for Other Senses and tally them up."

It didn't take long for nervous whispers to rise. "Did anyone have more Other Senses than they had Sight?"

No one responded.

"I wouldn't expect you to. Sight will be your number one asset. But, don't neglect your other senses.

"What you have so far are observations. I also asked you to make deductions about me based on those observations. My using a white cane is an observation. 'Steve Smiley is blind,' is a deduction you made from that observation. Write down the number of deductions you made about me."

It didn't take long before he asked, "Did anyone have more than seven things?"

"Yes, sir," said Heather.

"Anyone else?"

Silence.

"That's very good, McBlythe. Tell the class what you know about me based on your observations."

Heather took in a deep breath and began. "You're wearing a college class ring. At your age, which I judge to be just shy of fifty, I deduce you are a very proud graduate of your alma mater. Next, you're a dog owner. By the length and color of the hair on your pants, I'd say a golden retriever. You're very thrifty. I gauged this by the worn condition of your shoes, pants, and sport coat. Also, you needed a haircut two weeks ago. I didn't notice the smell of any cologne or aftershave, but I did notice a small amount of blood on your collar."

"And what did that tell you about me?"

"Two things. Your loss of vision occurred later in life and you're not fond of change. An electric razor would be more practical for you."

"Keep going."

"Your presence here tells me you miss being on the force."

"Anything else?"

"Your bearing is a little too slouchy to indicate a military background. You wear a wedding band, but your socks don't match. That, and the need of a haircut, tell me you're most likely a widower and you live alone. You have no desire for a new relationship and wear the ring as a guard against advances."

"Keep going. You're doing pretty good so far."

"There was one thing I found odd. You asked Recruit Bannon what she knew of the death of Ned Logan. That death hasn't been ruled a homicide yet. The lead story this morning was the murder of a cab driver. It received quite a bit of press coverage. The question I asked myself is why did you choose to question Ms. Bannon about the death of Ned Logan and not the cab driver?"

"And your deduction?" asked Steve.

Heather shrugged. "The death of Ned Logan is of particular interest to you."

"Excellent," said Steve. "Ned Logan was my college roommate. Anything else?"

"Yes, sir, but I think it best if I tell you in private."

"We all have our secrets, don't we, Ms. McBlythe? Very well. I'll see you after class."

He raised his voice. "Everything McBlythe said is accurate with the exception of my current ownership of a dog. He died five months ago. I haven't worn these slacks in nine months. Thus, Beauregard's hair remains on my trousers."

A voice piped up from the rear of the classroom. "What did you deduce from asking me my name?"

"Ahh, Hank Strother. I'll get to you in a few minutes. First, let me chat with Mary Bannon." He shifted to where he faced her. "Bannon, all it took was one sharp question and you turned to jelly. A series of quasi-accusations and I had you near tears. Here's what I deduced from our short conversation, Ms. Bannon. You have a fifty-fifty chance of graduation from this academy. Your chances of making it on the streets for more than a year are lower."

The room became graveyard quiet. Heather looked at the quivering jaw of the recruit. Here it comes.

"You have two choices, Mary Bannon: grow a backbone or find another line of work."

Pow. He nailed her.

A voice came from the back of the room. "You can't know that from one short conversation."

"Strother," said Smiley, his voice salted lightly with derision. "I thought I might hear back from you. I'm glad to see you're paying attention considering what you did last night."

"What do you mean?"

"When I passed your desk three strong odors assaulted me. The first, cologne. Old Spice, liberally applied. Breath mints came next, followed by last night's consumption of alcohol seeping through your skin. The Astros played last night. You spent an evening swilling beer at the ball park. Am I right?"

"I only had two beers."

Heather shook her head. Wrong answer, Bozo.

"Don't test my patience," snapped Smiley. "That 'two beers' fairytale won't cut it."

"You can't know where I was or how much I drank last night," challenged Strother.

Smiley raised his chin a little as his next words spilled out. Heather knew the signs. The red flag had been waved in front of the bull and it didn't matter that the bull couldn't see it.

"Strother, you have a voice like a megaphone and a mouth that needs a zipper. You were talking to the young man beside you about last night's game when I pretended to grope my way around the room. My suspicions of an alcohol-addled mind were further confirmed when you failed to stand before you gave your name and to address me as 'sir.' Add to that, you snickered when you heard a blind man was going to be teaching on observation skills. You mumbled a disparaging remark when Ms. McBlythe showed you up with the number of observations she'd recorded. You are not only a drunk, you're a belligerent and dangerous drunk."

"I still say you can't know where I was or what I was doing last night."

Steve lifted his hands upward in a sign of frustration. "You already stand convicted by your own words. Do you need more proof? All right. I'll be glad to give it to you."

"How?"

"The testimony of an eyewitness." Without waiting for a response, Smiley pointed with an outstretched finger. "The young man sitting in the last chair next to Strother, come up here."

A murmur of muffled voices rose and fell.

"Tommy Fletcher, sir."

"Tommy," began Smiley in a soft, fatherly voice. "You've been whispering back and forth with Hank since I arrived. You two are pretty good friends, aren't you?"

"Uh... good enough, sir."

He's baiting the trap.

"I'm going to ask you a series of questions. I warn you now not to lie or be evasive." He motioned with a tilt of his head. "Sergeant Holland is standing by the door, isn't he?"

"Yes, sir."

"He's listening to every word we say, isn't he?"

"Yes, sir."

"Lying to an instructor is cause for immediate dismissal, isn't it?"

"Yes, sir."

He's got a nibble.

"You went to the ball park last night, didn't you?"

"Yes, sir."

"You went with Hank, didn't you?"

"Yes, sir."

"You drank beer, didn't you?"

"Half a beer, sir. It got too warm for me."

"Hank drank the rest of it, didn't he?"

"Well..."

The voice of the instructor broke in with enough force to cause half the class to jump. "Tell him!"

Watch out, fishy.

"Yes, sir. Hank drank the rest of it."

"He got up every inning and bought a fresh beer, didn't he?"

"No, sir. He bought two at a time from the vendors who came down the aisle."

The hook is set. Now reel him in.

"My mistake," said Smiley. "One more question. Did Hank drive last night?"

The brief hesitation gave Heather the clue she needed to know the fate of Hank Strother. The delayed response mingled regret with conviction. "Yes, sir."

"Thank you, Mr. Fletcher. Have a seat."

The voice of the instructor came next. "Strother. Grab everything you brought to class and go to my office."

Fish landed, gutted, and filleted.

Heather looked on as the door closed with more force than necessary. Steve pointed again to Mary Bannon. "Bannon, was I too hard on Strother?"

"No, sir." The voice had more substance to it than her previous responses.

"Are you sure?"

"Yes, sir." Her words rang with conviction.

"Explain yourself."

"He's an alcoholic. He had at least seven and a half beers in a two-hour period. They stop serving in the seventh inning to cut down on drunk drivers. He was drunk when he drove home."

"You don't sound very sympathetic."

"I'm not."

"Congratulations, Ms. Bannon. Your chances of graduating and becoming a good cop are up forty percent."

His voice rose to address the entire class. "Train all your senses, not just sight. Ask questions, lots of them. Get over being shy about making people uncomfortable if you want to be a cop. This concludes my presentation."

Steve received accolades as recruits filed past on their way to lunch. The door shut and only Heather remained.

"Ah, Heather McBlythe, you didn't run out on me."

"No, sir. That was an impressive presentation."

The compliment passed with a simple nod. "Miss Bannon needed to find her backbone while Mr. Strother didn't belong." He paused. "You had something for me you didn't want to share with the class. What is it?"

"Before I tell you, I noticed you failed to pronounce your deductions concerning me. I'd be most interested to hear them."

"Are you sure?"

"That sounds ominous, but yes. Don't hold anything back."

"Very well. Your placement in the room intrigued me. You sat on the front row but against the far wall. This told me you were intent on getting the most out of the training but you wanted to remain inconspicuous, under the radar, so to speak. Next, I detected a slight accent in your voice. I had my suspicions when you gave only your name, but these were confirmed when you spoke later in complete sentences. Boston, I believe. You've done a good job in hiding your accent by purposefully slowing your speech and drawing out certain vowels, but that particular dialect is a tough one to shed."

"So far, so good," she said.

"A slight scent of perfume came to me. I can't remember the name, but I once splurged and bought Maggie a small bottle for her birthday. You, Miss McBlythe, have expensive taste."

"Keep going," she said.

"Based on the sound of your voice in relation to my ears, I'd say you're five foot six. I didn't detect any odor of makeup. Based on Troy Franks' interest in you, I'd say you're a naturally attractive woman of approximately thirty years of age."

"How did you come by my age?" asked Heather.

"Your skills in observation and deduction are too advanced for someone younger than that."

"I'm twenty-nine."

Steve acknowledged the one-year mistake with a slight bow.

"What else?"

"You're starting over. You've already been a detective somewhere. The cadence of your speech and the specificity of your words have 'detective' written all over them. No raw recruit ever comes up with over thirty-five observations, nor do any but a few regular cops."

"Any final deductions?"

"You're very well-educated and poised. I'm guessing Ivy League. For some reason things didn't end well for you when you were a detective. You have something to hide. Why else would you be starting over?"

She purposefully kept her voice flat and emotionless. "Most interesting. May I finish my observations and deductions concerning you?"

"By all means."

"You believe the death of Ned Logan will be ruled a homicide and you're trying to find a way to solve the case."

"Ned was on the university swim team and he stayed in good shape. The pool he drowned in is only about four-feet deep." He paused. "Sorry I interrupted. You were saying?"

Heather had to regather her thoughts. Her words came out slow but soon gained speed. "You were a superb detective and you're completely adrift without the job you loved. You believe these infrequent training classes are a form of charity from the department and you don't like that feeling. You also lost the only woman you ever loved."

Steve issued a tight-lipped smile. "If things don't work out for you here, look me up."

Heather lowered her voice and leaned in. "I might have to do that. Where do you live?"

"If you can't find me, McBlythe, I can't use you."

———

Smiley and McBlythe Mysteries are available in paperback and ebook at your favorite online retailer.

About The Author

Drawing from his extensive background in criminal justice, Bruce Hammack writes contemporary, clean read detective and crime mysteries. He is the author of the Smiley and McBlythe Mystery series and the Star of Justice series. Having lived in eighteen cities around the world, he now lives in the Texas hill country with his wife of thirty-plus years.

Follow Bruce on Bookbub and Goodreads for the latest new release info and recommendations. Learn more at brucehammack.com.

Just for mystery lovers!
Receive a free mystery short story when you sign up for Bruce's newsletter at brucehammack.com

---

Thank you for reading one of my books. I hope the mystery and suspense kept you turning the page to see what happens next. If you enjoyed the book, please take a minute to leave a review at your favorite retail site, Bookbub or Goodreads. Reviews help other readers discover a great read and also help your favorite authors keep churning out stories for you to enjoy.

Happy Reading!

Bruce